different kinds *of* fruit

different kinds *of* fruit

KYLE LUKOFF

Dial Books for Young Readers

Dial Books for Young Readers
An imprint of Penguin Random House LLC, New York

First published in the United States of America by Dial Books for Young Readers,
an imprint of Penguin Random House LLC, 2022

Copyright © 2022 by Kyle Lukoff

Visit us online at penguinrandomhouse.com.

Library of Congress Cataloging-in-Publication Data is available.

Printed in the United States of America

ISBN 9780593111185

10 9 8 7 6 5 4 3 2 1

CJKB

Design by Cerise Steel
Text set in Berling LT

To the old friend who gave me the beginning.
and the new friends who gave me the end.

chapter 1

Okay, I know that the sunset is majestic and timeless and awe-inspiring and everything, but also there was some ice cream dripping onto my hand and it was extremely important that I tend to that at once.

And yes, the light did spread out over the water like sparkly popcorn, and yes, it *was* cool the way the sun hovered trembling above the horizon. However, I also had a big scoop of Nutella ice cream, which is my absolute favorite, in a waffle cone, which is also my absolute favorite, and my ice cream was melting fast in the hottest August on record. The sun would set again tomorrow but my hand might be sticky and gross for the whole ride home because my dad, unlike my mom, doesn't carry a purse filled with wet wipes.

"Told you to get it in a cup," Dad said. He was taking leisurely bites of his mint chocolate chip, gazing out at the Pacific. Little bites, like he had all the time in the world, which I guess he did because even if his ice cream melted into soup (which is great, I love ice cream soup in an appropriate container), he wouldn't have the whole sticky-hands problem that I was currently struggling to prevent. Not to mention that I was wearing one of my cutest dresses, cream-colored with a halter top and a swishy skirt, and I did not want it to have a sticky brown splotch forever. Even if I was about to outgrow it.

I grumbled at him, working my tongue into that space between my ring finger and pinky.

"What'd you say?" he asked.

"I *said*, grumble grumble grumble!"

"A compelling point," said Dad, and turned his attention back to the sunset. I turned back too, and noticed that the railing came up to his belly, and it hit me right above mine. I was almost as tall as my dad now. When did that happen?

Dad came up with this tradition when I was seven. He would pick a last day of summer, when it would stay warm and bright for hours and hours. Drive the two of us down to "the city," also known as Seattle, but my parents always called it "the city" like they were describing a bodily function that's perfectly natural but also embarrassing to do in public. We'd get dinner at a restaurant that doesn't exist in our town, usually something I've never had before (this time it was fancy ramen, which would be my first choice for a cold winter night but maybe not my first choice for a hot summer day). Then we'd wander around the little tourist shops, find some cool street performers and give them dollars, and end by watching the sun set over the Sound.

Dad always called this "father-daughter bonding," but I

wished he wouldn't. Calling it "bonding" made me worry that I was doing something wrong, like instead of scouring novelty stores for those smashed-penny machines we should be having intense heart-to-hearts about how fast I'm growing up and how glad he was that I'm his daughter. I wished he'd say "Hey Bananabelle"—(yes, that's what he calls me sometimes—) "have you ever had tandoori? You should try it, it's delicious" or "There's a new exhibit on raptors at the natural history museum! I love raptors, want to go with me?" That way we could do the same fun stuff, eat dinner, have a good time, and not feel like we were doing something meaningful to cement our father-daughter relationship. He's my dad, I'm his kid, I didn't get why he wanted to make it into such a thing.

Anyway, so we were watching the sunset, or at least he was watching the sunset and I was sneaking peeks of it while avoiding an ice cream catastrophe. He was probably thinking deep thoughts about the universe and how fast I was growing up and how the sun is eventually going to explode, which will kill us all, if climate change doesn't get us first. I was thinking about all those things and also how I should have gotten a cup *and* a cone. That would have been genius.

I glanced up at the sun again. Ouch. "Shouldn't we be wearing sunglasses or something?" I asked. "Don't you care about my eyes?"

"You'll be fine," Dad grunted. "Strengthens your retinas."

I was almost sure he was joking about that. I knew you

weren't supposed to look directly into the sun, but also I couldn't tell what kind of mood he was in. Sometimes he liked to joke around, would tease me and I would tease him back and it was great. Sometimes he got prickly, and grimaced every time I tried to say something funny. He had started out the day in a good mood but had gotten quieter and quieter, and I knew better than to try to bring him back. It was almost time to go home anyway. Phew.

Finally I looked up from my Nutella-stained hands, just in time to catch the sun slipping below the water like magic, and I really did get why the sunset was such a miraculous thing. Even though it happened every day. We turned away from the railing without speaking and started the long trek towards the car.

As we walked, I tried to soak up the last few minutes of being in the city. My parents always acted so freaked out by it for no good reason. Seattle is *amazing*. Before dinner we had found a store selling nothing but fancy olive oils and olive oil–related products. And we got to pick between a million restaurants with a million different kinds of food, as opposed to our boring suburb of Tahoma Falls, which had a McDonald's, a Taco Time, an okay diner, and a Red Robin for the nights we wanted something fancy. The light posts on every corner were always thickly papered over with advertisements for parties, music, shows, and benefits for extremely cool people.

In fact, there was an interesting flyer pasted onto a pole

right above eye level. I stared at it as Dad and I waited to cross the street. It showed a woman with eye-popping makeup in a bright zigzag-striped dress, surrounded by shirtless boys. The rainbow text was yelling at me to go to a "Pre-Pride Drag Brunch," and even though I didn't know what any of those words meant, it was a very convincing advertisement.

Well, okay, I did know what all of those words meant, but not necessarily in that order. "Pre" means before, and "pride" means, like, feeling good about yourself. I knew what brunch is, we got it sometimes on Sundays at the diner. It's breakfast but later. And "drag" means to pull something behind you. Or something hard and bad, but that's mostly old-fashioned slang, like "don't be a drag, man." So that meant "pre-pride drag brunch" was a late breakfast you kind of pulled yourself into before you felt good about yourself. That maybe made sense? But I wondered if there was some context I was missing. My teacher last year always talked about using context clues to improve your reading, so I decided to ask my dad. Literacy is important.

"Dad? What's a 'Pre-Pride Drag Brunch'?"

I already knew his mood had gone from good to . . . something else, so it wasn't a surprise to see his jaw tighten. He glanced at the poster and widened his eyes, his nostrils flaring slightly. "Pre-pride brunch is why we don't come into the city much," he said. Then the walk signal changed from a red hand to a walking man and he bolted across the street, his not-very-long legs pounding his dismay on the crosswalk.

I skipped to keep up. I knew it would be useless to ask any follow-up questions, but I couldn't help myself. "What does 'pre-pride' mean? I know what 'pride' is, but I've seen that word all over the place lately. Is everyone constantly overjoyed to be a Seattleite?"

I liked that word, Seattleite. I wanted to be a Seattleite someday. Much better than being stuck as a Tahomaite forever, and people from our town didn't even call themselves that. Which made sense; "Tahomaite" sounds like a disease.

Dad pinched a little bit of beard between his fingers and tugged on it. He always did that when I asked him a tough question, or when he was unsure of something. After a minute he released the poor tortured hairs and said, "Well. You know what 'gay' and 'lesbian' are. Right?"

Oh. Yeah. *Pride* pride. How had I missed that?

"Right," I agreed. I didn't really need him to explain any more, but I hoped he would. I was curious what he would say. My parents didn't talk about stuff like this much.

"Pride is for them," he continued. "For those kinds of people. A parade. It celebrates an important day in their history. It happens in June, so all these posters and signs are out of date. They should get someone to take them down."

That seemed like all he was going to say. Brief, and correct, and not nearly enough information, which was about right for my father when he didn't want to talk. But there were still some parts I wasn't sure about, so I risked a few other question.

"So, is 'drag brunch' brunch with drag queens? I've seen drag queens on TV, are they also waitresses? That's cool, I want a drag queen to bring me pancakes, can we do that sometime?"

He shrugged, which was probably a "no" to that last question and an unsatisfying answer to the others. I wanted to run back to the flyer, not for the shirtless boys but because I realized that the woman in the bright dress and amazing makeup was a drag queen and I wanted to examine her more thoroughly, but we were already a block away and there was no way he'd let me go back. Oh well. Someday I'd come down to the city on my own and no one could stop me from doing whatever I wanted.

I had other questions, but I could tell he had said all he was going to. If Mom were here I would have asked them; she always gave me much more helpful answers. Like when I asked where babies came from, Dad stuttered and turned red and played with his beard while Mom told me everything about sperms and eggs and uteruses and all that. People always say I look exactly like my dad, but I have my mom's sense of humor and love of bright clothes and accessories, so being a mixture of both parents made sense to me. But if I asked Mom to tell me more about Pride, she might tell Dad. And then they'd wonder why I was so curious about the topic. So I had to be satisfied with that tiny bit of information.

I said a silent goodbye to "the city." It's about a forty-minute drive from Seattle to Tahoma Falls. An hour and a half if traffic is bad. But it would feel ten million hours long if Dad insisted on listening to his sad-girl-with-guitar music or talk radio the whole way, and that would be intolerable while I was buzzing from ice cream and the city and the poster and maybe some nerves about the first day of school. "Father-daughter bonding time" was his idea, so he would have to deal with the fact that I could not be quiet and introspective the entire ride home. I waited for us to get in his pickup truck (hot as an oven inside, I yelped when my thighs touched the fake leather of the seat), and started talking once Dad got onto the freeway heading north.

"I can't believe it's my last year at the Lab!" I began. My school was called the Tahoma Falls Collaborative School, but we called it the Lab for short. "I remember when I was a kindergartner and the sixth graders looked so huge. Like, basically grown-ups. And now I'm going to be one of those basically-grown-ups, but I feel like exactly the same person that I was in kindergarten! And everyone in my class seems the same too. It's so weird. And now I'm like, 'Wow, middle school students are so big and old,' but I bet that once I get to middle school I'll have the soul of that same kindergartner. Does that ever go away? Will I get to college and still eat my broccoli pretending that I'm a dinosaur eating trees? Or is there some magic point where you become an adult and stop feeling like a kid inside?"

I on purpose left that as both a question and a comment

to see if Dad would take the bait and start talking, and if not I could keep going without making it awkward. He let out a "mm," so I decided to keep going. I didn't think it was a mad "mm," maybe an I-don't-know "mm." Or even an I-do-know-but-I'm-not-going-to-tell-you "mm."

"Although I guess I did start feeling older last year," I continued. "Because you know how we mostly stay in our classroom but we also move around for, like, P.E. and music and library? We started calling those 'first period' and 'second period,' it even says that on our schedule. That did make school different, saying 'What do we have for second period' like high schoolers do on TV. Even though the boys laughed at first because we were talking about periods. Do they ever get more mature about that, also?"

That was definitely a question that he could and should respond to, being a boy and all, but it was maybe unfair because Dad got embarrassed talking about those kinds of girl things. Like when Mom bought me my first training bra a few months ago, we were at the mall and she told him why we had to stop by the Target. He stopped dead in his tracks, saying that he had to go to the hardware store and would meet us at the car.

And sure enough he tugged on his beard, cleared his throat, and said, "Not as far as I can tell. Sometimes guys get comfortable talking about that kind of thing, but that won't happen for a while. And plenty never get there at all. Sorry about it."

"It's okay," I said. "And actually I can see this being a good thing? If there's ever a guy bothering me and I want him to go away, I can say 'Oh man I got my period yesterday, so funny how it's blood but also doesn't hurt, you know?' and then he'll run away like a scared little bunny. Ooh, this could be a lot of fun, what if I started doing that? Not even if they're bothering me, just to make them uncomfortable? No, that's mean. Oh well."

Dad hadn't stopped tugging on his beard, and I felt a little bad. He was obviously one of those guys who would have run away.

He cleared his throat. "Have you, uh, started. Yet. Or would that be a joke?"

"Omg. Dad. You don't even know? I promise that once I get my period, I'll tell Mom, and she'll tell you. Did you think that had happened and you didn't know?"

He shrugged, both hands on the wheel. "It's your business. Didn't want to assume you'd tell me. But you can. You don't have to go through your mom."

"Really?" I tried not to sound so surprised, but his lips quirked up in a smile; he had to see why this was a shocking development.

"Really," he said. "I know you're growing up. You'll be a teenager soon, and I want you to be able to talk to me too. About anything." He cleared his throat. "Like your feelings, your friends. Any boys you have crushes on." I've always loved his voice; it's light and reedy, but I'd never heard it like that, almost rough.

There was something I could have said then. About boys, and crushes on them. How I might never have one. And that I didn't know why. But I held back. "Well, thanks, Dad. I'll probably value Mom's opinion about pads and bras and that kind of thing more, but I'm sure we'll find other important coming-of-age topics to bond over! Maybe once I hit high school, there will be boys worth having crushes on, and your male insight will come in handy."

Probably not, a little voice whispered at me, but I told it to hush. Because Dad smiled and nodded, then turned up the radio. Because we finally did "bonding" right, for once, and I wanted to keep it that way.

chapter 2

"**What** do I wear on the first day of school of my last year at school?" I yelled down the hall.

"Clothes," barked Dad, unhelpfully. But I wasn't asking him.

"Moooooom! Help me pick out my outfit!"

"You don't need my help, Annabelle, you'll look beautiful no matter what," Mom called back. "And we have to go."

"Please?" I hollered. "I am suddenly overwhelmed by choices!"

Yes, I should have figured out my first-day-of-school outfit before the first day of school. But in my defense, there were so many first-day-of-school decisions to make. What kind of binder to get, whether or not I needed a new backpack (I said yes, Mom and Dad said no, we compromised and Mom helped me sew some cool patches onto my old one: unicorns and shooting stars and emojis), and also since I didn't have our class schedule yet, there were so many unknown factors! What if I wanted to wear the shirt that goes with my green Converse but I also wanted to wear my green Converse tomorrow because we'd have gym class, but I didn't want to wear them two days in a row? Or what if I decided to wear my absolute best outfit today but everyone else dressed normally and it looked like I was trying too hard? But what if there was a cool new kid and this was my only chance to make a first impression?

Well, that last one wouldn't happen. People didn't move to Tahoma Falls often, and the kids that I'd be graduating with had been my classmates since kindergarten. A few joined in first or second grade, but the rest of us had known each other since we were babies. Our class used to be twice as big, but the younger grades are always bigger than the older ones. People move away, or go to different schools, and I guess "small class size" is something that parents think is important, but I wouldn't mind more choice when pairing up for group projects. So the odds of someone new joining in the sixth grade? Maybe in a movie, but not in real life.

I pulled a bunch of things off the hangers and threw them onto my bed. Mom thumped down the short hallway, and of course when she came in my room she was already perfectly dressed in a knee-length orange sun dress, bright red lipstick, and my favorite pair of her glasses, the magenta cat-eyes with rhinestones.

My mom and dad are total opposites in every way. And I know they say that opposites attract, but they're *so* different that it was hard to imagine them ever attracting each other. Like, my dad only ever wears dad jeans, which means "out of style." He might wear a T-shirt if he's working in the garden, but otherwise, it's jeans and a button-down. Button-up? Anyway, a plain shirt with buttons. So boring. Whereas my mom always, always, always wears dresses. I think I've seen her wear pants three times in my entire life. And the dresses she prefers are like lush tropical flowers, eye-catching and surprising and able to turn any room into a party.

And they're the exact opposite physically too. For most of my friends, the mom is shorter than the dad, and the dad is generally bigger than the mom. Not in my family! My mom towers over my dad, especially when she's in heels. And it's not only that Dad is short and Mom is tall. My mom is like one of those old paintings of rich ladies, all hips and belly and boobs. While my dad is like a blade of grass, sharp shoulders and a sharp jaw and a belt always cinched to the last hole.

I was waiting to see which one I'd take after. For now, in addition to having my dad's eyes and nose, I was also on the smaller side, hoping for a growth spurt. I've always wanted to fill up a room the way my mom does, but I guess there's more than one way to do that.

"You haven't let me dress you since you were four!" Mom remarked as she came into my room. "What's going on?"

"I don't need you to *dress* me, but this is a special occasion and I could use your expert eye! Is that too much to ask?"

She laughed. "I suppose not. And it's nice to know I'm not irrelevant yet. But everyone in your class has known you since kindergarten, so I'm not sure why this is such a big question. Pick one of the new outfits we got for you over the summer, they're all perfectly nice."

"Mom!" I huffed. "Don't you get why it's important to start off on the right foot? It's a new year in the oldest class in the whole school! A new me! I don't know exactly *how* it's a new me, but I *want* it to be, so let's pretend anyway."

"Okay, okay," said Mom, putting up her hands in surrender. "So the question is, do you want to go in and make a big statement right away? Or begin as more of a blank slate, so you can evolve into a style as the year progresses?" She walked over to my closet and started pushing hangers aside.

I mulled over my choices. That was a good question. No wonder Mom always looked perfect. "Can I go with something in between? Not a boring blank slate but also not 'Annabelle Blake, fashion icon'?"

Mom groaned. "You couldn't have thought this over yesterday? Okay, we're going for interesting but with plenty of room to grow. How about your denim skirt and this flouncy top?" She held out a shirt that I would describe as more ruffly than flouncy.

"The denim skirt has not fit me in six months, you know that!"

"I didn't buy you a new one?"

". . . Also I didn't like my denim skirt."

"Fine. Okay, your pink overall dress and a white shirt underneath."

"No, that screams that I'm a girly girl, which would be

okay as one outfit out of a lot of outfits, but not as the first one of the year." I hopped off the bed to join her in front of the closet, frustrated that nothing seemed quite right, and then inspiration struck. "How about my yellow capris and the forest shirt?" I pulled them both out and held them against me.

"Perfect. Beautiful. See, you didn't need my help after all. And now you have two minutes to get your yellow-capri'd butt in the car."

I threw on my outfit, which was super cute, grabbed my backpack, bounded down the porch steps, and was in the car in three minutes. Mom was already waiting for me, engine idling, and Dad waved at us from the door.

I started walking myself to school last year; it only took twenty minutes, there weren't any big hills, and driving is bad for the environment. But the Lab was on the way to one of my mom's early clients, and she said that her baby only started sixth grade once. She worked for a program like Meals on Wheels, helping old people keep themselves fed, which meant that my lunch was always balanced and nutritious.

And honestly, I was glad for the ride. It was the hottest first day of school I could remember. Not that I had a cataloged memory of every first day of school and how sticky I was on each one, but global warming is a thing. I told myself that one short car ride wouldn't make much of a difference in the overall life of Planet Earth, and I didn't want to sweat through my deodorant before the day even started (I started using deodorant this summer, I hoped everyone else did too).

I watched the same old scenery scroll past me, trees and ivy-covered ditches and identical split-level houses, and sighed. School was fine, mostly. We called a lot of teachers by their first name, and parents were encouraged to volunteer in the classrooms or even teach special lessons. In the second grade we learned about embryology by hatching duck eggs, and also learned about how farm-to-table restaurants work because some kid asked what happened to the ducks we sent back to the farm once they got too big for the classroom. That was a sad day for Peepers, Quackers, Spots, and their siblings, but also my mom made duck for dinner once a year around Christmas, and ducks are delicious, so I couldn't feel too bad about it. We only ever took tests when we had to because the state made us for funding or whatever, and we never had to do boring stuff like reading a textbook and answering questions at the end. I only knew what textbooks were because sometimes teachers talked about how lucky we were not to have them.

The Lab was started by a bunch of parents a million years ago. Back then, there wasn't a public school in the area, and they didn't want to drive for hours every day. Now there is one, of course, but the Lab is smaller and closer to our house, and when it was time for me to start kindergarten my parents talked to people who had kids there and they liked the set-up.

Sixth grade was supposed to be fun. Rumors had circulated for years about what our last year at the Lab would be like—ice cream parties every week, unlimited library books, more field trips, generally being the bosses of all the little kids. Caroline, the sixth grade teacher, had been there since before I was born, and everyone talked about how nice she was.

But I was more excited about the end of sixth grade than the beginning or the middle. I wanted to graduate, and get out. The Lab was fine, but I was getting tired of fine. In the same way that Tahoma Falls was a perfectly nice place to live, but "perfectly nice" had started to become code for "boring." If I was too young to go to Seattle by myself, I at least wanted to start middle school, where some things would be different.

But before I could work myself into a funk Mom pulled up to the collection of low, flat-roofed buildings that didn't quite fit together but would be my educational home for one last year. She kissed me on the cheek, I grabbed my backpack, and I zoomed out the car. The year couldn't end until today started, and I was more than ready for it.

chapter 3

As I approached the classroom door, the tiniest part of me held out hope that *something* interesting would happen. Like maybe a swirl of blue jays and hummingbirds would accompany me into the room, or I would all of a sudden learn how to walk in slow motion with the wind dramatically blowing my hair back. Or I'd open the door into my face and start the year with a bloody nose, because at least that would be a story. Instead I walked through the doors without a problem, and discovered that the sixth-grade classroom looked exactly like the fifth-grade classroom: desks arranged into groups of four, a library nook, a rug in front of the smart board, a big closet for teacher supplies. I hadn't been expecting a space-age set up, but they could have spruced it up a *little*.

"Good morning!" a voice chimed from behind me. "What's your name?"

I turned around. Instead of staring up at Caroline, who was very tall and usually wore blouses and skirts, I was right at eye level with a woman with hair cut in a cute bob, a bright orange scarf twined around her neck over a dark purple shirt, and black jeans.

"Where's Caroline?" I blurted out, before remembering that it was probably a bad idea to be rude to the person who was going to be grading my homework for the rest of the year.

But she didn't seem offended. Her laugh sounded like the bubbles you blow in a milk carton, delighted and fresh. "I'm Amy. Caroline got sick over the summer, unfortunately, so I'm her replacement. We sent an email to the families, did your parents miss it?"

One thing my parents loved to complain about was how many emails my school sent. "When I was a kid my parents figured school would keep me alive and that was about it," Dad griped sometimes. I don't think he'd set foot on campus since dropping me off for the first day of kindergarten. Mom paid attention, sometimes, but she only went to the parent-teacher conferences they scheduled twice a year, no school board meetings or parenting discussion groups or anything, so I wasn't too surprised to hear that they had entirely missed some big announcement.

"I guess so! But, it's okay, I like surprises. I mean I don't like that Caroline is sick—that's sad and I hope she's okay—but we've all known each other forever, so it's cool that there's at least one new person in the room."

Amy smiled. I couldn't tell how old she was because she looked like an adult, not a teenager or a senior citizen. She was definitely either older or younger than my parents. Maybe thirty? Or forty? Probably in between those two numbers. "You never did tell me your name," she reminded me.

"Oh! Sorry. Annabelle."

She picked up the class list from her desk. "Annabelle Richards or Annabelle Blake?"

"Blake. Annabelle B. That kind of sounds like Anna Belby, which I don't want to be called, so maybe you could call her Annabelle R.? Sometimes teachers call both of us by our full names but that's a lot of syllables to say every time. Maybe she's decided to go by Anna or Belle or her middle name over the summer."

I hoped so. Us having the same name always bugged me. Not because she's a bully or a teacher's pet or anything that bad, really, she just never seemed quite *here*. It's hard to explain, but talking to her always made me feel uncomfortable. She was so clearly in another world, you could never tell if she understood what was going on. And I don't want to sound mean, but she chewed her hair a lot, so it was always kind of wet and clumpy. She never paid attention, so whenever she asked questions it was usually something the teacher had *just* said. It wasn't a big deal, no one ever got us confused, but I still wanted to be the only Annabelle in my class.

And right on cue the other Annabelle walked in. She always dressed like her mom picked out her clothes, without realizing that her little girl had grown up. Sixth grade didn't seem to be any different. She was wearing orange sweatpants, and a yellowish shirt that used to be white with a bunch of Disney princesses on it. Amy introduced herself, and the other Annabelle blinked a few times, said hi, and that her name was Annabelle (dang it) and looked around for the desk with her name on it.

"Where am I sitting?" she asked slowly.

"Oh, I haven't assigned you seats yet!" Amy said. "I want to get to know you all first. We can figure that stuff out as we go along. Go ahead and find a spot anywhere." The other Annabelle put down her Frozen backpack, the same backpack she'd had since third grade, at the desk closest to the back of the room. I was glad I hadn't picked a seat yet, so I wouldn't have to sit at the same desks as her.

I put my backpack down at the desk diagonal from Sadie, closer to the front. Sadie wasn't my best friend or anything; my best friend had been this girl named Franka, but she moved away last year. So now Sadie was my favorite person in my grade. We had gone to the mall a few times over the summer, and she was wearing one of the outfits we got together.

"Annabelle! Hi! How was the rest of your summer? Can you believe Caroline is gone?"

"Sadie! Hi! Good! Yes!" I said, answering her questions in order. We compared new school supplies as the other kids in my class started to trickle in.

Johnson set his green backpack topped with a fin of dinosaur scales on a desk across from the other Annabelle, then came over to ours to say hello.

"Hi Johnson!" Sadie exclaimed. "What did you learn about over the summer?"

"Well," said Johnson, "I got a Lego set for my birthday that forms an M22 Locust, a lightweight tank used during World War Two. They were airborne and weighed only seven-point-four long tonnes, a British unit of measurement that is one thousand kilograms. Sherman tanks were the most popular, but I decided that M22s are more interesting."

Johnson's lecture probably sounds annoying, but there was something deeply delightful about his excitement. He articulated each letter perfectly, only sometimes spitting on the "s"s. He sometimes sounded like a robot reading from an encyclopedia, but he also laughed a lot, and was a good person to team up with on group projects. He was definitely weird, but in a way I liked better than the other Annabelle's version of weird.

As opposed to Dixon, who strutted in right after him. Dixon wasn't weird at all, and that is *not* a compliment. He was wearing what looked like a brand-new outfit from one of the more expensive stores in the mall. A red polo shirt, crisp black jeans, white sneakers that I would probably recognize if I was the kind of person who paid attention to boy sneakers.

He was objectively the cutest boy in class, or at least the one who looked the most like a magazine cover with his curly blond hair, dark blue eyes, a nice chin, and dimples that came out when he smiled. Also, I hated him.

Adults are always saying "'Hate' isn't a nice word!' and I *know* that, which is exactly *why* I use it to describe my opinion about Dixon. He's the type of boy who knocks things out of girls' hands and then have a nearby grown-up say, "Oh that means he likes you." My parents say that that's the kind of liking I can do without. Once, he decided that random words like "doughnut" or "tadpole" were insults, and then spent days calling Felix and Jonas and Patrick doughnuts and tadpoles until they exploded, and then defended himself saying "but those aren't even bad words" even though he knew it was going to upset them. He's the worst.

Dixon dropped down his backpack at an empty pod and yanked his desk out a little bit, so it wasn't touching any of the others. Then he sat down in his chair and immediately tipped it onto the back two legs, which teachers always tell us not to do.

"'Sup?" he said, nodding in our direction, in a tone of voice that he clearly thought sounded cool. And maybe it did sound cool; I didn't know and also completely didn't care. But maybe he got nicer over the summer? Like he had some transformative experience at camp where he learned the true meaning of friendship and why you should be nice to other kids even if you can get away with being mean.

"Hi, Dixon," said Sadie, not quite looking at him.

"How was your summer?" I asked. I was not, in fact, curious about his summer but figured that starting the year off on the right foot couldn't hurt. Especially in front of a new teacher.

"It was great!" he said. "My parents took me to Europe. I loved Athens and Rome. They're the birthplace of civilization, you know."

"If you say so," said Sadie, rolling her eyes. Her parents had moved here from South Korea, which definitely has civilization and is very far away from those random cities. So much for the right foot. I waited for Dixon to ask us about our summer vacations or what we thought of the new teacher or literally anything, but he just wandered over to Johnson's desk, probably to try and outsmart him about something. After a minute, we heard Johnson interrupt Dixon to lecture him about different theories surrounding the fall of the Roman Empire, which cracked us both up.

We had a few minutes before the day officially started, so I decided to get my desk in order. I placed my new binder with its colorful subject dividers in the center, and arranged my pencils, pens, and erasers, and a package of multicolored Post-its around it. I was deciding what to do with my highlighters (I literally never use them and also they're important to keep on hand in case I find something that needs highlighting) when I heard the door open again. I looked up reflexively, curious about who had shown up, and did a double take. The kid coming through the door was no one I had ever seen before.

My brain spent a few seconds ricocheting around the question "Is that a girl or a boy?" First I was like "Oh my gosh there's a new boy, where did he come from?" And then I was like "Wait, hang on, I think that's a girl with short hair? She looks so cool!" But then I wasn't sure, about anything.

Except I was sure that their shoes were amazing. They were white, and made of some shiny fake leather or whatever, and the new kid had clearly decorated them at home with markers. The shoes didn't match, exactly, but they both had eyeballs and rainbows and peace symbols and shooting stars, things like that. Definitely the coolest ones I had ever seen.

The new kid was also wearing a T-shirt with the words "Hedgehogs: Why don't they share the hedge?" and a picture of two hedgehogs standing next to a strip of green, with a word bubble coming from one of their mouths saying "no." Before the kid even introduced themself to Amy I burst out into laughter.

"That is the best shirt I have ever seen!"

"Thanks!" they said. "I love your forest shirt!"

"Yeah well, I also love your shoes, and my shoes are fine but not nearly as cool as yours, so I win the compliment battle. So there."

"I'll take it," said the new kid, and their laugh was like a rare bird had flown into the room and perched on my desk.

Amy glanced down at the attendance sheet. "What's your name, friend?"

"Oh, hi, I'm Bailey. Bailey Wick." Of course they would have the coolest name I'd ever heard.

"Oh, you're the student who enrolled over the summer, right?"

"That's me! We just moved here. My parents heard good things about this school and figured one year at the Lab was better than none."

"We'll have to compare notes," said Amy, bubble-laughing. "This is my first year teaching here. Choose any seat you like."

Bailey came over to our pod. I wriggled with excitement.

"Hey, I'm Bailey. I mean, I know you heard me say that to the teacher, but it's the best way to start a conversation with people you don't know." They put their hands on the desk across from me. Purple polish adorned their neatly-trimmed, square fingernails.

"I'm Sadie," said Sadie.

"I'm Annabelle! How long have you been in Tahoma Falls? Where did you move from?"

"We got here a few weeks ago," they said, sliding into the open seat. I tried not to stare. Tried to look at them like I would any new kid, not an especially cute one that I couldn't tell was a boy or a girl or—"From Seattle. My parents wanted a change of scenery, I guess? I'm not sure why they picked Tahoma Falls over, like, Bellingham or Snohomish or Issaquah, but this place is fine so far."

"My parents always act like Seattle is on the other side of the world," I said. "Did you grow up there? That must be so cool."

"I guess it's cool? I already miss Seattle but my friends and I talk a lot, and it's not like we moved to Wenatchee or Spokane. We can still visit each other. Honestly, it feels weird to not be on Capitol Hill surrounded by ramen shops and drag queens, it's all I've ever known."

Drag queens. Hang on. "Have you been to drag brunch?" I blurted out. "What's it like?"

Bailey did a double take, which made sense because that wasn't exactly a normal question to ask when you're getting to know someone on the first day of school.

"Um, yeah, a few times? It's just brunch, but with drag queens as waitresses giving shows and stuff. Why?"

"The last time I was in the city with my dad," I said, trying to sound casual and sophisticated, like we went to Seattle all the time, "there was an ad for something called 'Pre-Pride Drag Brunch' and he refused to explain anything about it." It's hard to sound casual and sophisticated when you don't know something.

"Oh! Yeah, drag brunches happen all the time at Cherries, but a lot of other places have them during Pride. It's fine, I guess, but honestly I don't want a show when I'm eating. Gotta focus on my waffles, you know?"

"Totally," I said, because waffles are serious business. Sadie also nodded in agreement, but I bet you anything she had also never been to a restaurant that had a drag queen showtime.

I was going to ask another clarifying question about what exactly happened during a drag queen show in a restaurant, but a chime rang through the classroom causing the chatter and motion to die out all at once. The rest of my class had shown up while I was talking to Bailey, and Amy was standing at the front of the room. It was time to begin.

"Good morning, sixth grade!" she said. "Let's get started. Everyone find a spot on the rug."

It turned out that even sixth graders had morning meeting. When we were little it was pretty basic, going around the circle and saying good morning to everyone, reading the schedule for the day, checking the weather, that sort of thing. It got more interesting the older we got; sometimes we'd talk about current events or have a show-and-tell or play fun games to start the day. I wondered how different it would be this year.

All twelve of us found a spot on the rug. I sat between Bailey, who smelled pleasantly like Cheerios, and Jonas, whose curly brown hair stuck up several inches above his scalp. There were no other surprise classmates. Loud Olivia, who always acted like she was in charge. Amanda, who used to throw a lot of tantrums, but in third grade started helping Jonas recover from his. Patrick, who always got upset when something was unfair, know-it-all Audrey, bookworm Charlotte, and Felix, who was always goofing off. And then I wondered how they would describe me—Annabelle who talked more than the other Annabelle? The girl who knew way too much about hungry old people because of her mom's job? Annabelle with the cool, colorful outfits? Or maybe what they thought about me were things I didn't know about myself. Huh.

Amy sat cross-legged on the floor and took a deep breath. "Welcome to the first day of school," she began. "I know you were all expecting Caroline to be your teacher. She was the sixth-grade teacher when I went here, believe it or not. So it's a little strange to try and follow in her footsteps, but if we all work together, I know we can build our own special community."

"Wait, you went to school here?" asked Charlotte.

"Sure did! I was a Lab lifer, kindergarten through sixth.

I've only ever taught in public schools, but I'm familiar with how this place is run. Maybe too familiar," she added with a chuckle. "Let's start off the year by going around and sharing your name, the best part of your summer, and one goal you have for this year. Patrick, would you go first?"

Patrick was sitting directly to her left. "Uh, okay," he said, his cheeks turning red. "My favorite part of the summer was when we went hiking at Mount St. Helens. And my goal for the year is to . . . um . . . not eat anything with palm oil in it. Because to get palm oil you have to cut down palm trees, which is bad for orangutans, and I care about orangutans."

"Thanks Patrick, that's great. Audrey? You're next."

I'd probably spent a million hours of my life being part of a circle-go-round where we each say one thing. It totally made sense why teachers had us do this kind of thing. The problem is that instead of listening to the kids who go before me, I always spend the whole time rehearsing and planning what I'm going to say. And then after I share I spend the rest of the time going over what I had said, wondering if I could have said something better, and worrying that I had forgotten to say the most important thing, whatever it was. So it doesn't matter if I go first, last, or in the middle, I never pay attention to what anyone else was saying. By the time it was my turn, I vaguely remembered Charlotte saying that her goal was to learn calligraphy, and Dixon repeating again something about the birthplace of civilization, but I hadn't thought of anything interesting to say.

"My favorite part of the summer was going berry picking in Carnation and then making pies and jams and stuff with everything we got," I began. If I was being honest I'd say, "I don't have a real goal because all I want is to get out of here," but that would be a downer, so I said, "My goal for the school year is to get ready to move on to middle school," which was practically the same thing but a nicer way of phrasing it.

Bailey was up next, and, for once, instead of worrying about what I just said, I focused on their every word.

"Hi! My name is Bailey. My parents and I moved here three weeks ago, so I guess my favorite part of the summer was the goodbye party we had in Volunteer Park. My goal for the school year is to be more of an animal advocate—Patrick, I want you to tell me more about palm oil! Oh, also, my pronouns are they/them."

I had no idea what that meant and cocked my head curiously without meaning to. Bailey glanced in my direction, then quickly turned away. For the first time since striding into a brand-new school with brand-new kids, they looked nervous. Confusion spread over a lot of faces, but not Amy's. She was grinning widely.

"Bailey, thank you for sharing that. I'm noticing that some of your classmates could use an explanation about what you mean. Do you want me to try to explain, or would you prefer to?"

Bailey narrowed their eyes. "How about if you go first, and I'll add anything you miss?"

Amy laughed. "I love a test. Okay. But first, who can tell me what a pronoun is?"

Johnson, Charlotte, and Dixon raised their hands, but Olivia yelled "He, she, or it!"

Amy ignored her. "Johnson, can you share what a pronoun is? Olivia, raise your hand next time."

"A pronoun," Johnson enunciated carefully, spitting a little on the "p," "is how you refer to something or someone when you are not referring to them by name. A chair's pronoun is 'it,' so you could say 'Can you pick up your chair and move *it* to the rug' instead of 'Can you pick up your chair and move the chair to the rug.' For people we use 'he' or 'she' instead of saying their names all the time, because it is a more efficient use of language."

"Correct," said Amy. "So, the pronoun 'they' can be used for a group of people, but it can also be used for one person, if you're not sure what pronouns that person uses, or if that person's gender isn't easily described as 'he' or 'she.' Bailey, how'd we do?"

My head was spinning. This might have been the most educational morning meeting of my entire life. Even though I was left with a million more questions than I started with. Meanwhile, a huge grin spread across Bailey's face as they said, "You got it! I'm nonbinary, so I go by 'they' because I'm not a boy *or* a girl."

I looked around to see what everyone else's reaction was. The other Annabelle was picking at something stuck to the sole of her shoe, shoulders hunched up around her ears. Sadie and Patrick were nodding like this was something they already knew about. Everyone else looked either confused or interested. Dixon was the only one with a Look on his face, like he was saying "yeah, right" on the inside.

What did my face look like? Probably more confused than Audrey, who always pretended to know the answers even if she didn't. Hopefully nicer than Dixon's. At least I was paying attention, unlike the other Annabelle. But honestly? I still didn't understand. Did Bailey mean that they were, like, born some kind of way that wasn't boy or girl? Or that they didn't feel like either? Did they feel like a little bit of both or nothing at all? Is that why I couldn't stop staring at them? But as these questions popped up in my head Bailey was still talking, so it was probably a good idea to shut myself up and listen.

It turns out that Bailey wasn't answering any of my burning inquiries. They were saying that they started going by they/them pronouns last year, and that a few of their friends in Seattle were nonbinary too, and then their turn was over.

As Felix started sharing, I realized: I hadn't thought of Bailey as "he" or "she" at all! My brain was like, oh you don't know that person's deal? Better go with "they" till you find out. And then I found out! And I was right! My brain is a genius sometimes. I mentally high-fived my brain and then wondered what it would feel like to physically high-five your brain. Probably sticky. Ew.

Anyway, sorry to Felix, but I did not listen to a word he said, and I also didn't hear what Audrey's goals for the school year were, but it was probably something ridiculous like "Build a garden on the roof" or "Memorize an entire Shakespeare play." Then it was back to Amy.

"Thanks, everyone. I'm so excited to get to know you all better during the year!" She twisted to the smart board to look at the schedule. "Okay, the first part of our day is math. We're going to—"

Before she could say more, Dixon cut her off, which usually would be okay because I love any excuse to avoid math, but I could tell from the impatient way he raised his hand that it wasn't going to be good.

"Quick question," he said. "Bailey, which bathroom are you going to use? I mean, I know you say you're not a binary or whatever, but on some level you really *are* a girl or a boy, so. Which one? Just so we know."

"What are you *talking* about?" yelled Olivia, before Bailey or Amy could respond. "Every classroom has its own one-person bathroom, and then there are one-person bathrooms outside the gym and the library and everything. You *know* this! You've been here almost as long as the rest of us!"

Usually teachers shut Olivia down when she starts calling out, but Amy looked amused. "That's true, Dixon, so there's no reason to worry. I'm sure Bailey appreciates your concern for their well-being."

"Yeah, thank you for your concern," said Bailey archly, one perfect eyebrow raised. "That was one of the reasons we decided that I should go to this school anyway, the public school only has one bathroom that isn't gender-segregated. And also, you obviously want to find out what I was assigned at birth, like whether I have an 'M' or 'F' on my birth certificate, but that's *so* none of your business. Sorry not sorry."

And just like that Bailey proved that they were the amazingest person ever. Not because of the gender thing, but because anyone who could make Dixon turn that shade of bright red was someone I needed in my life. But also, some guilt wormed its way through my stomach because I kind of had been wondering what Bailey was. I mean, I knew they were nonbinary, but like—and then my brain started yelling that it was rude of me to wonder, and that it wasn't any more my business than it was Dixon's, and I should probably shove all of those thoughts into a box and pay attention to the math lesson that had just started.

By the end of the period it had become impossible to imagine my new classroom without Bailey. My eyes kept wandering over to them; they already seemed familiar, but it was still exciting to see a new face.

After second grade we were allowed to eat anywhere in the classroom, not only at our desks. I weighed my options and decided on the corner that had bookshelves, a softer rug, and pillows. A few kids stayed at their desks, but everyone else spread out in that general area of the room.

"Olivia, your hair looks so good with that color," said Amanda, reaching out to stroke a lock dyed bright pink.

"Thanks, babe," said Olivia. Those two had switched between best friends and worst enemies for as long as I could remember.

"So, Bailey!" Audrey exclaimed. Her eyes were magnified behind her thick glasses, which matched her constant, aggressive curiosity. "It's so interesting to have someone new in our class! The last person to join was Dixon, and that was four years ago. There used to be more kids, but obviously people move away, go to other schools, you know. What was your old school like?"

"So far? Not too different from this one," they said, carefully peeling a string cheese with nimble fingers into the thinnest possible strands. "We had morning meeting, and our schedule looked a lot like yours. Small classes, except we always had two teachers. We also had a lot of groups! What kinds of things do you all have here?"

"What do you mean?" I asked. "We have library, and art, and gym, and . . . I don't know what else."

"I mean, what kinds of . . . I dunno, not-school things do you have? Clubs or whatever? Like, two years ago I started the Cool Animal Friends at my school. We met once a week at lunch and talked about whatever cool animals we learned about, like pygmy jerboas and slow lorises. And we had a bunch of after-school groups, a makerspace, a chess club. An affinity group for kids of color, of course. And I was also part of the Rainbow Club, for all the LGBTQIAP+ kids." There was a lopsided smile on their face, like some good memories were washing over them.

"Ell . . . gee . . . what?" asked Jonas, his brow furrowed.

"I know what LGBT stands for!" exclaimed Audrey. "Lesbian. Gay. Um . . . bystander? Transgender."

Bailey started laughing. "Bisexual! Not bystander. And then queer, intersex, ace, pan, and everything else in the rainbow."

We Lab lifers looked at each other, and all you could hear was chewing. That sounded so different from our school. Amanda was the only Black girl in our class, after Liana's family moved away two summers ago. And Felix was the only Latino kid. There was an Asian girl named Jamie who graduated last year, and teachers called Sadie "Jamie" more often than they should (which to be clear is never, and not only because Jamie is Vietnamese and Sadie is Korean). There were other kids of color, but they were either in younger grades or graduated earlier, and no one had ever talked about a group for them. And Audrey never let us forget that she was the only Jewish kid in the whole school.

And the way Bailey said "LGBT—" whatever, "kids." Like they knew lots of kids like that, and not only ones with two moms or two dads. Like that was something you could be. Something you could call yourself. Something that wasn't a big deal. Only something to have a Rainbow Club for. My stomach twisted in jealousy or anxiety or maybe something else. I stared at their shoes again, too overwhelmed to look anywhere else, and noticed for the first time that they weren't wearing socks. Their ankles looked like smooth, tan marble.

"We don't have anything like that," Patrick finally said

reluctantly. "Last year I wanted to get everyone to do a better job of recycling, and we even got a compost bin after I asked Principal Quinn, but I didn't form, like, a 'Green Club' or anything. Maybe I could, though!"

I wanted to hear more about the Rainbow Club but didn't want to be the one to ask about it. Patrick was onto something, though. "Could you?" I piped up, my face suddenly hot. "I don't know about you all, but I don't remember the first day of school being this hot. And remember last year when the forest fire smoke made the air all gross?" Everyone nodded solemnly. That had been bad. "Maybe there's something we can do."

I glanced over at Bailey. They were looking at me like I was someone worth looking at, and jumping started in my stomach like I had swallowed grasshoppers for lunch. "My old teachers always told me that we couldn't fix all the big problems in the world, but we could start by making things better in our community," they said. "Maybe we could do that here."

The last five minutes of lunch were more subdued than usual. It had been so long since we had a new kid, and I had never seen my school through someone else's eyes. It was a little uncomfortable.

I didn't want to think of myself as completely sheltered. We got a newspaper delivered to our front door; I read it sometimes, and when I had to ask my parents questions, they almost always answered. But it always seemed like the problems in the world only ever happened somewhere else, to other people. And that they had nothing to do with us. But maybe that wasn't true. Maybe my goal for the year would be more than getting it over with. When Amy rang the chime to signal the end of lunch, the room was already mostly quiet, all of us thinking our separate thoughts. The first day of school had never been so educational.

chapter 4

"**Honey,** I'm home!" I yelled as I walked into my empty house after school. That was a joke I picked up from my parents, who sometimes said it when one of them arrived home. I'm not sure if they also did it when the house was empty. That was probably a "me" thing.

My parents started letting me come home alone last year. At first it was kind of scary, and I spent hours planning what I would do if I had to run away from burglars (answer: Sneak into the garage and then out through the garage's back door, run like the wind), or if I lost my key and couldn't get in and the ancient cell phone my parents gave me was dead and it was snowing (answer: Go to a neighbor's house, or dig a fort and cover myself with leaves and pine needles).

When I was younger my parents staggered their work schedules so someone could get me from school, or they made sure I went home with a friend. Sometimes they would enroll me in after-school classes. But musical instruments were expensive and I didn't practice enough, I've never been into sports, and there isn't much else to do around here. So we decided as a family that ten years old was old enough to walk home alone, and spend a couple hours by myself while they were both at work. It made me feel very grown-up to be home alone, and know that I could do anything I wanted but mostly made good choices.

And sure enough, when Mom banged through the door and yelled "Honey, I'm home!" I was sitting at the kitchen table finishing our first assignment of the school year, a book report on any book we read over the summer, while eating a reasonable snack of several Oreos and a handful of cheddar bunnies.

She snagged one of my cheddar bunnies and popped it in her mouth. "How was the first day?"

"Good!" I said. "We have a new teacher, her name is Amy, and I like her a lot so far. Caroline probably would have been fine—millions of years of sixth graders survived—but Amy seems cool and nice. Question: Do you guys *ever* read emails from school? She said they told you there was a new teacher, but it was news to me."

Mom pursed her bright red lips. "I did get an email labeled 'Community News,' or something, but that's usually about book drives or asking for September Picnic volunteers, so I deleted it. It must have been in there. Sorry, cupcake." She opened up the pantry and started poking through it.

"That's okay, it was a cool surprise. And speaking of surprises!" I took a deep breath, a little nervous for no reason that I could figure out. "There's a new kid in my class! Their name is Bailey and they moved up here from Seattle." I had never called someone "they" before, but after literally one day of practice it was the easiest thing. I waited for Mom to ask me about it. She was looking in the pantry, but her body had stilled. I kept going. "They're so cool! You would LOVE their shoes. They're white with rainbows and things drawn on them, Bailey designed them themself!" I almost tripped up wondering whether I should say "themself" or "themselves" instead, but that second one sounded wrong so I went for the first one.

I stopped talking to give Mom a chance to respond. The next step was for her to ask about the pronoun and then I could explain that Bailey was nonbinary, and . . . and . . . I didn't know why, but the idea of talking about this stuff with her made me feel like my brain was full of fizzy soda. But Mom didn't ask me anything. Didn't say anything. The fizzing in my brain started to subside. Mom took something out of the pantry, moving with a strange gravity, then turned around. I looked at her face and it was calm. Too calm. Because there was nothing going on that she needed to be calm about. Nothing was wrong, so why did she have to *pretend* that nothing was wrong?

She was holding a package of ground corn, shifting it up and down so the fine meal ran through the bag in her hands in a stream. "That's great, sweetie. I hope the other kids are . . . well, I know how hard it can be to make new friends, especially in such a small class. Is everyone being nice?"

"Yeah! I mean, Dixon was kind of a jerk but Dixon is

always kind of a jerk, and Olivia stepped in and did her Olivia thing to get him to shut up."

"Good. How does chicken and polenta sound for dinner?"

"Fine! So long as there's cheese in the polenta. Anyway, Bailey was also saying that at their old school they had all sorts of cool clubs, for the students of color and a makerspace and a Rainbow Club, which I think has to do with . . . they said a bunch of letters, LGBT but then some, for kids who have two moms or two dads. Or kids who are nonbinary like Bailey. Or, you know, gay or lesbian or something." I rushed through the last part of that sentence double-quick, and I had already been talking even faster than usual. Sweat began to collect under my arms; my deodorant must have worn off. I was on the edge of my seat, literally, toes braced against the floor, waiting for Mom's response.

It was weird. Instead of asking me follow-up questions, like she usually did, Mom took off her glasses and rubbed the bridge of her nose. "Sweetie, I'm glad you had such a good first day, but I have a headache. I'm going to go lie down before dinner. Why don't you go play outside?"

All the air left my body in a rush. I almost told her that I was too old to "play outside" and she knew that, but stopped myself when I got a good look at her face. She was wearing a new expression. It didn't look like she had a headache, it looked like someone had died, and she was only now remembering. "Okay," I said. "Feel better." She poured herself a glass of water and walked heavily to her bedroom.

We had a little plot of vegetables in the backyard. Well,

mostly vegetables, with strawberries along the outside. So a vegetable garden with a fruit frame. I didn't like "playing outside" by myself, but knew it would make them (the plants and my parents) happy if I weeded, and it would make me happy if we had fresh strawberries in a bowl on the counter. As I worked I started to think about Bailey again, and how much I liked their nail polish, and how strong their fingers looked, and then shook that thought out of my head like a dog shaking water out of its coat. Thinking about Bailey's hands made my stomach hurt, kind of, in an unfamiliar, low-down sort of way.

I forced myself to think about starting a compost bin, so we didn't put so much food waste into the garbage, which then went to landfills, which then . . . well, I didn't know what happened when landfills ran out of space, but it was probably bad. After I finished pulling up weeds and piling ripe strawberries in the grass I filled up the big green watering can, even though it was my least favorite chore because water is the heaviest thing despite being clear. Then my brain went back to Bailey, specifically how nice their shirt looked on their shoulders, and how I had never noticed a person's collarbones before but theirs were distinctive, and then I replayed the birdlike lilt of their laugh in my memory, over and over and over. When I finally heard the familiar sound of Dad's truck in the driveway I dropped the watering can on the ground and ran around the side of the house, grateful for the distraction.

"Dad!" I said, almost tripping over my feet as I skidded to

a stop by the front door. He looked surprised; I usually didn't rush over to see him like a puppy that's been left alone all day. "Mom got home a while ago and I was telling her about my first day of school but she said she had a headache and had to go lie down. I'm not convinced it was a headache, but maybe you should go see if she's okay? Or maybe leave her alone, I'm not sure."

Dad narrowed his eyes. "Did she say anything was wrong?" he asked.

"No. Well, she *said* she had a headache, which is kind of something wrong? But also she looked upset, but she didn't tell me anything."

"Okay. Thanks for the heads-up," he said, his eyebrows meeting with concern, and went inside.

I thought maybe it was a good idea if I stayed outside until they called me in for dinner. If Mom really did have a headache Dad might cook instead, or we would order a pizza, but it was probably best if I let them figure it out. There was nothing left to do in the garden, so I went around the yard picking buttercups and clovers and arranged them in a pattern around my dead hamster's grave, or at least in the general area of the yard where I thought my dead hamster was buried. Nibbles died when I was seven, so the memory of his funeral wasn't exactly fresh. Then I remembered about clovers and looked for a four-leafed one, planning on giving it to Bailey as a "welcome to town, have some good luck" gift, when I heard Dad call "Annabelle! Dinner!"

I could have used a four-leafed clover myself. Mom's

headache didn't seem to have gone away. If it was a head-ache. But now both their faces looked tense and strange. Headaches weren't contagious, which proved that something else was wrong.

Mom and Dad talked about their days. She got some new contracts with local farmers. He helped people fix their Internet. Nothing unusual. Nothing half as interesting as my day. I kept waiting for them to ask me about it. My first day of sixth grade, my last first day of elementary school. But they both kept up the most boring conversation imaginable, punctuated by unnecessary details and some uncomfortable pauses. I sat there, spooning cheesy polenta into my mouth until our bowls were almost empty, and then I couldn't help myself anymore and blurted out, "What is wrong? And don't try and say 'nothing,' because something is obviously up."

They looked at each other, and clearly had a whole con-versation with their eyes. Finally Mom sighed with her whole body and said, "We heard from some of our old friends in Arizona. It wasn't good news. You don't need to worry, it's no one you know"—(I didn't know why she said that, they moved here when I was a newborn and I didn't know anyone from their time in Arizona)—"but your father and I are tak-ing it in."

"Oh. Did someone die?"

"No, sweetheart, no one died. It's . . . it's hard to explain. But we're fine, everything's fine. We just need some space tonight."

I glanced over at Dad. He was twisting his napkin in his hands, staring down at his lap. I could see his nostrils flare with each breath, and decided that pressing either of them for more information would be a bad idea.

"Okay. I'll clear the table. Can I watch TV?" I usually wasn't allowed to watch TV on a school night, but I had a hunch they'd say yes. I was right.

Mom usually puttered around the kitchen until late into the evening while Dad would watch the news, or work on whatever home improvement project he was in the middle of, varnishing an old cabinet or tinkering with a broken type-writer he found at a yard sale. But tonight they both went into the bedroom and shut the door. I heard them switch on their TV, but the low murmur of conversation told me that they weren't watching it.

Weird weird weird. But also, none of my business, I guessed. Whatever it was didn't sound like something I could help with.

Sometimes I wondered if my parents wished they had more help. It had always been just the three of us. No grand-parents, no aunts or uncles or cousins. Mom's parents died in a car accident when she was in college. She sometimes talked about them, and showed me pictures from when she was a little girl. Dad's parents were also dead, but he wasn't the type to pull out an old photo album, and I never asked. I had never seen a picture of my dad as a kid; all the pictures they had around the house were from after I was born. But somehow it was one of those things that I knew not to ask about. No one had to tell me, it was clear without anyone ever saying it.

Sometimes they'd mention bits and pieces of their lives before Tahoma Falls, before each other. But I had never heard about old friends from Arizona. They never talked about any; how can you be friends with people but you never visit and you never talk to them on the phone and never talk about them at all? That didn't make sense. But this was between my mom, my dad, and their past. I was their present and their future, so I decided to butt out.

chapter 5

On the second day of school, which was exactly as hot as the first, we came in from outdoor P.E. class sweaty and panting after a spirited game of freeze tag. It was apparent that we all mostly learned to use deodorant over the summer, except for the other Annabelle and Jonas. Hopefully they'd get the hint once no one wanted to sit next to them after gym.

I peeked at the schedule on the board. Social studies was next, which we usually had every day but skipped yesterday because the outplacement counselor came to talk to us about the applying-to-middle-school process. Not a big deal for me, since we had decided I'd go to the regular public school next year, but a bunch of my classmates looked anxious. They wanted to go to Snohomish Day School, in the next town over, which was competitive and didn't always take kids from the Lab.

Anyway, I liked social studies. We spent all last year on Washington State history, which included a lot of field trips to Seattle. Caroline usually taught the sixth graders about super-old places, like Greece and Rome, but I had a hunch that Amy might have something different up her sleeve.

Of course I was right. "All right, everyone, I'm going to be honest with you," she announced, as we all sat down at our desks. "As you probably know, the sixth graders usually do a whole ancient civilizations study. Mesopotamia, Greece, Rome, the whole deal. Caroline has been teaching it for years, if not decades, but didn't leave behind any notes. I literally got this job two weeks before the school year started, so I don't think I'll be able to re-create her year-long unit from scratch."

Audrey raised her hand. "Does that mean we won't be learning about ancient Greece this year? I reread all the Percy Jackson books in preparation."

"You would read those anyway!" Olivia called out. "I like the Jason ones, I have such a crush on him."

"Okay, but Magnus Chase?" Bailey added. "Alex Fierro is my hero."

Amy clapped her hands to get our attention. "Reading is never a waste of time, Audrey. But, yes, that's correct, I don't think we'll be doing a big ancient civilizations study like last year's sixth graders did."

"So what will we be doing?" asked Felix, the king of only asking questions that the teacher was about to answer anyway.

"I'm getting there!" Amy said, in an exasperated-but-good-natured voice. "I want to know what social studies topics you all think we should learn about this year. I checked in with Paul—I mean, Principal Quinn—and he said that it's fine if we don't follow Caroline's set curriculum so long as we cover, quote, 'topics related to human society that will help enrich and inform your understanding of the world.' That means we can learn about whatever you want, within reason."

Principal Quinn replaced our old Head of School, Carrie, five years ago. Before him everyone in our school, including teachers, went by their first names, but now it was a mix of first-name teachers who had been there for a long time, and last-name teachers who were mostly hired later—except for Amy, obviously.

Dixon's hand shot up. "I think we should keep the ancient civilizations study. After all, how are we supposed to understand anything about where we are now if we don't understand where we came from?"

"Not sure who you mean by 'we,'" said Amanda softly. Dixon either didn't hear her or decided to pretend that he didn't hear her.

"Hold on, people," said Amy. She dragged an easel out in front of the room, the kind with a big pad of sticky paper like a huge lined Post-it note. At the top she wrote "Social Studies Ideas" in that handwriting that looked exactly like every teacher's handwriting ever. Is that something you learn in teacher school? Not only perfect handwriting, but the exact same kind of perfect handwriting? Anyway, when she was done she looked around the room expectantly.

"Like I said, ancient civilizations," Dixon called out again. Amy shrugged and wrote it down, but I think the rest of us knew that was only to be fair.

"I want to learn about world religions," said Audrey, and Amy wrote that down too.

Sadie raised her hand. "Popcorn out your ideas," Amy encouraged. "If it gets out of control, we'll go back to hand-raising, but I think sixth-graders can handle a discussion without having to be called on."

"I was going to say that maybe we could learn about American history," Sadie said. "We don't cover anything except for a little bit about the Revolutionary War in fourth grade, and we talk about slavery and civil rights during Black History Month, but that's about it."

Amy wrote down "American history." "That was my major in college," she added as she was writing, "so I'd be happy to focus on that."

"I want to learn about climate change," I said. "Like, what's causing it, and what we can do to stop it." Patrick made a vigorous "me too!" gesture.

Amy muttered something that sounded like "capillism." I wasn't sure what that meant, but she wrote down "climate change" and then added an arrow that connected it to "American history."

"Immigration," said the other Annabelle. I looked at her in surprise, and I wasn't the only one, because that was a good, relevant, important idea and she wasn't exactly known for coming up with stuff like that. Amy nodded seriously and wrote it down, with another arrow pointing toward "American history."

"I want to learn about American history too," said Amanda, "but . . . I don't know how to explain it. My parents talk to me a lot about how you can't trust everything in books, and how they always leave out the important stuff. That's what I'm interested in."

Amy put an asterisk next to "American history." "What I'm hearing," she said slowly, "is that you all want to learn about the larger context we're living through. Dixon, you want to understand how our particular society developed. Sadie and Amanda, you do too, but from a different starting point and a different angle. Patrick, Audrey, and both Annabelles are all curious about particular themes, or strands, that affect us and our country. Does that sound about right?"

Nods all around. I didn't love being one of "both Annabelles," but the other one did have a good idea, so it was only fair.

"All right. I'll do some thinking about how we can structure the year. But now, the library is open, so let's head there as a group. I want each of you to check out one fiction book and one non-fiction book."

I sidled up next to Bailey on our way to the library. They walked like a strong gust of wind, like nothing could get in their way, and it gave me a little thrill to match my pace to theirs. "What was that series you mentioned?" I asked them. "The one by the Percy Jackson guy." I had read the Percy Jackson books and liked them a lot, but never picked up any of the others.

Their deep brown eyes lit up. "Magnus Chase! I love most fantasy books, but that series is my favorite. There's a gender-fluid character that I want to be when I grow up." We all filed into the library, a hushed room with flickering fluorescent lights and shelves that looked like they stretched up to the ceiling when I was little, but now were practically at eye-level.

I took them over to the Percy Jackson section. I mean, there were other books there too, obviously, but I figured that's where more adventure books would be. Audrey was standing nearby grumbling a bit about how all her preparation was for nothing. "Here, read this," said Bailey, pulling a book off the shelf and putting it in her hand. "It's about this girl whose best friend is a pelesit, this evil ghost that gets jealous of her for making a new friend."

"Ooh, cool!" Audrey exclaimed, and sat down at a table to read.

Bailey then pulled out a thick book with a blond teenage boy on the front. "Here you go, the first book in the fourth series. Magnus Chase. You don't meet the genderfluid character until the next one." They plopped the book into my outstretched hands, and I know you're not supposed to judge a book by its cover but in addition to the boy I assumed was Magnus it had a flaming sword against a creepy-looking tree, so I was sold.

I decided to grab the second book so I'd be ready, and Bailey looked proud. I flushed with pleasure and immediately started plotting how to get them to smile at me like that again.

Johnson's dad was volunteering in the library that day, so he buzzed around helping kids find their own books, suggesting non-fiction topics since Amy said we had to. I had picked one on Norse mythology, because it has the word "ology" in it, which meant it counted as non-fiction, to go along with the Magnus book.

The library didn't have to be a quiet place. When we were little we ran around and fought over pop-up books and Where's Waldo?, but today, as everyone found their books and sat down, a hush fell over the room. Sadie joined me and Bailey at our table and we all become absorbed in our books, each of us wrapped up in our own worlds.

The next day I got to class early, waited by the door, and the second Bailey walked in I pounced on them. They looked amazing again, in red Converse sneakers, green shorts, and a white shirt with daisies on it that perfectly matched my sunflower-yellow dress. That had to mean something good. "Bailey! You were right, this series is amazing, I'm *obsessed* with Alex Fierro and also Samirah and the dwarf and the elf and also obviously Magnus. Thank you so much for getting me to read them!"

They looked shocked. "Wait, you're already on the second one? Didn't you take them out yesterday? Those books are a million pages long."

I ducked my head. "Well, I'm halfway through the first one. And I peeked ahead in the second book and read some of the parts with Alex—I love her. It's just, there wasn't much to do last night, so I sat on our porch and read for a few hours. It's such a 'fast-paced' story," I said, putting air quotes around "fast-paced" because that sounded like something a commercial would say, "that it was impossible *not* to get sucked in. The pages practically flipped themselves."

I sounded like a movie announcer or an overeager librarian because I didn't want to mention that it had been another strange night at home. I made myself finish my homework before starting to read, more excited that Bailey suggested it than the story itself. But it turned out to be really good. When Mom got home I told her about the book, and that Bailey had recommended the series because there was a genderfluid character, and how awesome was that? But then Mom looked weird and sick, again, and said I could keep reading as long as I wanted and she would put dinner together. Then Dad came home, and before I could tell him what I was reading, Mom rushed onto the porch, wearing her frilly apron that would look fancy if it wasn't always covered with grease stains, and asked if he would help her with something in the kitchen. I kept my eyes focused on the book but could tell there was something else going on and I should let them be. Dad spent dinner telling us about the different clients he visited that day and the strange things he saw in their houses, not letting me say *anything* about my day, and I spent the whole meal chafing with discomfort. Keeping so much inside was almost physically painful. Did being in middle school, or close enough, mean that you always wanted to explode around your parents? I hoped not.

Anyway, by lunchtime I was done with the first Magnus Chase book because before lunch we had sustained silent reading. I bolted down my sandwich and string cheese and asked Amy if I could go to the library to get book number three, so I wouldn't have to wait once I finished number two.

"Can I go with her?" Bailey asked. "I'm almost done with mine too." I caught a glimpse of where their bookmark was and they weren't being entirely honest about that. They were coming up with an excuse to spend more time with me! I squirmed with excitement.

"Sure, but come right back when you're done," Amy said.

An incredible plan hatched in my brain as we strolled to the library, chatting about which mythological creature we'd most like to hang out with (I voted for a jackalope because they seemed cute, and Bailey decided on a friendly were-wolf). I practiced what I wanted to say while Bailey browsed. They eventually got a graphic novel about a boy starting at a new school, and I exchanged book one for book three, and we started back toward the classroom. "Hey, do you want to come over after school today?" I asked all in a rush, then held my breath waiting for their reply.

"I'd love to!" they exclaimed, and tiny, sparkly explosions went off in every part of my body. "I haven't been over to anyone's house since we moved here."

I swept a slightly trembling arm in front of me in a courtly bow (even though I was wearing a dress and could have curtsied, a bow was clearly the right choice for that moment). "Well then, I shall be the first to welcome you to the amazing destination that is . . . uh . . . my house."

The last couple hours of school were the longest hours of my entire life. Bailey. With the smile, and the laugh, and the hands, and the everything. Was coming to my house. I wondered if they were going to be my new best friend. If that's why I felt the way I felt. I pictured the two of us walking home together and in my mind's eye we were cast in this golden-yellow tone, like we had our own private sun hovering right above the horizon. It made me shiver, even though every part of me was warm.

chapter 6

I should talk about the thing that happened last year. See, it's Lab tradition for the fifth graders to go on an end-of-the-year field trip to the roller-skating rink. The first few times around the rink I was a wobbly mess, but I eventually got the hang of it and mostly stuck with Franka and Sadie. But then the DJ put on a slow song, the lights dimmed, and before I realized that anything different was happening, boys and girls were holding hands and skating in lazy circles, heads turned to each other, talking quietly.

I went to the bathroom. And stayed there until I heard the Chicken Dance song come on.

Because who was I going to hold hands with? Dixon? Barf. Johnson? I like him, but couldn't imagine *like*-liking him. Patrick has nice hair and nice eyes, but that wasn't a reason to put my sweaty hand in his sweaty hand, ew. I knew that girls could hold hands with girls, in a boy-girl way if that makes sense (I don't think that makes sense), but when I held hands with my friends it didn't feel like anything special.

I knew, instinctively, that this was different. And I didn't want to stand off to the side, by myself, and have people wonder why.

The next day all the girls were buzzing about who they got to hold hands with, and the boys were all in little clumps, giggling and looking over their shoulders. Something had changed, for everyone but me.

But as Bailey and I walked to my house, I thought back to the roller rink and wondered again what everyone else had felt last year. If it was like looking at someone, and *wanting* something from them. Like being a rough piece of wood and they're a piece of sandpaper. Or like you're a cold hand and they're a blast of hot air.

Probably not. This must be something else, like new-friend energy. I hadn't made a new friend in a long time. Anyway, I didn't think this was the sort of thing you were supposed to say to another person. Especially someone I couldn't like in a boy-girl way, because they weren't a boy. So as we walked along the sidewalk, instead of babbling about my feelings, I pointed out every landmark that had been a scene of triumph or tragedy throughout my life.

"And *that's* the tree I threw up on one Halloween when I ate every piece of candy I got instead of putting it in my pillowcase. Sometimes I apologize to it when I walk by. Sorry, tree!"

"How do you know its name is Tree?" Bailey pointed out. "Maybe it goes by Doug or Greenling or Spidery or something."

"Hmm, well, I've never asked. That's rude of me, oops. But, I bet that if trees did have names, they would be some whooshy sound that we can't even pronounce."

"Ah, good point," said Bailey. "She's sorry, Wsshhh-wshhhhwshhhh!" they yelled in that tree's direction, and I giggled. We stopped by the Circle K for some snacks (pretzels for me, a doughnut for them), and soon we were at my house.

In third grade I read some of the Boxcar Children books, and spent the next several months pretending that I lived in a boxcar. My house kind of looked like one—a small, compact rectangle, like a shoebox placed in the middle of some grass and trees. The two bedrooms were at one end, and a short hallway with a tiny bathroom led to the living room and kitchen. It used to seem so big to me, or at least normal sized, but now it felt like I could stand in the center, stretch out my arms, and touch my parents' room and the front door at the same time. But it was also surrounded by trees and flowers and snakes that wriggled through the grass and squirrels chasing each other in the trees. Not as exciting as a busy city street lined with brunch places and souvenir shops, but it was home.

First stop was my room. I panicked briefly before opening the door, half "Did I leave any dirty underwear on the floor?" and half "Will they like my posters?" But my room was tidy, they squealed over my posters of cute animals, and pointed out the ones they'd talked about in Cool Animal Friends at their old school. We had a brief but spirited debate over which was more adorable, sugar gliders or pygmy marmosets, and then we got ourselves glasses of iced tea and went into the backyard to look at the garden.

"I used to pretend I was a farm girl," they said, crunching on a sugar snap pea. "We didn't have a garden in Seattle, but sometimes on hikes we'd find patches of huckleberries or blackberries or whatever. Back when I used to wear dresses, I would, like, hold on to the bottom of it so I could put berries into it, instead of a bag or a jar or something. Every dress I had was covered in purple stains."

"Oh! Were you a—did you used to be—I mean, I wasn't sure which—not that I was wondering but—"

I stopped myself. They had answered the question I had tried not to ask myself the day we met, a question that I knew was rude but wondered about anyway. I should have pretended like nothing happened, like it was just a normal thing to learn about a new friend, a normal conversation topic, but I had to go ahead and turn it into a whole thing.

I forged ahead. Maybe if I pretended like nothing had happened, they would too. But from the look on Bailey's face, I knew it was too late.

"Um, I used to pick huckleberries too, but there aren't as many of them! Our science teacher said it's because there are fewer pollinators around. Not good. Right?"

They shook their head. "No, not good." An awkward silence fell. Why did I have to say anything? Why couldn't I have been cool about it? I tried desperately to think of more to say about pollinators, but my face must have been telling a different story, because Bailey sighed. I wanted to throw up.

"Annabelle. It's okay." They didn't seem mad. But something in their eyes looked far away.

"What? What's okay? Fewer bees?" I asked nervously. I couldn't stand it if they were mad at me.

Bailey plopped down right into the dirt, their face dappled with sunlight and shadow. I hesitated for a second, then joined them among the vines. "It's okay that you're curious. But . . ." They picked a twig off the ground. I was briefly distracted watching their long fingers delicately peel away a layer of bark, but snapped to attention when they asked, "Do you know a lot of people who identify as trans or queer or whatever? It's okay if you don't, I just want a better idea of how much I need to explain versus how much you might know already."

I ripped a leaf off the vine nearest me, and slowly shredded it down its veins. My short, stubby fingers were nothing like theirs. "Well. The answer is somewhere in between 'so many!' and 'like two or three, maybe.' There used to be kids in my class who had two moms or two dads. But the last family like that left after fourth grade. They moved to Seattle, actually. And also I don't go around asking random people 'Excuse me, are you part of the LGBT-whatever community?' So maybe I've met a lot and don't know it, but that probably doesn't count as knowing them, you know?"

I wondered if there was a word to describe me. Someone who didn't like boys, but didn't like girls either. It was bad enough not being able to keep those letters straight, let alone not knowing if there was one for me. I kept my eyes on the leaf.

Bailey dropped the twig, now stripped bare, and dug their fingers into some loose dirt. It was a warm day, and the soil was dry and crumbly. "Okay. So I was assigned female at birth, which is also called AFAB, which means that my parents guessed that I was a girl, but they have tons of queer and trans friends, so they never made too big a deal of it. For as long as I can remember I knew that my gender could be whatever I wanted it to be. So when I told them I was more nonbinary, and that they should use 'they' instead of 'she,' they went with it. I'm one of the lucky ones. Privileged, I guess. Sometimes I go—or at least, used to go—to a support group for trans kids, and a lot of them are staying with friends or homeless."

Something twisted in my stomach. That would never happen to me. Right? My parents loved me. I flopped back onto the ground, not caring that there would be dirt in my hair. "Gosh," I said. The sun was in my eyes, so I shut them tight, feeling the earth spinning beneath me.

I lay there thinking, for probably too long, but when a bee buzzed by my face, I waved it away and sat up. "Thank you for explaining. I don't want to keep treating you like an information vending machine, so how about if now we talk about ourselves in a normal way, and maybe if you know of any books or whatever about being trans, you could tell me about them, and also I'll keep this to myself unless you want me to tell other people?"

"Sounds good! Please keep it to yourself, mostly because I don't want Dixon to think he got something out of me."

I laughed, and promised, and we continued to hang out in my yard. We practiced cartwheels and headstands, and when they helped me up into a handstand their hands around my ankles were strong and warm and confident, and the slight squeeze they gave before letting go ricocheted all over my body. When I toppled over, they caught me and set me gently back down. I sternly told myself to stop noticing things like that, but clearly noticed anyway.

An hour or so later we were looking for a snake that had slithered into some bushes when Mom's baby-blue sedan purred into the driveway. We ran over. "Mom!" I exclaimed. "This is Bailey! That new kid I've been telling you about?"

"You've only known me for three days," Bailey teased. "What could you possibly have told her about me?"

"Your shoes, mostly," I said, pointing them out to Mom. "Aren't these exactly as cool as I promised?"

Mom had slammed her car door shut and was leaning against it. She looked tired, as always, but there was a tight-ness around her mouth, cracking her red lipstick. Normally she greeted my friends, even new ones, with a hug, but her hands were busy digging through her purse.

"Bailey, it's nice to meet you," she said. Her normally musical voice had a flat note behind it. "Your shoes are so creative, did Annabelle say you made them yourself?"

"Yeah! Well, I mean, I didn't sew them together, I don't know how people *make* shoes, like cobblers or whatever, but I decorated them myself."

"Very nice." She paused. "It's getting late, Bailey, your parents must be expecting you home soon. And I'm hoping they know where you are? My darling child didn't mention your visit"—she shot a look at me, not playfully stern, but something I couldn't read, and I squirmed until she moved her eyes away from mine—"so I'm hoping no one thinks you've been kidnapped."

"No worries, Mrs. Blake, I texted them after school. My dad said to call when we were done and he would come pick me up." There was a hesitance in their voice that I hadn't heard before.

"You can call me Hannah. We're going to be having dinner soon, so it's probably best if you call your dad now." She stopped short, struggling with something, and I hugged my arms to myself. When Sadie or Amanda came over after school she'd usually invite them to stay for dinner, or offer to drive them home, or at least generally treat them like my friend. I couldn't figure out why she was being so rude.

And then it got worse.

"Annabelle, here's an idea," Mom said in a rush. "Instead of having Bailey's dad drive all the way over here, why don't you walk with Bailey in that direction? You can meet him halfway."

"I guess?" I said uncertainly. She didn't even know where they lived, why was she acting like it was hours away? I wanted to ask why we couldn't wait here for Bailey to get picked up, it was a perfectly normal and reasonable thing to do, but Mom had started rummaging in her purse again, not meeting my eyes. Bailey got out their phone gingerly, looking uncertain.

I hugged myself tighter. Maybe there was a good reason for all this. Maybe she got more bad news about their old Arizona friends and wasn't up for entertaining. But before I could say anything, Dad's battered brick-red pickup pulled into the driveway. Mom closed her eyes, and I saw her chest rise and fall with a deep breath. My heart sank, but I didn't know why.

Dad walked over to where the three of us were standing. He looked at Bailey, from their hair to their shoes and back again, and crossed his arms. "Who's this?"

Bailey stuck out their hand. "Hi, Mr. Blake, I'm Bailey! It's nice to meet you."

Dad extended one hand for the quickest handshake in the world, then went back to holding his elbows. He didn't say to call him Mike. He didn't say *anything*, and I squirmed.

"This is our daughter's new friend," Mom said carefully. And I realized that, given how weird he and Mom had been acting lately, I hadn't told Dad anything about Bailey. Only Mom. She must have told him.

"Yeah, Bailey started at the Lab this year! They moved up here from Seattle, and their parents want to make friends in Tahoma too. Maybe we could have them over for dinner sometime. Bailey, are you guys vegetarian or anything?" I was chattering to fill what would otherwise be an awful silence.

"I'm mostly vegetarian," they said. "My parents aren't, but I like animals too much to eat them. We usually try to eat organic but aren't too strict about it, and dairy and gluten and everything else is fine." They didn't sound excited by the idea of coming over for dinner, though, maybe because my mom and dad were acting as if I'd invited over a family of mostly organic and vegetarian hyenas.

"You should go home," Dad said curtly. "Time for Annabelle to do her homework."

We didn't have any homework that day, but neither one of us was going to tell them. Bailey stared down at their phone, typing away. "My dad will come get me," they said. "Probably like fifteen minutes?" They looked uneasy. I was too.

"We'll wait out here," I said. "I'll come in after." Dad jerked his shoulders in a motion I couldn't interpret, and brushed past us into the house.

I turned back to Mom, hoping she would say something to make it better. Maybe she and Dad had talked earlier and he had had a hard day at work. I hadn't done anything wrong, and they didn't even know Bailey, so it wasn't our fault they were being like this. But Mom said, "Bailey, it was nice to meet you. Annabelle, you can give Bailey's father our address.

Come inside once your friend has been picked up." She followed my dad into the house, her steps slower than usual.

And then it was the two of us again. We slowly wandered over to the edge of the driveway. My heart was racing like when we were chasing that snake. "I'm so sorry. My dad is sometimes a grouch, but my mom is *never* like that, I have no idea what's going on but that was SO rude and I'm so so so sorry." I wanted to apologize over and over again, but they stopped me.

"What did you tell your parents about me?" they asked. They were squeezing the fingers of their left hand with the fingers on their right, thumb to pinky and then pinky back to thumb.

I scrunched up my face, scanning my memory. "Not much. That first day I told Mom that there was a new kid named Bailey, you had cool shoes, and you moved here from Seattle. But I didn't know much more about you, so there wasn't anything else I could say."

"Did you tell them I was nonbinary?"

I mentally replayed as many of the details of the conversation as I could. "I don't think so? I mean, I know I used the right pronouns for you. And I kept waiting for Mom to ask what that meant, but she didn't. And then . . . well, they've been acting different these last few days. Mom said it had something to do with friends they had from before they moved here, back in Arizona, but she wouldn't tell me what. And Dad has barely talked to me. I didn't tell him anything about you, at all, but my mom must have." I remembered Mom and her sudden headache that first day. When she stopped me from telling Dad about the Magnus Chase book. I didn't want to think this sudden, strange behavior had anything to do with Bailey. But a sick thrum in my stomach told me that it did.

"Huh." They lowered their voice to an anxious whisper. "Do you think . . . I mean, I'm sorry to even ask this, but do you think they're transphobic or nonbinary-phobic or whatever? Because it honestly seems like your dad decided to hate me for no reason."

I wanted to leap to their defense. To say, no way, my parents aren't transphobic or nonbinaryist or anything. But I couldn't.

I mean, I didn't know that they *were*. They never said anything specifically *against* gay or trans people. But they had also never talked about it, at all. Like, not once. Not even when there was something in the news. Or on TV. Sometimes in the checkout line I'd read the headlines of those celebrity magazines, and one time I asked my dad what a "Sex Change Shocker" was. He literally didn't say a single word until we were in the car, halfway home, and then all he said was "That's not for you to know about." And when I first started at the Lab, this one girl, Lily, had two moms. I remember asking my parents how that worked, where Lily came from, and Dad shrugged while Mom said something about respecting people's privacy, and we never talked about it again.

This is why I had never told them. About me, about

that roller-skating trip, about questioning who I might have crushes on, boys or girls or no one at all. Because I had no. Idea. How. They. Felt. But I did know they were avoiding the topic. And I knew that you didn't avoid topics if you didn't have a problem with them. So in a way, I already had my answer.

I took a deep breath, my chest tight. "Bailey, I'm so sorry." They scuffed at the dirt with a toe of their sneaker, and I started to cry. Quietly, so my parents wouldn't hear, but my tears darkened the ground around my feet.

Bailey typed something on their phone, which was a basic one like mine but covered in rhinestones. Together we walked out to the center of the yard, then stretched out on the grass. We looked for shapes in the clouds, neither of us wanting to talk about anything closer to home, until their dad pulled up. I waved at him, and he leaned out the window saying something about how happy he was to meet his kid's new friend, how I'd have to come over to their house soon. Bailey hugged me, and I didn't want to let go, they felt so sturdy and warm. But I had to. They got into the car, their dad drove away, and I tried to pull myself together enough to face my parents.

I had expected, maybe hoped for, another strange dinner where they talked about basically nothing and I didn't say anything. But no sooner had I sat down at the table, heart pounding rapidly, than Dad got going.

"That's your new friend?" he asked bluntly.

I nodded and speared a green bean on the end of my fork.

"Don't think that's good for you. The kid is obviously

confused about something." I gripped my fork until it hurt. The truth was coming out, and I hated it.

"Bailey's not confused," I said, in a small voice I barely recognized. I looked at Mom, wanting her to make this better somehow, but she was carefully twirling a strand of spaghetti around a single tine of her fork. "They're just nonbinary," I added, interrupting Dad, who had opened his mouth to respond. My voice grew stronger as I continued. "It's something they've known since they were little, and it's not even a big deal."

Dad snorted. "What is it with this 'they' crap? If Bailey knew that . . . if Bailey was actually transgender, Bailey would want to be a boy. He would know, without a doubt, that he was a boy, and he wouldn't want anyone to know otherwise. With those shoes, that nail polish, that kid clearly doesn't want to be a boy. She should stick to being a girl."

"Bailey ISN'T a boy!" I yelled, throwing my fork onto my plate. Green beans scattered everywhere. "They're not a girl, either. They're just Bailey, I don't get why you're being such a jerk about it! Are you . . . are you transphobic or something? Why do you have a problem with them being nonbinary?"

Dad slammed his fists on the table, and I jumped. Mom had her head in her hands; she wouldn't look at either of us but I saw a drop of water fall onto her plate. She was crying.

"Mom? What's wrong?" I asked, distracted for a second. She shook her head, pushed back from the table, and rushed toward their bedroom.

"Now you've upset your mother," Dad snapped.

"*Excuse* me? *You* are the one who was awful to my friend, and now you're saying terrible things about them and saying they're not good for me, nothing about this is my fault!" Dinner was clearly over. No one was going to eat now. I cleared the table noisily, resisting the urge to spill Dad's plate of spaghetti into his lap. What I really wanted was to hurl all the plates and glasses into the wall, the muscles in my arms burning to do something dramatic, but I didn't know how to come back from that. Dad didn't move, and the pressure in the kitchen grew until I wanted to scream it away.

I was furiously washing the pasta pot, rage and fear and terror and anger and other synonyms for those feelings rushing through my body as the hot water washed over my hands, when Dad finally got up from the table. He came around to lean against the counter, and I braced myself for him to say something else terrible. I had never yelled at him like that before. I had no plan for what would happen next.

"Look, Banana," he said. My shoulders were hunched up around my ears. "I know you think I'm being closed-minded. But I promise, all I've ever wanted, since the day you were born, is to keep you safe. Bailey's choices are going to make . . . their . . . life so much harder. The world can be a cruel place, especially for people who are different, and right now Bailey doesn't understand what this means for the rest of their life. I don't—" he swallowed, like he was fighting to keep something at bay. "I don't want you to get any wrong ideas from them. Ideas that might make your life harder too."

At least he was using the right pronouns. My shoulders

eased down, just a bit. And the shrieking in my head was quieting to a grouchy mutter. But nothing he was saying made sense. "I'm not going to get any wrong ideas. And Bailey is fine." I paused, then added, shakily, "They even know people who are homeless or whatever because of their gender, but their mom and dad are totally cool with it." Now was his chance, to tell me that he loved me no matter what, that it was horrible that some kids suffered because their parents didn't accept them. But he shook his head, and shook me with it.

"Bailey is too young to make this kind of decision. And I don't want my daughter getting mixed up in things she's not ready for."

I dried my trembling hands on a dish towel without turning around. "Dad. I'm in the sixth grade now. I'm not a little kid anymore. You don't have anything to worry about."

His voice lightened with what might have been a smile. "I'm your dad. It's my job to worry. Been doing it since before you were born, and I'll do it till the day I die. Get used to it."

I got my face under control and turned around. He looked like my dad, but somehow unfamiliar. No longer safe. He hugged me, and I put my arms around him. Stiffly. Cautiously. Like we were strangers now, but I was the only one who knew it.

chapter 7

The next morning felt broken. Mom and Dad drank their coffee silently. I crunched a bowl of cereal but couldn't taste a thing. We moved around each other like the floor was covered in shards of glass and any misstep would slice us open. I hitched my backpack onto my shoulders and left without saying goodbye. For the first few blocks there was nothing inside me—no words, no feelings, just empty and still and calm. But then Bailey's face floated into my mind, the hurt look on their face while we waited for their dad. And the sound of my father's voice, not even his words, but the nasal pitch he got when he was upset. And my mom, how I usually loved how solid she was, but how last night she seemed like a block of stone, unable to move in any direction. Before I knew it I was outside my classroom door, and Bailey was walking up to it looking so nervous that all I wanted was to put my arms around them. But I kept my hands to myself.

"Bailey, I'm so sorry. We got into a huge fight last night, I told my dad that it wasn't okay to be so awful to you. He kind of apologized? And at first he called you 'he,' and 'she,' but then he started calling you 'they.' That's something, right?"

My voice sounded calm but my insides were curdled. I hated this. Hated knowing that Bailey wasn't safe around my parents. That I might not be, either. That if they found out I . . . I blinked, hard, and turned back to Bailey. Couldn't think about that right now.

"Thank you for standing up for me," they said, not quite meeting my eyes. "I'm sorry you had to."

"It's not your fault." Really, really not. "Do you still—I mean, are you mad at me?"

Their warm, beautiful eyes locked onto mine. "Of course not," they said. "Your parents aren't your fault. But I don't think I want to hang out at your house again."

"Oh. Yeah," I said, and I had never been punched in the stomach before but got an idea of what it must feel like. I also didn't want to be in a house with people who hated me for no good reason. So I couldn't blame them.

"But you can come over to mine!" they went on. "I decided not to tell my parents what happened. They worry enough about me without having to learn that my first good friend in Tahoma Falls has transphobic parents."

Equal parts fire and ice rushed through my whole body. Fire, like blushing warmth that Bailey called me their first good friend. Ice, because there was no way around what we had learned about my mom and dad.

Amy chimed the bell, we went to our seats, and the boiling within me settled to a gentle steam as the familiarity of my surroundings washed over me. For once I was grateful that this place, at least, hadn't changed. Now that it was the fourth day of school we had mostly settled into a rhythm. Math was math. Then we went to the art studio, a brightly-lit basement room crowded with origami paper and scraps of fabric and weird scissors and every kind of glue imaginable, and started working on different projects. After art, Amy gave us a reading assessment. It didn't feel like we were big important sixth graders; it was school, again, same as always.

For most of the day my brain was back home, churning through what happened the previous night. Even during lunch I was quiet. I just ate my sandwich and half listened to everyone else talk.

We had all gathered in the library corner again, and a couple people, mainly Olivia and Patrick, noticed that I wasn't talking as much as usual. But every time they started to ask me what was wrong, Bailey would distract them with some question about what happens at the Lab, the field trips we go on and what graduation looks like, that sort of thing. They didn't know all the reasons why I was keeping to myself, but they could tell that it wouldn't be good for my classmates to grill me for details. Once they even leaned against me, briefly, and for the next few minutes I forgot about my fear and anger because all I could think about was how nice their arm felt against mine.

Sometimes the hours after lunch stretched on for a thousand sleepy years, the second hand clicking forward so slowly I would wonder if it was broken. But today, when I didn't want to go home, the minutes raced by, and before I was ready it was three-thirty, we were packing up our bags, and I wished desperately that I was in some afterschool club.

I slowly zipped up my backpack, one tooth at a time. Amy gave me a funny look; I usually threw my stuff together and skipped out, but she didn't ask why I was taking my time today. Outside the door Bailey and I hugged before going our separate ways, and I inhaled their orange-slice scent. "Good luck," they said.

"Thanks." They headed off, and I planned out what my afternoon would look like. I decided to walk home as slowly as possible, maybe climbing some trees along the way since I was wearing leggings under my skirt, stopping to smell whatever flowers I happened to pass. Every dog I passed needed to be petted. I wanted to put off seeing my parents for as long as possible.

But I stopped in my tracks when I reached the driveway to my house. Both of their cars were there. And they were making that ticking sound, which meant they were cooling down after being driven. My parents must have just gotten home. At the same time. This never happened.

I opened the front door slowly. They weren't in the kitchen, or sitting on the couch. But the door to their bedroom was closed, and the light was shining through underneath.

I tiptoed over, not even breathing. You can tell so much from the tone of someone's voice. From how much one person talks and the other listens. The way quieter words are uttered in the midst of lengthy pauses.

My mom sounded low, and calming, and soothing. It was her "I promise everything is going to be okay" voice.

My dad, though. I had never heard him like this before. He usually spoke in short, clipped sentences, not the tumble of frightened words spilling through their bedroom door. But now his words started low, then got higher and louder. I knew that if they caught me listening I'd get in big trouble, but we were all already in trouble. I put my ear against the door, careful not to make a sound.

"If this gets out," I caught, and "had to leave it all behind." Then Mom broke in, whatever she was murmuring calming him down, and then he made noises that I'm almost sure were "I know, I know."

And then: "We have to tell her." That was my mom.

"I don't know how." My dad.

Pause. Then, "She'll be home soon." My mom.

A wiser daughter than I would sneak away and then make a big show of coming home noisily. But I have never been that daughter, so I hollered, "I'm home now!"

A shocked silence, then feet pounded toward the door and it was flung open. My parents stared at me, and then at each other, and made a decision.

"Get in the truck, Bananabelle," my dad said. "We're going for a drive."

chapter 8

You hungry?" he asked as we sped toward the highway, my hands gripping the shoulder strap of my seat belt. I nodded, so he stopped by a gas station. While he filled the tank I ran in and got a plastic-wrapped chocolate croissant and a can of ginger ale. Once we were moving again I took a bite and made a face. "Ick. This is like wet paper towels around a melted Hershey's Kiss."

He chuckled. "Did you expect fine French pastry?"

"Well, I knew it wasn't going to be good, but I was hoping for something slightly better than a wad of used Kleenex."

He shook his head, smiling, and I turned to look out the window. A little bit of tension drained out of my body. Maybe we would be okay. He was my dad. Whatever it was, we had to be okay.

Twenty wordless minutes later I asked him where we were going. "Are you taking me to a watery grave or something?" I joked, hoping I hid the nervousness in my voice.

"Something like that." He had gotten off the freeway and we trundled along through a suburb that I had never been in before. Then we pulled into a parking lot, and it turns out I had been kind of right. About the watery part, not the grave part. We were at a lake.

Was this an attempt at father-daughter bonding? Him explaining, again, why the coolest person I'd ever met was somehow going to make my life worse? We were so far from home that if I lost my temper and started yelling at him we'd be in for the most terrible car ride home imaginable. I started planning what I would do if that happened, maybe call Bailey and see if their parents could come get me. But even then I'd have to go home eventually, right? It was probably for the best if I kept my cool no matter what he said, but I wasn't sure if I could. My whole body was coiled like a spring.

We were at a trailhead, and the rough map at the edge of the parking lot indicated that the path looped around the lake. We started walking, and I picked a few lingering huckleberries off a bush to get the sour taste of gas station croissant out of my mouth. There were some ripe blackberries too, still hanging plump on the vine, and I gathered a few. Dad selected one from my palm and tossed it into his mouth, and we both smiled. I took a deep breath for what felt like the first time in days.

A few bees bumbled along, and I wondered if they were more likely to live around a lake than in our neighborhood, and thought about looking into what kinds of plants could attract them to our garden. Before I could bring that up as a not-terrible topic of conversation/distraction Dad cleared his throat.

"I don't know how to tell you this," he said abruptly. "I

don't want to. I've never wanted to. But now I have to. So you understand. I'm not perfect, and have only ever wanted the best for you, but sometimes I let my own fears get in the way of that. And while I still think I'm right, your mother has convinced me that that's what's happened here. And that it's something we need to talk about. Because this issue isn't going away. You're only getting older, meeting more people."

" . . . Okay," I said, uncertainly. I had no idea what he was talking about. Bailey, obviously, that whole situation, but this sounded like the start of something else.

He took a deep breath and words spilled out of him, like a dam reluctantly breaking open into a choppy river. "There's no easy way to explain this. I don't know how. So the only way is to say it. I'm your father. I'm transgender. And your mother didn't give birth to you. I did."

I stopped dead in my tracks, the huckleberries spilling out of my palm. My dad is transgender? He wants to transition, so I'd have two moms? That would be cool, I guess, but why was he—

But then the second part of what he said hit me. That my mom didn't give birth to me. That he did. That meant . . .

"You're trans?!" I exclaimed, the truth dropping on me like a weight. Or freeing me like a balloon. Somehow both, at the same time. I started laughing in relief.

But Dad winced, whipped his head around to make sure no one was nearby, and I realized why he picked this empty trail to tell me. He wanted to keep it a secret. Had been keeping it a secret, and wanted it to stay that way. I knew a little something about that.

But this was different. I was bubbling over with questions, and they poured out of me in an impossible rush. "How long have you—I mean, when did you—I mean, so you were pregnant with me?? Why didn't Mom—wait, were you going to be my other mom and then—that's why I look more like you than Mom? Is Mom—" I could have kept going forever, never finishing an entire question, but Dad held up his palm and I let the bubbles pop. Sometimes too many questions made him clam up, and now of all times that couldn't happen.

"We are going to walk once around this lake. It's about two miles. I'll tell you about it. And answer your questions. When we get back to the truck, we will be done with this discussion. Is that clear?"

I nodded immediately, even though there was absolutely no way that this was going to be a one-time conversation. But if I didn't agree he wouldn't tell me anything right now, and maybe not for a while, and I would die of curiosity before then.

"Okay," he said, and took a deep breath. He was staring straight ahead, his hands thrust deep in his pockets. "I started living as a man not long after college. I was back in Cleveland then. That's where I started hormones—what that means is that I inject testosterone into my body. That's how I'm able to grow a beard, why my voice is deeper, why my body looks more masculine. That's also where I had what we call top surgery, where I got a flat chest."

I wanted to ask, "You got your boobs cut off?" but he probably said it like that because he didn't like talking about his boobs. So I kept my mouth shut, and listened.

"I moved to Arizona because I wanted a change of scene," he continued. "A lot of people in Cleveland knew me from before—knew my old name, what I used to look like. And they never let me forget that. I wanted to go somewhere where people would see me, Mike, without the ghost of who I used to be layered beneath."

That made sense. I nodded, but he didn't notice. He was still staring at the path in front of us. The water was to my left, and I wondered how much farther we had to walk. How much time I had with this new man I was learning about.

"Your mother had also moved to Arizona, with her former partner, but they had broken up. We met through something called a butch/femme society. It's hard to explain, but before I came out as transgender I identified as something called butch. It's like a kind of lesbian. I've only ever been attracted to women, to women like your mother, but when I was new to being a man I didn't know how to date straight women. And while I've always been comfortable around other men, it was also important to have places where I didn't have to ignore the other parts of myself. Your mother and I met at a dance, and it was love at first sight." For the first time a small smile curled across his face. I had asked before how my parents had met, and they always said "through friends." This was much more of a story.

"After we got married—not legally, but we had a wedding and everything—we wanted to have a kid. We wanted to have you. We assumed your mother would be the one to carry, but she has something called PCOS, and wasn't able to get pregnant. We looked into adoption, but there were too many hurdles for a couple like us, and it's expensive. So we agreed that I would."

This might be the part that I had the most questions about, but the smile had left his face and his jaw was tight. "I don't . . . I don't want to talk much about that part. It wasn't easy, but we had you at the end. The important part is that it . . . Annabelle. You need to know that you are the best thing that has ever happened to me. To us. You were worth all of it, and then some. But it was hard.

"I knew some other trans guys in Arizona. We had a brotherhood, almost. We played soccer together, went hiking with our girlfriends. Being among men like me . . . it was a special feeling. The only times I could truly relax. But when I told them what I was planning on doing, they told me I wasn't welcome anymore. That I would make them look bad in front of non-trans people. That if I wanted to be a man I wouldn't do this to myself."

I stopped walking. "What? Those jerks! How could they think that?!" I had half a mind to hop a train to Arizona and kick some old trans guy butt.

But Dad kept walking, and I had to run a few steps to catch up. "I . . . I understood," he said. He pinched his nose, right between his eyes. Like he was struggling not to cry. "I didn't at first, but then . . ." He sniffled, and there was a long pause as he struggled to get his voice under control. "Well, like I said, I left home so no one would know that I hadn't always been a man. I quit the soccer team, wore baggy clothes. I was figuring out what to say to my coworkers if anyone asked, but somehow they found out. I still don't know who told them, or why. I had hoped that people would assume I was getting a beer belly, but soon it became common knowledge that I was . . . that I was going to have you. A few people were understanding, but most weren't. I got stared at. People starting calling me 'she' instead of 'he.' Referring to me as a mother. People from different churches started coming by the house, inviting us to join, saying they could free us of our sin.

"Your mother and I decided to leave. You were born, and six weeks later we moved here. We left it all behind, everything, to make a fresh start. To be a normal family. And we did it. I never wanted to tell you any of this. About anything related to . . . to who I am. What my life used to be. I thought it would never come up. But when you brought home that friend of yours, it's like it knocked down our door."

We were halfway around the lake. A few precious minutes trickled away as I waited for him to say more. But he didn't.

"Can I ask questions now?" I asked. Dad nodded.

But I didn't even have any questions. Not real ones, not pieces of information that needed to be slotted into place.

What I wanted was for him to tell me that story again, and then again, over and over until it became something I truly understood, not in my brain but in my body. In my heart. Until it became something that was part of my life, part of our lives, something that could work itself into the rhythm of our days instead of being hidden away for the rest of them.

But that would take time. So I focused on the only real question that affected my life—what happened next, that is, and not what happened before. "Why were you so upset that I became friends with Bailey?"

"I already explained that," he said tightly, but he ducked his chin. He looked embarrassed.

"Well, you kind of did," I said. "But you said it was because you were worried about me, not because it had anything to do with you. I thought . . ." I took a deep breath. "I thought maybe you were transphobic. And probably homophobic. Like, you didn't want me being friends with them because you didn't believe in people being LGBT."

He was silent for so long. So was I. We were rounding the last bend of the lake when he choked out, "I'm sorry, Bells. I wish I could be another kind of father." He cleared his throat, which had gotten rough again. "But I can only be who I am. I wasn't lying last night. I do worry about you, and I do think that being friends with Bailey might . . . impact you, in ways that you aren't aware of yet."

"What do you mean 'impact'?" I asked carefully. I knew that Bailey was already impacting me, but in a different way from what he probably meant. "Are you afraid that I'm going to think I'm nonbinary because my friend is? I know that sometimes I want to get outfits if they look cute in a commercial. And sometimes I make you buy me snacks because someone else had them and they look good. But I don't think I would change my gender because my, um, friend did."

He snorted, which was almost a laugh. "Well. If you only knew how many people I know who started with 'I'm not trans but a lot of my friends are' and then were on hormones a year later, you might not be so sure."

"How many?" I asked. He was hinting at a world that I hadn't known existed until a few days ago. But he shook his head.

"Annabelle. I know, better than anyone, how hard it is to be different, and I would give my life to protect you from those experiences. And with Bailey . . . how can I explain it. It's like I'm playing for keeps, and they're kicking a ball around."

I must have looked exactly as confused as I felt. "I've known a lot of nonbinary people," he explained. "When I was in college the word was 'genderqueer.' We would all go to the same trans support group, and later the same bars and parties, the same larger social world. But there was always a difference between those people and guys like me. Or trans women. We had to work to be seen as who we are—doctors, surgeries, getting whatever documents changed that we could. But for them it was always . . . not putting on a costume, exactly, but more like an experiment. It wasn't about being who you were, it was talking about what you weren't. People like Bailey . . . they can stop any time they want. That's what I mean when I say I'm playing for keeps. I don't trust people who aren't. You never know what they're going to pretend to be next. And I want you to *know* who you are, not slap a label on yourself because it's trendy."

Well, there was my answer. Eventually I would tell my dad that I was . . . well, eventually I would know the right word. But until I was *sure*, he would say I was following a trend. Slapping on a label. And maybe that I wasn't taking it seriously enough. That it would make my life harder, and he didn't want that for me. It could be worse, I guess, but I didn't want to go there with him yet.

The lake was still glinting to my left, but the gravel of the parking lot opened up in front of us. Our walk was almost over. We approached his truck from the opposite side, and if my dad had his way the conversation would be over when we slammed the doors. But I knew this wasn't going to be the end. So instead of squeezing any last bits of information out of him, I decided to end the conversation, for now, by giving *him* something to think about.

"You told me about the guys you knew in Arizona, the brotherhood. How they kicked you out. And said that, like, you were making the rest of them look bad, and that if you wanted to have a baby maybe that meant you weren't really trans. Isn't that . . . how is that different from what you're saying now? About Bailey? Aren't you treating them the way those guys treated you?"

Dad stopped next to his truck and dug his keys out of his pocket. I hopped into my side, he got into his. He put the key in the ignition, but before turning it he said, "No. I was a man by then. Living as a man. Nothing could take that away from me. This isn't like that at all." With that he started the truck and we drove home, the only voices coming through the radio.

chapter 9

Mom was sitting on our tiny front porch with a glass of iced tea when we got home. She was still in her work clothes, a nice red dress, and looked like a round rose planted firmly into the floorboards. Dad put a hand on her shoulder as he walked into the house and she smiled at him, warm and sad. Then she patted the chair next to her and said, "Sit, Banana." There was another iced tea on the side table, I picked it up and took a long swig. It was cold and sweet, and helped calm my twitching nerves. That wordless ride home with Dad, after everything I learned, felt like I had swallowed a whole Fourth of July's worth of firecrackers and they were all exploding inside me with no wide sky to sputter out into.

"You learned a lot this afternoon," she said. "I know your father isn't always the best at communicating, so I can also answer any questions you might have. There are some things he'd rather keep private, but for now, kiddo, what do you want to know?"

"I don't know where to begin," I confessed. "But first I should probably begin in the bathroom. Don't move, okay?"

"I won't," she promised, so I darted inside.

I didn't actually have to pee. Well, I did, a little, but it could have waited. What I did have to do was stare at my face in the mirror. The face that everyone said looked like my dad's, but that I always thought had a little bit of my mom in it. Around the smile, maybe, or the chin. I stared into my eyes for so long, looking for myself in them, this new Annabelle who was now, in some ways, a mystery to me. I wasn't sure where she came from. I wasn't sure what that meant. But staring at my reflection wasn't going to help, so I stuck my tongue out at myself and went back to the porch.

"Okay, where to begin!" I exclaimed, and draped myself over the arms of the chair dramatically. Then, not feeling dramatic enough, I rolled off the chair onto the floor of the porch, making sure I didn't knock over my iced tea. There, sprawled out like a starfish, my body language could accurately describe the amount of overwhelm in my soul.

There were so many equally pressing questions. Not only about who I was, but how I came to be. "I guess . . . okay. I'm so so so curious about how he got pregnant and what that was like and everything, but I bet a million dollars that's on the list of things he wants to keep private. Right?"

Mom nodded wryly. "You know your dad well. I will tell you, though, that all the details you already know—like, how you were a C-section, we were worried the cord was wrapped around your neck, you were a remarkably big baby—those are all true."

"And why couldn't you get pregnant?" I asked. "Dad said something about you not being able to. Something called peasus? Maybe?"

"P-C-O-S," she spelled. "It stands for polycystic ovarian syndrome. Doctors don't know much about it, but it affects my hormones, and ovaries, and meant that if I wanted to get pregnant we'd have to spend thousands of dollars on treatments that might have failed anyway. Whereas to get your father pregnant . . . well. I don't think he wants me to go into details, not quite yet, but it was much simpler."

I nodded. To be honest I wasn't sure if I wanted to know that much about that whole situation. It made me a little squeamish. There was another human being involved in the process, there had to be. I knew that you needed an egg and a sperm, and if my dad had the egg, then someone else provided the sperm. Someone I didn't know, someone I might never know. Was that person taller than my dad? Fat like my mom? Is that why my hair was curlier than either of my parents? Mom must have understood where my brain was spiraling to, because she dipped her finger into her iced tea and flicked a cold drop onto my face. I startled, then laughed.

"You are every inch my daughter," she reminded me. "No matter how you came into this world. Never forget that." I nodded, firmly, and wiped my face.

Lying there, flat on the floor, I thought about what else I wanted to know. But first things first, like when a genie offers you three wishes and you wish for more wishes. "Dad told me all this while we were walking around a lake, and he said that he would never talk about it again. Do you have the same rule? Like, once we go inside the house, I can't ask you any more questions for the rest of my life?" I didn't mention that I didn't believe Dad and planned on bringing it up again. For now I wanted both of them to think I was going to go along with that plan, and then maybe catch him by surprise.

But I knew Mom would be different. She looked square into my eyes, or at least as square as possible when she was sitting on a rocking chair and I was on my back. "Annabelle, I have always told you that you can talk to me about anything. And that you can ask me a question, any question, and I'll do my best to answer. That hasn't changed."

"Okay, phew. For now, I guess, I'm more curious about you. Dad said you met at some society? For guys like him? So that means you knew he was trans when you started dating, right?"

Mom smiled, but not at me. She was staring out at the grass, but I was willing to bet that whatever she saw in her mind's eye, it wasn't our yard and the scraggly line of bushes at the edge. "Yes, the Butch/Femme Society. And yes, I knew he was trans. There wouldn't be any non-trans men there, it was only for . . . well. I used to think of myself as a lesbian. Then I met my first trans male partner, and realized that that word might not quite fit me as well as I had thought. But I've only ever been attracted to people like your father, whether they're trans men or butch women."

Okay. Okay. My mom had been talking for like twenty

seconds? And already it was so much information that my brain was in the middle of its own personal earthquake. I was glad I was lying on the floor because my thoughts were working overtime and I'm not sure I could have sat up if I tried.

Bailey had asked me if I knew any queer people. I had said no. And it turned out that I was living with two of them. And those lessons I internalized about what my parents didn't want to discuss and why, kids with two moms and trans celebrities in magazines, they were all completely backwards. I started to laugh. Not a little chuckle, not like at the punchline of a joke, but as if someone was holding me down and tickling me and I was too out of breath to tell them to stop. I laughed until tears rolled down my cheeks and my stomach was sore. Mom looked at me amused, and then concerned, and I think I caught a glimpse of Dad peeking through the screen door, but I couldn't stop. Eventually I curled up into a ball on my side, pleased with my choice of the floor, little hiccups and guffaws escaping as I slowly, slowly got myself under control.

"What happened, sweetheart?"

I flopped over onto my back again, hands over my aching stomach. I closed my eyes, hoping that if I didn't see my mom's face, I'd avoid another outburst. "Bailey asked if I thought you guys were transphobic, and I said yes. They also asked if I knew any gay or lesbian or trans people, and I said no. I . . . have never been so wrong about anything in my entire life."

Having gotten through that without laughing, I cracked

my eyes open. But Mom wasn't even smiling. She took her glasses off, the ones with the green frames, and wiped her eyes. Her fingers came away smeared black with mascara, and each breath caught in her throat. While I had been laughing, she had started to cry.

"I'm so sorry, my girl," she said in a whisper. I held my breath. Seeing my mom cry, not at a sad movie, made me feel like the floor was about to open up underneath me. Each shuddering breath she took reverberated in my own stomach, telling me that before she was my mom she was a whole human being, who met my dad and had hoped for a certain kind of life and then got something entirely different. The corners of my eyes started to prickle with tears of their own, but I blinked them rapidly away. I didn't want to make her feel worse.

Mom found a tissue and dried her face. "I promise you that we can talk about this some more. But right now . . . right now I can't. There's so much that I haven't let myself think about, haven't let myself remember, for so many years. I want to tell you, but it's going to take some time. Okay?"

I pushed myself up, wincing a little at my sore stomach muscles. Got to my feet and wobbled over to my mother. I put my arms around her, loving as always how soft and huge and warm she was. The sweet smell of her perfume was twined around my oldest memories.

"Of course, Mom," I said. "I'm not going anywhere, and neither are you. We've got time."

* * *

Dad made dinner that night. Oven-baked salmon, broccoli, rice. Both my parents were good cooks, and I found myself thinking about the stereotype that men didn't cook. I had always liked that my mom and dad did chores equally, cooked equally, that sort of thing, and now I wondered if that was because they were . . . whatever they were.

For a while the only sounds came from forks and water glasses. I had almost gotten used to awkward dinners, but this one was the hardest yet. Now I knew that those first couple nights were odd because they didn't know what to say about my new friend. Didn't want to say too much, maybe, or didn't want to say anything at all. Then there was that awful dinner after they met Bailey for the first time.

But this one was even weirder. Because we were all thinking about the same thing, and knew that we were all thinking about the same thing, plus our own added secrets, but no one knew how to bring that up.

But there was one thing I needed to get out, a decision that had sprouted in my brain in the hours since he told me. "Dad. You have got to let me talk about this to Bailey. If you don't, they'll keep thinking that you and Mom are terrible people and that I'm suffering in a household run by movie villains." He opened his mouth to respond, but I barreled ahead. "Honestly, letting them believe that would make me feel like I'm lying, and I'm a terrible liar! Remember that time I snuck a cookie into my bedroom? And then hid it in my closet, but then when you came in to say good night I got so afraid you'd find it that I started crying? But couldn't tell you why until you promised I wouldn't get in trouble? That's going to be me this entire year, and even if I don't mean to tell them, I will probably let something slip eventually and make everything even worse."

That was all true, but you know what's weird? I *was* bad at lying and secrets, but the questions I asked myself on that roller-skating trip had been growing inside me for so long that they had become a part of me. They were something I was keeping to myself—not a lie, not even a secret, but a corner hidden out of sight. I was proud of myself, actually, for being able to hold something in my heart for so long and not let it spill. Especially now that I knew that it was going to be okay when I figured it out and *could* tell them, there was something delicious about having this bit of knowledge that I could sit with and wonder about in private. Something that was for me and me alone.

Dad kept his eyes fixed on his plate, but I could see a tiny turn at the corner of his mouth that meant he was amused. Phew.

"Annabelle has a point, Mike," Mom said. Yes! I knew she was going to take my side. "When have you ever known our daughter to keep something bottled up for any period of time?"

"Never," said Dad, reluctantly.

"Hey, that's not fair!" I exclaimed, pretending to sound more outraged than I felt. They had no idea. "I never told you about the time I got lost on the way home from school and the mailman had to give me a ride."

They exchanged panicked looks. "Wait, when did that happen?" Dad asked.

"Last spring! And I never told you about it because I knew you'd worry and wouldn't let me walk home anymore. But it only happened that one time and I kept it a secret until now!"

"Well, then. You've proved you can keep a secret," Dad declared. "Your argument is invalid."

I tossed my hair. We were playing a game, and I was winning. "But now I've told you, so I *didn't* keep it a secret. Also I forgot about it until now, so it doesn't even count."

"Hm." He narrowed his eyes at me, but couldn't hide the glint of laughter in them.

Mom came to my defense, again. She put her hand over his, and he curled his thumb across hers. Bailey's hands floated into my mind for some reason and I blinked the image away. "Michael. This is huge knowledge that our daughter will be carrying. And yes, it's about your life but it's also, very literally, about hers. You and I both needed a lot of support early on. So does she, and she needs it from her peers, from her community. You and I aren't enough for her right now." Something rippled across Dad's face as he took that in, but he didn't speak. "And it's also only fair to Bailey," Mom continued. "You of all people should know what they're going through right now. If Annabelle believes that Bailey is trustworthy, we should trust her on that."

They looked into each other's eyes for a long, long time.

Dad had made it clear that he wanted to leave everything behind and start a new life, but what had Mom wanted? She left everything too, but did she wish there was something she could have brought with her? I put those questions away to ask at a better time.

Whatever wordless debate passed between them, my mother's side must have won out. Dad squeezed her hand, then faced me. "Invite Bailey over after school tomorrow. You can tell them, but I want that to happen here. With me. We'll make it clear that this is private, and that they are not to share it with anyone outside their family. Is that clear?"

I tried not to let any kind of gleeful expression cross my face, because that wouldn't be appropriate given the seriousness of the situation. I must have looked like I had eaten a sour candy dipped in hot sauce, my mouth and cheeks were twitching like a rabbit eating a carrot. But I managed to say "Yes, that's clear," as gravely as possible, and then set about shoveling all the food off my plate and into my mouth.

Dad wasn't quite done yet. He put down his knife and fork, and stared intently at his water glass. He started to form words, then bit them back, then tried again.

"Annabelle. Bailey can know that I'm—that I transitioned. But not that I . . . had you. Understand? I can't talk about that again. I don't want them, or anyone, to think about me that way. I'm sorry. But I can't. You won't tell them either. Right?" His eyes flicked up to mine. I had never seen him so afraid. So vulnerable. I knew I had to promise, and mean it.

"I won't," I said. And held up my pinky, for the unbreakable bond of a pinky swear. He was going to share so much about himself, so much that he had planned on taking to the grave. I couldn't blame him for holding on to some of it. And I was sure that they had never told me because Dad was afraid I would blab about it to everyone. I had to prove them wrong.

Dad wrapped his pinky around mine, tight, like all his strength was in his littlest finger. The rest of dinner was quiet, again. But a full quiet, instead of an empty quiet. Like we all knew there was more to say, and we were saving it till later. I couldn't wait for tomorrow.

chapter 10

Of course the day I needed to talk to Bailey before school started was the first day I was late. I had had a nightmare, something about drowning in the ocean except it was also on fire, and I missed my alarm. Mom had to get me up but was running late herself so couldn't drive me, and Dad had already left. If I'd jogged the whole way I would have been on time but it was too warm for that. I only made it a few blocks before slowing down to a brisk walk that became less brisk as I started to sweat. I made sure there weren't stains under my armpits as I approached the Lab, creaked open the door to the classroom, and darted into my seat as Amy went over the day's schedule.

"First period today, we're heading over to the science lab. I think you might be doing an experiment! And after lunch we have social studies again. We'll be discussing what the rest of this year will look like. I'm excited about what's to come. Now, get moving."

I sidled over to Bailey as we walked down to the science room, a little discombobulated (the BEST word) but determined. "Hey!" I said. "Are you doing anything after school today?"

They stroked their face like they were thoughtfully pulling at chin hairs, and it reminded me of how my dad always played with his beard when he was thinking hard. They looked extra good, in brick-red shorts and a blue shirt with a complicated paper airplane diagram on it. Instead of their cool homemade shoes, they had on a pair of battered black boots with green laces that went halfway up their calves, which for some reason were hard to stop staring at. In my morning rush I had thrown on plain khaki shorts and a baby-blue tank top, mature and boring, and I made a mental note to retire that outfit so I wouldn't accidentally put it on again. I hoped Bailey thought I looked nice anyway. "My busy social calendar has some availability," they said. "Do you want to come over to my house?"

"Actually . . . my parents were wondering if you could come over today." I ran my fingers through my hair, curlier than usual in the humidity. "They want to apologize. And also explain something to you." Okay, to be fair I couldn't remember if Dad said anything about apologizing, but I knew he was going to. Or Mom would. I hoped.

They grimaced, like I had invited them to a hot tub full of leeches. "Are you sure? It was pretty obvious that they never wanted to see me again."

"I know, but we talked about it yesterday. It turns out that . . . well, it's complicated. I'll tell you more at lunch, can we have lunch together?" I pleaded.

"Okay," they said, sounding unsure. And I couldn't blame them. But before I could work on convincing them any more we were at the science lab.

The science teacher was this woman named Sarah, who'd been at the Lab for exactly as long as us sixth-graders had been alive. But she acted like every scientific topic she taught us about was something she had just learned, and was as awed and excited by it as we were.

On Tuesday we had gone over lab safety, and so before she even introduced the experiment we were suited up in lab coats, safety gloves, and goggles. And the entire experiment was . . . boiling water.

That's right, we put a glass beaker of cold water on a Bunsen burner, and took notes as it heated up. Sarah flitted around the room, asking us what we noticed, and it turns out I had never paid attention to how boiling water went from tiny bubbles to bigger bubbles to an actual boil, which I guessed was a lot of bubbles all at once. I hoped that someday we'd do actual experiments, a dissection or some kind of explosion (not an exploding dissection, though, ew). Or maybe we could do a unit on climate change and what we could do about it. Or about pollinators in the Pacific Northwest. Anything more important than boiling water. But maybe we had to wait until we were older for that sort of thing.

After science was math, and after math was lunch, which meant that I spent all of math rehearsing what I was going to say to Bailey to convince them to come over without spilling the beans. I raised my hand a couple times early on to make Amy think I was an "engaged and attentive student," like they say on report cards, so I could tune out for the rest of class and figure out my plan.

But of course my entire plan was based on me talking, and Bailey only saying exactly what I imagined them saying, instead of a real conversation with a real person with their own brain and mouth. We grabbed our lunches and I ushered Bailey over to the windows on the other side of the room, wishing our classroom wasn't so small. It wouldn't be hard for anyone to overhear what we were saying. I'd have to be careful.

But before I could even start talking, Bailey spoke up. See, that's why I'd rather have conversations with people in my head—they never beat you to the punch.

"I know your parents aren't your fault," they began. I could tell they didn't want to hurt my feelings, and were choosing every word as carefully as possible. "And I would love to have you come over to my house." The word "love" jolted through me like a static shock. "But," they continued, "it's not safe for me to be at yours. Not for me, and also not for you. Back home I knew people who got in trouble for having queer or trans friends, because their parents worried it was contagious, or something. I wouldn't be comfortable spending time around your family right now, and I also don't want to make things harder for you."

Tears welled up in my eyes. I was all prepared to promise

them that my parents weren't going to be rude to them again, but I hadn't expected them to be thinking about *my* well-being. I wiped my eyes and managed to avoid crying for real, but Bailey looked worried. "You've been down these past couple days, are you okay?" they asked.

I took a deep breath, and quickly glanced behind me. The rest of the class was buzzing with conversation. No one was paying attention to us. "I'm fine," I said, honestly. I might have been blushing a little, because they had noticed my mood, they were paying attention to my feelings. "I wasn't fine at first, but now I am. Really. I swear. But I need you to trust me."

They pulled back a bit, confusion written all over their face. "I promise my parents aren't mad at you. Or me," I added in a rush. "They—my dad, especially—talked to me yesterday. I learned a lot about my family, things that I never imagined. At first Dad told me that we would never talk about it again, but Mom convinced him that I could tell you about it. Because you would understand, in a way that none of them would." I jerked my thumb towards the kids behind us.

Their brow was furrowed with confusion, but there was some curiosity mixed in. "Wait, what did you talk about? What did they tell you?"

"It's private," I said, looking down at my lap. "Something they've been keeping from everyone, even me. But Dad finally told me, and said that I could tell you, but only if you came over and we all talked about it together. I know this sounds like some ancient curse or like we have a dead body buried in the back yard, but I promise it isn't anything bad! You have to come over. It's okay. I promise, cross my heart and hope to die, everything else. Please?"

They removed a round Granny Smith apple from their lunch bag and tossed it up and down a couple times. It made a satisfying *thwap* every time it hit their palm. Then they put the apple down resolutely and looked at me. "Pinky swear?" they asked, and stretched out their right hand, pinky finger extended.

"Pinky swear," I confirmed, and wrapped my little finger tightly around theirs. My second-most important pinky swear in twenty-four hours. We stared into each other's eyes until I had to look away.

"Did you know that the word 'apple' used to mean any kind of fruit?" they asked, unhooking their finger.

"Wait, what?" I said, feeling like I tripped and fell into a whole different conversation.

"Yeah, bananas used to be called 'apples of paradise,' and even though Bible people like to talk about the apple in the Garden of Eden, it could have been any kind of fruit. Like a pomegranate or a pear or even an avocado or whatever."

"Huh, I didn't know that. Did you know that"—I cast around for a random fact to pull out—"that in *The Very Hungry Caterpillar* he turns into a butterfly after going into a cocoon, but that butterflies actually come out of chrysalises? Only moths come out of cocoons."

Bailey's eyes lit up. "I didn't know that! Where did you get that from?"

"Our librarian told us after she read us that story! I was in kindergarten, and it stuck with me. It's weird to think that authors could put mistakes in their books."

"Well, did *you* know that—" And then they were off telling me butterfly facts, and I countered with fun facts about how Dr. Seuss was kind of a jerk, and by the time Amy rang the chime I had almost forgotten to be nervous about later.

"Please join me in the meeting area," Amy announced, once we were all cleaned up. We gathered on the rug.

"I thought about your ideas for our social studies curriculum," she said once we had settled. "You all want to understand the world we live in today, how we got here, what needs to change, and how we can accomplish that. You're interested in a variety of topics, some of which are related to how you identify, and others are related to what you believe.

"On the one hand, there's no way that, over the course of a single school year, we could learn everything about everything that you all are interested in. Even getting to the bottom of one single topic could be the work of a lifetime. And as your sixth-grade teacher, I believe that it's not my job to teach you everything you need to know, but instead to help you learn *how* to think, and learn how to identify your own interests and explore from there. I've decided that we can use this school year to introduce a lot of different topics, using different awareness and history months as our guide."

The other Annabelle raised her hand. "Like Black History Month? That's usually when we learn about Martin Luther King."

"And Women's History Month," Audrey added, "we learn about voting and also famous women."

Amy had a downright mischievous look on her face. "That's exactly right. Except instead of learning about whatever it is you've always learned about, we're going to go about this in a different way. A better way, if I do say so myself. Annabelle, you mentioned Black History Month, but have any of you heard about the Black Lives Matter Week of Action?"

The other Annabelle shook her head, and everyone else looked confused too. Except for Bailey, who was nodding along enthusiastically.

"Bailey, did you learn about that in your last school?"

"Yeah! It's a week where we learn about the Black Lives Matter guiding principles. It's cool."

"And Audrey, you mentioned Women's History Month, but have you ever heard of Stormé DeLarverie? Do you know about what Helen Keller did *after* she learned the word 'water'?" Audrey furrowed her brow like she was thinking hard, then gave up.

Amy looked pleased. "My favorite thing about history, about social studies, is how every single topic is related to every single other topic. And that no matter how much you think you know, there's always more to learn. That is what we will explore together this year. You will probably graduate with more questions than answers, and that's how I'll know I did my job."

Dixon raised his hand, and a little voice went "Oh, no" in my head. "You mentioned Black History Month and Women's History Month," he said, in a voice smooth as a weatherman's. "But is there a White History Month or a Men's History Month?"

Amy nodded seriously, and I noticed her take one long, full, deep breath before responding. "Dixon, are you worried that you don't know enough about men, or about white people?" The whole class went so silent, you could hear a pin drop. "Are you having a hard time finding white people, or men, in the books you read, movies you watch, or video games you play?"

He opened and closed his mouth a few times, but instead of answering her question he said, "It's not fair, that's all."

Next to me Bailey snorted delicately, but Amy responded as if he was being reasonable, probably because that was her job. "In that case, I think we've found an excellent educational goal for you. By the end of the year perhaps we can come to an understanding of why it *is* fair. There are reasons, good ones, but instead of telling you now, I think that's something we can discover as a community."

Dixon was staring out the window and nodded, barely. He pulled a quarter out of his pocket and started fiddling with it, and some of the tension lifted.

"What month is this?" Amanda asked. That was a good question.

"I had planned on starting in earnest next month," Amy admitted. "I want to make sure we've planned and prepared in advance. But let's find out!" She started up the smart board and searched for "September Is." A whole list popped onto the screen.

"Let's see," she said. "Disease Literacy Month—we could always talk about chronic illness and invisible disabilities. Better Breakfast Month? Mortgage Professional Month? Wow, I didn't know about any of these."

"Hispanic Heritage Month!" Felix pointed out.

When Amy scrolled down more I saw "Polycystic Ovarian Syndrome Awareness Month," and before my brain could tell my mouth to shut up, I chimed in with, "My mom has that!"

"What does she have?" Olivia asked.

Too late for me to pretend like I hadn't said anything. "That," I said, pointing, "PCOS. I didn't know she had a whole month to herself." I hoped no one would ask anything more about it. Luckily everyone else was reading all the random events that happened in September.

"I have to admit," said Amy, "I didn't realize how many months they packed into each month! Not to mention all the different weeks and days. But Hispanic Heritage Month starts soon, it's half of September and half of October. And Annabelle, do you think your mom would want to come in and talk to us about PCOS?"

Ugh, what made me blurt out my mom's personal business? "Um . . . I don't know. I can ask." I wouldn't ask.

"Well, there's so much we could do for each month," Amy

said. "But instead of me talking at you, for now let's have you break up into small groups to talk about what you want to learn about, and how you want to learn it. Not only books or movies, but guest speakers, field trips, that sort of thing. I can't promise that we'll be able to use all of your ideas, but it will help me get a sense of what to plan for."

Before we broke up, she wrote out some months on the board—Native American Heritage Month, Asian American & Pacific Islander Heritage Month, and Human Rights Month, among others. We moved into different parts of the room, and I tugged Bailey over to our window spot so that we wouldn't have to sit with Dixon. He sat down next to the other Annabelle, who was near Felix, and while the two of them chatted with each other he played with his quarter.

"Can I sit with you guys?" asked Audrey, and Patrick came over too.

"Do you think we could come up with a project for Earth Day?" asked Patrick.

"Yes, definitely," I said.

"Would you want to do something for our classroom, or for the whole school? Or something else, like a bake sale where the money goes to an environmental organization?" Bailey asked.

"The teachers' lounge has one of those coffee machines that uses pods, those create so much waste! Maybe we could make them get a better coffee pot," Audrey suggested.

"That's a good start," said Patrick, "but not enough. I don't know how much you guys know about climate change, but we need more than recycling bins in the classroom."

We brainstormed for a while: using reclaimed water for the toilets, using part of the yard as a community garden, strapping the kindergartners onto treadmills and using that as a source of alternative energy. When we came back to share as a group, Amy said that she could help us with any of our ideas except the kindergartner one.

For a few minutes I was excited about saving the environment, but then all my immediate concerns came flooding back, which fell into two categories: what my dad might say when Bailey came over, and what Bailey might say back. Luckily P.E. was the last period of the day, and running relay races is a good way to take your mind off that sort of thing. But by the end of the day those squirgles in my stomach came slithering back.

I was worried that Bailey was going to use the walk home to press me for details about what, exactly, they were about to learn, but they started complaining about Dixon.

"'*Why isn't there a Men's History Month,*'" they sneered. "Where did he even get that from?"

"He's such an entitled brat," I agreed. "He's always asking stupid questions like that. It's like he thinks it makes him sound smarter than us, when it's actually a big waste of time. One time he spent an entire math class making the teacher *prove* that one plus one equals two, and wouldn't accept anything she said. He just likes to argue. And then wonders why no one is particularly excited to hang out with him. I don't get it."

"I bet you anything he hangs out with racist gamers online. He's, like, two steps away from becoming a men's rights activist."

I nodded even though I didn't know much about racist gamers online. I played Minecraft sometimes but never got that into it. And I wasn't sure what a men's rights activist was. I knew what all those words meant and could piece it together, but there was probably more to it than that. But I wanted Bailey to think I was worldly and smart and cool. They probably realized that I didn't know as much as they did, but I hoped they didn't realize just how *much* I didn't know.

"I like Patrick's idea," I said. "I saw a magazine cover that had the Earth in an ice-cream cone, and it was melting. I don't want the world to melt before I grow up—there's so much I want to do! But also reading articles that are like 'Hey the world is going to melt before you grow up' make me panic and I have to pretend like it's not happening and everything is fine. Maybe actually doing something about it will make me feel better."

"Ugh, you're so right," said Bailey. "I know that being vegetarian doesn't do anything big to help the environment. And all the same animals are going be factory farmed and eaten anyway. But I don't know what else there is to do!"

We were almost at the Circle K, which meant we were

almost at my house. "Let's get some snacks first," Bailey suggested. They got a bag of chips and a box of Lemonheads, but I was too nervous to eat, so I just got myself a cherry-and-Coke Slurpee. By the time we got to my house, I had already given myself two brain freezes.

Mom and Dad were sitting out on the porch when we arrived. They must have rearranged their schedules again to focus on this whole situation, and my sudden pang of guilt was swallowed by a rush of anger. If they had been honest with me from the start, there wouldn't even *be* an issue. Maybe if Dad hadn't been so scared of people finding out we could have moved to Capitol Hill instead of boring little Tahoma Falls, and been Bailey's neighbors, and I could be half as cool as them. But no, my parents wanted me to stay some ignorant little kid who had to struggle through figuring out who she was all by herself.

Speaking of being half as cool as Bailey, if I was the one walking into a conversation with people who, for all I knew, hated me because of how I identified, I would be an incoherent puddle of anxiety. But Bailey marched confidently up the porch steps, head high, back straight, and said, "Hi, Mr. and Mrs. Blake! Do you like Lemonheads? I got these for you," and put the box down on the table between them, without even a quaver in their voice.

Mom and Dad both looked surprised. "I love Lemonheads. Thank you, Bailey," Mom said.

Dad nodded. "Thanks. Call me Mike." He ripped open the

box and popped one into his mouth, then shook some into Mom's hand. "Let's go inside," he said.

Once indoors, he pointed at the kitchen table. There were four glasses of water set out. We all sat down as the silence stretched out, past a moment, past a pause, past a comfortable amount of time for four people to sit without a word. But it wasn't my job to start. It certainly wasn't Bailey's. It wasn't even Mom's.

Finally—finally—Dad took a sip of water and clasped his hands together. "Thank you for coming over," he said, looking down at his knuckles. "What did my daughter explain to you today?"

Bailey shook their head. "Nothing. Yesterday she apologized for the way you both treated me when I came over. Today she said that you wanted to explain why you acted that way. Something about your family history. She promised that it wasn't about me, but something going on with you. And that you didn't hate me."

They were looking at my dad the whole time, but it wasn't until that last sentence that he met their gaze. I had never seen my dad's eyes like that, red-rimmed and watery.

"I don't hate you, Bailey. I'm sorry I made you think that. I can explain everything, but before I do, can you promise to keep this between us? I can't ask you to keep secrets from your parents, but I need to know that you won't tell Annabelle's classmates, or your teacher, or anyone else."

Bailey kept their eyes locked on my dad and extended their

hand. "Pinky swear." Dad smiled a tiny bit, and locked his pinky around theirs. Connected, Bailey kept talking. "When I first came out as nonbinary, my parents and I started going to a group for all kinds of queer and trans families. Confidentiality was the number one rule. Some of the kids who found their way there couldn't be out to their families because they'd be hurt. Sometimes there would be kids who went to the same school and neither one of them was out at school. Or someone would share about something serious and scary and have to trust that no one else would find out. I trusted people there, and they trusted me. I have a lot of practice."

Dad nodded, and put his hand back down.

"We moved here from Arizona," he began. "And I moved to Arizona from Cleveland. In Cleveland and Arizona I was also in support groups like that. For trans men. Some people said they were genderqueer—we didn't have the word 'nonbinary' back then—but we were all in the same group. The ladies had their own group. Sometimes we would all hang out together, but not often."

Bailey had been about to take a sip of water, but set their glass down with a *plink*. I watched understanding break over their face like the dawn.

"You're trans," they said, like I had. But softer. Warmer. Dad nodded. "Wow."

Next, I thought, Bailey was going to start asking questions like I did, wondering when he did all this, what it was like back then, why it was something he kept to himself. But instead, they sat back in their chair and stretched out their arms, then put their elbows on the table and cupped their chin in their steady hands. And waited. Quietly.

I knew my dad could quietly outwait anyone; I'd tried that trick before. But Bailey was better at it than I was. They didn't crack. And after longer than I would be able to last, my dad started to talk again.

"I learned a long time ago," he said, "that you can't trust anyone with this issue. Non-trans people don't get it. They see us as talk show freaks. And other trans people . . . you think they'll be there for you, but we all want the same thing. To pass, to fit in, to be seen as normal. And the second someone gets that, they leave it all behind. And they'll leave you behind, if they think you threaten that."

Across the table Mom took a deep breath, maybe about to say something, but then let it out slowly. Like she knew it wasn't her time to step in.

But, "Cis," said Bailey.

"What?" Dad asked, taken aback. Mom and I both looked at them curiously.

"If someone isn't trans, the word for that is 'cis.' You said 'non-trans' people—is that what you used to call it?"

"Oh. Uh. Yes," said Dad. "When I was first coming out we would say 'bio,' like 'bio-man' or 'bio-girl,' but a lot of us thought that was wrong because . . . well, a lot of reasons. So we started saying 'non-trans.' What does 'cis' mean? Must be new."

"It literally means 'not trans' in . . . I don't know, Latin or

Greek or something. So it's not new. How is it that you've been trans for—how many years?"

"Twenty-three," Dad said. He didn't even have to count.

"For more than twice as long as I've been alive," Bailey continued, without skipping a beat, while Mom grinned mischievously in the background, "and you've never heard that word before?"

Dad bristled. "When we moved here, I gave all that up. I knew everything I needed to. Now I'm a husband and a father. I spent a lot of time arguing about language with people, and that didn't do me any good. Now I'm just living my life."

Bailey shrugged. "So am I. And part of that is being friends with whoever I want. Are you going to be the first adult to kick me out of their house for being nonbinary?"

The silence that fell over the table was nothing I'd ever heard before. I knew my dad, could tell that he was one step away from getting up from the table and walking away, away from the conversation and also that whole part of his life. I couldn't let that happen.

"Dad, if Bailey isn't welcome in this house, then that means I'm not, either." I was surprised by the sound of my own voice; I hadn't known I was going to say anything until the words were out.

Dad snapped his head to look at me, like he had to remind himself that I was sitting there at all. That it wasn't only him and Bailey at the table, and Mom and I hadn't faded into the background. "What do you mean?" he asked, his voice flat.

I wasn't entirely sure what I meant, but started putting

words together, and the more I talked, the more right they felt. "Well, you and Mom have always told me that I can be whatever I want. That you'll love me no matter what. But you're saying I shouldn't be Bailey's—that I shouldn't be their friend. Right? Which means that there's at least one thing you hope I'm not, and that's not even a bad thing, like a murderer or bank robber. Just someone's friend. It makes me wonder what else you secretly hope I don't grow up to be."

Dad looked like he had been slapped across the face. For a second I wished I could take it back, but I knew I was right. Mom stepped in before I could apologize.

"They're right, Mike," she said. "Both of them. I've made my own decisions, but Annabelle was born into this. And Bailey has to be themself. You can make whatever choices you want about your own life, but you can't ask your daughter to change who she is because of it. And you can't expect Bailey to go away, to lose a friend because of your own fear."

Mom and Dad locked eyes. Bailey had the good sense to keep their mouth shut, and I followed along. Finally Dad crumbled.

"Bailey," he said, his voice rough. "We invited you over here today so I could tell you about myself. And apologize. You're welcome in our home. But please understand how hard this is for me. How different it is for me than it is for you. And how important it is to believe that I can trust you."

Bailey raised their eyebrows. "Mike, no offense, but do you honestly think I'm going to go around saying 'Hey guess what everyone, Annabelle's dad is a trans guy'? Even if I didn't care about other trans people's privacy, I wouldn't talk about you. No one talks about anyone else's parents! We don't care! You're the people who drive us to the movie theater and shush us during sleepovers."

"They're right," I chimed in. "In the grand scheme of things, other people's parents aren't very interesting."

"But this is different," he argued. "It makes sense that I would be concerned."

Bailey crossed their arms but smiled a little. "Maybe, if you were the only other trans person I had ever met and I was dying to talk about it. But that support group I told you about? It was usually run by trans adults. Kids at my old school had trans parents. My parents are friends with trans people. It's not a big deal to me. Now, can Annabelle and I go outside?" They cocked their head sassily.

I didn't mean to laugh, but a huge guffaw broke out of me. That was *such* a power move. Dad looked like he had been run over by a truck, but Mom had tears in her eyes, glittering over the biggest smile I'd ever seen. "You two go have fun," she said.

Bailey and I rushed out, giddy with triumph. "That was *amazing*," I said, once we were away from the house. I did half a cartwheel in the grass out of excitement and fell, like I always did when attempting cartwheels. "You completely ruled back there! We won!"

"You were great too," they said. "What you said about how

you weren't welcome either, if you couldn't be friends with me? And we haven't even known each other that long! You're amazing."

Their eyes were shining, cheeks flushed, we were both breathing heavily. If this were a movie or if I were more sure of myself, this would be when we started kissing. Because in that moment I realized that I had wanted to do that since the second I met them, that all of my "oh wow, a cool new friend" feelings were actually that I really really really liked Bailey in a way that I had never liked a boy and never liked a girl and thought that maybe I would never like anyone. So that meant that I was. I was. Something. I didn't know what. But I was someone who wanted to kiss Bailey, more than anything in the world. I was about to lean forward, to find out if they wanted to kiss me too, but before I could get there they kicked up into a handstand, then toppled over onto their back.

I remained stiff as a statue. Feelings broke over me like waves, this sudden need to put my lips on their lips but also the questions of what if they don't and what am I now and what does this mean and what do I say. Too much. So I lowered myself down next to them, not caring if I got grass stains on my boring shorts.

"Well, I guess I should be getting home?" they ventured. "I mean, I don't have to. We could hang out for longer, if you want. But it seems like the right thing. Give you some time with them to get back to normal. And we do have homework, I guess."

"Yeah. Right. Normal. Homework." I didn't sound right, no doubt about it, but Bailey would probably assume it was because of everything that had happened. The parts they knew about, with my parents, not the parts they didn't know, about how I wanted to kiss them. I stretched out on my back, avoiding their eyes, but every nerve in my body was alert to where they were, how they displaced the air next to me. I didn't say anything. Neither did they. We looked up at the clouds again, like we did the first day they came over, but this time we didn't talk about what shapes we saw. Before long Bailey went home to their family, and I went in to mine.

chapter 11

"Ugh, Monday" is something adults say a lot, but when Monday came it was like the start of vacation. It had been a long weekend, and I was glad it was over.

It wasn't bad, exactly. Or at least, nothing bad happened. Nothing *happened*. Another weekend in the same house and same yard and same town. Not too busy but not too boring. We worked in the garden some, I did my homework, finished another Magnus Chase book, helped make dinner, watched some TV. There weren't any more big life-changing discoveries, I didn't learn that my parents were also aliens from the planet Zborx, nothing caught on fire, whoever my sperm donor was didn't stop by for afternoon tea. Mom and Dad and I didn't fight at all. If anything, they were extra sweet with each other. I even caught them smooching in the kitchen when I padded in for a pre-bed snack.

But suddenly, everything *felt* different.

When I looked at my dad, I didn't see the dad I always knew. I looked at him and saw everything that he told me, and everything I still wondered. My mom wasn't just my mom anymore; she was this whole other woman too. One that wasn't even *related* to me, but who wasn't straight in the same way I wasn't straight.

Realizing that I had a crush on Bailey made everything make sense. And also made everything more confusing. All at the same time. I didn't like boys because I wasn't straight. But I also didn't think I was into girls, so I probably wasn't a lesbian. Was there a word for people who were only into people like Bailey? Or would Bailey be the first and last person I ever had a crush on? I didn't want to tell them, because what if they didn't like me back? Or what if they *did*? Both possibilities were terrifying.

I spent all weekend wrestling all my thoughts under control like they were a pack of wild dogs on a leash, lunging after new questions and new ideas and being jerked back by the throat. When I went to bed Sunday night I was so glad that the next day I'd be back with my class, mostly people I've known since we were all little, no big secrets hiding in plain sight. We had all changed as we've grown up, but on some level we were the same as we'd always been.

Like, during morning meeting, Amanda mentioned that she went to the beach over the weekend, and Olivia asked why she hadn't been invited, and then they didn't speak to each other all day. And during snack, Dixon started bugging Jonas, but in a whisper, so when Jonas snapped and started screaming at him, Amy at first thought that it was Jonas's fault, but quickly gathered that Dixon had to go have a conversation with Principal Quinn, which was about as "in trouble" as anyone ever got at the Lab. I'd never been sent to the principal's office before, but I couldn't imagine that it was anything that serious, because when Dixon came back, he was grinning. Nothing new, nothing unexpected.

Except for Bailey, of course. When they sat down next to me that morning I named the helium-balloon feeling in my stomach "crush." When they plucked at the carpet with their square-tipped fingers I knew the reason I couldn't look away. I wanted those fingers intertwined with mine. And when they laughed, and my heart soared, I understood why.

It was a gorgeous day, warm and sunny. Amy said we could eat our lunch outside if we wanted to, so Bailey and I used that as an excuse to sit by ourselves against the classroom wall, while everyone else spread out on the play structure. My heart was beating fast as I took out my caprese sandwich and grapes, I could feel it in my chest and my throat, but understanding why made it easier to handle. I told myself to relax. I wasn't going to tell them yet. When the time was right, I'd know.

"So. Did anything else happen with your parents?" they asked.

I shook my head. "Nope. They're both acting like nothing happened. Like nothing's changed."

"*Has* anything changed?" Bailey asked curiously.

"Yes?" I said. "And no. Ugh, I don't even know how to explain it!" I waited for them to ask me to try and explain it anyway, but they didn't. They methodically unpacked their lunch, and it felt almost like they were holding their breath, waiting to see if I was going to go ahead, or stop and talk about something else. I wondered if they were hoping I'd change the subject, but if they didn't want to talk about my family stuff anymore, they would tell me that, right? So I went ahead.

"It's like . . ." I slowed down, and organized my thoughts so they wouldn't come out as a mess. Took a bite of my sandwich, the soft mozzarella squishing against the chewy bread. "I see him differently now, you know? He's my dad, I don't think of him as not-my-dad, but now instead of being my dad, he's also this guy with this whole history and life and stuff that's . . . *different*, and I want to know about it! Like, I want to see pictures of him when he was my age. And I want to know how he came out as trans, what his parents were like, what his name used to be and who he dated before my mom and so many other things!"

Bailey was focused on their seaweed chips, nibbling them into circles, and didn't meet my eyes. Maybe I should have stopped talking, but there was no one else who would understand what I was going through. Words kept popcorning out of me, hot and sharp and all over the place. "But also the reason he never told me is because he didn't want me to see him as something different. He wants people to see him as normal, so everything that I'm thinking about is his worst nightmare and exactly why he didn't want to tell me in the first place, which makes me a terrible daughter and a terrible person and probably transphobic and I don't know what to do!"

A bunch of heads turned in our direction—my voice had gotten way too loud. I lowered my head and stopped talking. I took out a grape and started picking off the skin, not sure how to continue. I hadn't even gotten to my mom yet, how we weren't related biologically. I knew it didn't matter, but I also didn't know what it meant. And, oh man, that my mom and I both got crushes on trans people, and that for a split second I thought Bailey and I were going to kiss, but I sure couldn't get into *that* during lunch.

Bailey was peeling a clementine, slowly, so all the skin came off in one piece. "Okay," they began in a voice so soft, I had to lean forward to hear. "Honestly? I have to ask you something. Do you have the same questions about me? Like, are you dying to see pictures of what I looked like back when I thought I was a girl? Have you been wondering this whole time if my name used to be something else?"

There was an unfamiliar edge to their voice. I could tell that this mattered a lot to them. I thought it over, hard, for a long time. They deserved a truthful answer. I put the now-skinless grape into my mouth, and let the sweetness burst over my tongue as I thought about how to respond.

"No," I said finally, sitting up straight again. "Honestly. I never stopped to wonder about whether you had a different name. And now that I am thinking about it, I don't care. I guess if we ever look at baby pictures of each other, I'll see them, and I bet you were the cutest baby ever, but if you don't want to show me, that's fine too."

They nodded, looking relieved but cautious. "Well, I'm not a therapist or anything. But I know a lot about my mom and dad, I've seen lots of pictures of them, I know a couple stories about who they dated before they met each other and what happened in their lives before they had me and also two of my grandparents are alive and they talk about the dead ones a lot. It's normal to want to know about your family, and in your case, it means learning about what your dad was like before he transitioned. If you had this much curiosity about some random trans person, that would be messed up and invasive and transphobic, but . . . well, it's your family."

For a minute there I thought we were on the verge of a fight. I must have said the right thing. We spent the last couple minutes wordlessly finishing up our food, trading grapes for seaweed chips, then Amy called us back in.

"Hey, you should come over to my house after school," Bailey said, right before we went inside. "You want to?"

That helium feeling came back, like I had swallowed a dozen balloons and they were lifting me up to the sky. "Ooh, sure! Your parents won't force me to leave early when they find out that I'm not trans, right?"

Bailey laughed. "No, they're cis too. They understand what it's like to be part of that community."

As soon as school was over I texted my parents to let them

know my plans. Mom sent me a thumbs-up emoji, and Dad responded with a curt "k." Together, Bailey and I turned left out of the parking lot instead of right, and began the walk to their house.

Their hand, I noticed, was dangling right next to mine. Had they always walked so close to me? I wondered what would happen if I casually started holding their hand—friends held hands sometimes too, right? But before I could make a move, they shoved their hands in their pockets and started chattering, faster than they usually talked. "Remember how I said we used to live on Capitol Hill? My parents bought our apartment a thousand years ago, back when Seattle was super different, and they said when they bought it they couldn't even imagine what the city was going to turn into. I loved that apartment and it's always going to be home, but also it was so small! My bedroom was the size of a walk-in closet. Actually, it might have *been* a walk-in closet. And sometimes the windows leaked and it would smell mildewy after a lot of rain, which meant it smelled mildewy all winter, and *something* was always broken and when I was little there was a lot of crime in the area. Our new house is fine, but I miss where I grew up and as soon as I'm old enough I'm going to find a new apartment exactly like it."

I kept nodding, like I knew anything about buying apartments or selling them, but I couldn't understand why they were telling me all this until we walked up to their house at the end of a cul-de-sac.

It. Was. Huge. I didn't know if it was mansion-huge because it wasn't as if I'd ever seen a mansion before. But it had two stories, and a front porch that wrapped around one side, and it butted up against an actual forest. The top floor had four peaked windows looking out onto the road, and back behind it I caught a glimpse of something that looked like a whole separate little hut.

"Your house is gigantic!" I blurted out. "And what is that back there? For guests or something?"

Bailey craned their neck like they had no idea what I was talking about, and then said, like they had forgotten, "Oh. Uh, that's a hot tub. We haven't used it yet, though. It costs a lot of money to clean it and get it running and everything."

And then I got why they were nervously babbling about their Seattle apartment: Their parents were able to sell it for a lot of money, and buy this house that was three times the size of mine, and they didn't want me to judge them for being a millionaire or whatever.

Seemed like a funny thing to be embarrassed about to me, but I didn't mind them feeling awkward for a change. "Okay, well, you have to get it running before it gets too cold because I have only been in a hot tub, like, twice in my entire life. Ooh, but give me a few days' warning so I can go bathing suit shopping. I think I grew out of my last one." Then I blushed, thinking about the two of us hanging out in bathing suits.

They relaxed a little. "I used to take swimming lessons at

the rec center. They had an outdoor hot tub that was better in the winter. Sitting in a hot tub while it's snowing? Heaven."

"Fine. I'll use your hot tub whenever. I'm hungry, what kind of snacks do you have?"

We clomped up the wooden stairs to the front door and Bailey led me to the kitchen. A woman with long brown hair and glasses was sitting at a kitchen island with a laptop. She smiled as we came in.

"Hey kiddo, is this the famous Annabelle?" she said, getting up and enveloping them in a hug.

"Sure is," they said, grinning.

I had to be blushing. "Famous? Me?" I said.

"Of course!" said Bailey's mom. "You're the first friend they've made since we've moved here, and we've heard nothing but wonderful things about you. How welcoming you've been, what a good friend you're already being to our Bailey. Michael!" she called. "Come upstairs, we have a celebrity visitor!"

"Michael is my dad," Bailey explained. "My mom is Lindsay. What are you working on today, Mom?"

Lindsay sighed. "Some buggy code. The client wanted this done yesterday, but I'm not done combing through it. I'm a programmer, Annabelle. Not an exterminator. Though some days I wish I was chasing down actual bugs."

Bailey's dad joined us. "Annabelle! It's awesome to be formally introduced! I'm Michael, my pronouns are he/him/his. Can I get you anything? Water, a snack, do you have any allergies or food restrictions I should be aware of?"

"Dad!" Bailey exclaimed through gritted teeth. "We've *talked* about this! I told Annabelle about you, using your pronouns and everything, so you don't need to lead with them! And we'll get our own snack."

"Fine, but hey, you never know! I might have changed my pronouns since this morning," he said jovially. "Yours are still the same, right, B?"

"Yes, Dad, I promise I'll tell you if they change." They looked exasperated but cheerful, like this was something they'd argued about before.

"Okay, good. Annabelle, I'm guessing your pronouns are she/her/hers, because otherwise Bailey has been misgendering you this whole time and they should know better."

"You know, I've never had to think about my pronouns before," I admitted. "But, yeah, she/her, I guess?" The idea I could use different ones made my brain start to go a little fuzzy, so I changed the topic. "And my dad's name is Michael too! But everyone calls him Mike."

Lindsay laughed. "If I can't remember a man's name, I always call him 'Mike,' and I'm right at least thirty percent of the time. It's been one of the most common names for baby boys for decades."

"Really?" I wondered if that was why my dad picked it. Because it was the most basic man-name he could think of. And then I was struck by a sudden uncertainty: Dad said that Bailey could talk about him to their parents, but I wasn't sure if they had yet. Which meant I wasn't sure if I could say anything. I started getting flustered, but Bailey swooped in.

"If you're done giving my first Tahoma Falls friend the third degree, we're going to get some snacks and go outside. What's for dinner?"

"Bean soup, salad, bread," said Michael. "Annabelle, will you be joining us? There's plenty."

"I should probably be home for dinner," I said, "but thank you!" Bailey grabbed some baby carrots from the fridge and shoved a container of hummus in my hands, and we trooped outside.

After that ridiculously healthy snack I thought maybe we would talk more about my dad's past, or maybe what happened when they first told their parents about themself. Or we would talk about who we had crushes on, and they would say that they liked girls with long, dark, curly hair and an excellent fashion sense, and then I would know what to do next. But instead they spent about twenty minutes teaching me how to do a cartwheel. I crashed over every time, then got attacked by a giggle fit and couldn't stop laughing even when it hurt. They wanted to practice walking on their hands, so I helped, moving forward and backward in sync, their ankles quivering in my steadying hands. Then we were in the hot tub gazebo, peeking under the cover at the scummy water and coming up with scientific names for the new microbes we were sure to discover when their dad yelled that it was going to be dinner soon and if I wanted a ride home this was the time for it.

My phone had been buzzing in my pocket, but I hadn't

wanted to check it. There were several texts from Mom, wondering when I was going to be home. I let her know I was on my way, and then Bailey and I piled into their dad's car.

By the time we pulled up in front of my little shoebox house, my sides were literally splitting from laughter. Michael sure knew a lot of terrible knock-knock jokes. Dad came outside to say hello.

Michael got out of the car. "You must be Annabelle's dad!" he said. "Sorry we didn't get a chance to say hello the other day, I'm Michael."

"Mike," said Dad, shaking his hand.

"That's right, Annabelle said we had the same name! What are the odds, huh?" But that was obviously a joke, because my dad cracked a smile. I held my breath hoping that Michael wouldn't ask dad his pronouns, but luckily he said it was time to be getting home.

"My wife and I haven't had much of a chance to socialize since we've come up here," he added. "Maybe we could all have dinner sometime? Since our kiddos are becoming such good friends, maybe we will too."

Dad nodded. And why had I never thought about parents having friends? Mine didn't. No adult had every come over to our house for dinner. We had never gone to someone else's. Thanksgiving and Christmas we might spend with their coworkers, but those were always tense, awkward, and anxious. I assumed that most parents were like that; when you grew up and got married you stopped having friends.

But maybe that was another thing about my family that was different. Did neither of them *want* friends? Was our little family enough for them? Or was that another thing they gave up when they came here, me unaware in my baby carrier?

But, "That would be nice," my dad said, and he might have even meant it. Huh.

We walked into the house as they drove off. "You had fun?" he asked.

"Yeah! Their house is huge. And? They have a hot tub! It's funny, Bailey acted kind of nervous about bringing me over, I guess because they're rich and they thought maybe I'd be all judgy about that, and honestly I wouldn't mind living in a mansion, but I'd rather have a garden than a hot tub. Except maybe I'll change my mind once I get to use their hot tub."

Dad chuckled. "You want a hot tub, you can always take a bath."

I groaned. "Daaaaad! It's not the same and you know it."

"Heh. I guess. So what were their parents like? About . . . you know."

My shoulders tensed a bit. I didn't want to tell Dad how much better they were than him even though they were cis, but it was true. "Well they didn't say anything about you or Mom. I'm not sure if Bailey told them? I can ask if you want."

He nodded, stiffly, like that slight motion hurt his neck.

"And their mom seems cool. Super nice, but we didn't talk all that much. Their dad, though, he told me what his pronouns are and asked what mine were, and then Bailey made fun of him for it."

Dad snorted. "I remember doing that. 'What pronouns do you go by, make sure to share your pronouns.' People making up their own, 'my pronouns are *aye matey* because I'm a pirate!' What those people don't get is that the whole reason I did *this*"—he gestured at his face, his beard—"is so that people would look at me and assume I was a man."

I didn't want to argue with him, but that first day I saw Bailey popped into my head. "But . . . I mean. But what if someone doesn't want that? What if someone isn't a boy or a girl, like Bailey? I don't want to guess, what if I get it wrong?"

Dad shook his head impatiently. "Like I said before. A lot of guys I knew were also genderqueer. Some of them used other pronouns, 'ze' and 'hir' were popular back then. But most of them went on to be men. If Bailey's serious about being trans, they'll go that way too. And if it's too hard, they'll stop, which means they're not really trans anyway."

Maybe he was right about the people he met a zillion years ago before I was born, but I was not going to let him get away with predicting the future for someone else. I put my fists on my hips and looked him square in the eye. "What if it's only hard because people don't believe them? What if it was okay to be nonbinary? Maybe more people would be."

A spike of nervousness flashed through me. I didn't want a repeat of that first dinner, when he told me not to be friends with Bailey. But he just sighed, and looked away. "Annabelle, this is all new to you. Trust me. I know what I'm talking about. Now let's go eat dinner before it gets cold."

I wasn't sure if he knew as much as he thought he did. But at least he was talking about it now. That was a start.

chapter 12

When I was little I thought that teachers lived at school. That first time I ran into a teacher outside of school (Mrs. Marin, at the grocery store) it was a bigger shock than finding out the tooth fairy wasn't real. Teachers never seem human, you know? They all have perfect handwriting, and are always happy and calm and know the answers to everything. Like robots. But the next morning Amy looked tired, and her smile had another expression flickering behind it. I wondered if there was something going on in her personal life—maybe her mom was sick, or her house caught on fire?

But I didn't have long to wonder. "Good morning, friends. I have to tell you that there's been a change in our social studies curriculum. There has been a request to move back to the ancient civilizations study. We found an old binder full of lesson plans, so that's what I'll be teaching from."

"Wait, why?" Audrey asked.

"Yeah, do we have to?" Olivia whined. "That sounds so boring!"

"It turns out that there are some people in the community

who think that the ancient civilizations study is more . . . appropriate than what we had discussed," Amy said. But it seemed like there was a lot under her words that she wasn't saying. "As a new teacher here, there is some thinking that I shouldn't change too much right away."

I snuck a peek at Dixon. I figured he would be happy about this and I was right. He was leaning back on his elbows, a self-satisfied smirk on his face. But he didn't look surprised. Did he know this was going to happen? But how could he? Something strange was going on. I turned back to the meeting.

Patrick raised his hand. "But I wanted us to do things for Earth Day! Get compost bins for every classroom and make sure that none of our snacks have palm oil in them and—"

Amy interrupted him. "Like I said, Patrick, *I* have a curriculum that I am required to teach. But you, as a student, can also come up with ideas and share them with the community. Draft a proposal, find other interested students, and you can work on it together. In fact, if *any* of you have ideas for projects we can work on in class, we will find time for that, but it can't be part of social studies. We have to learn about the Greeks instead."

So we did. It was boring. A lot of words ending in "cracy" and "polis." We had lunch outside again, and this time we all sat together to complain. Well, most of us complained.

"I don't want to learn about a bunch of people who died a million years ago!" Jonas whined. "I thought this year was going to be different."

"Yeah," Sadie agreed. "We've literally never learned anything about Asia. I looked it up and that month is in April. I was already coming up with ideas."

"If we don't do *anything* for Black History Month, my parents are going to be so mad," Amanda added. "They're already mad that it's only one month, but now it's going to be old dead white guy *year*."

Dixon snorted. "Whatever. You're all complaining about missing out on your special interests, but this history affects all of us! I mean, our entire civilization is based on it. No offense, Sadie, but if we were in Korea we'd be learning about your culture, right? And that would be fine! But we're in America, and we should learn about the ideas that founded our country."

"What are you *talking* about?" I burst out. "We don't live in Greece! Or Rome! We live in America! At the very least we should be learning about, like, the Native Americans, since they were here first!"

Dixon shrugged. "Yeah, but they didn't have a civilization like ours, right? I guess we were founded by England, so it would make sense to learn about British history, but honestly we owe everything to the ancient Greeks. Sorry if that offends you, but it's true." He threw a handful of Pirate's Booty in his mouth like there was nothing more to say. A few of us started to argue with him again, but Bailey's voice cut through the chatter.

"It's not true, though," they said. "History doesn't belong to people like you."

Dixon started coughing. One of the booties must have swam down the wrong pipe. He managed to choke out, "What do you mean, 'people like me,'" through a spray of crumbs. I theatrically wiped some off my forehead and glared at him.

Bailey gestured at him. "Your whole deal. Privileged white boy who thinks you're the only one who understands the real world. You're so narrow-minded that you honestly believe there's nothing outside of what you've been taught."

"Don't label me!" he exclaimed, flushing red. "You don't get to call me names! How would you like if I started putting you in boxes too?"

Bailey rolled their eyes. "Okay, number one, I'm not labeling you, I'm *describing* you. And number two, you are doing that to me. And to the rest of us. You think you're the only one who doesn't belong in a box, but that's because you've been taught that your little box is the whole world." I cheered internally. Bailey was mopping the floor with him, I could watch this show all day.

Dixon sneered. "Yeah, well, you're welcome to your opinion, but the school is on my side. We wouldn't have to learn about this stuff if it wasn't important. And you heard Amy—if you want to come up with little projects about, like, your special interests, you can do that. So you don't have anything to complain about."

"Dixon, you—"

"He's not worth it, Bailey." Annabelle said that. Not me, the other Annabelle. She had been sitting quietly, like she always did, eating her lunch. Dixon spun around in shock.

"Excuse me?" he said, aggrieved.

"He's not worth it," she said again. "Don't even try. He'll keep arguing until you give up, and then he'll decide that he's won. It's a game for him, but you don't have to play."

I had never seen anyone turn such a bright shade of red. Dixon grabbed up the rest of his lunch and stalked off. We all waited for the other Annabelle to drop another truth bomb, but she went back to her Lunchable.

"I know Amy said we could come up with our own projects, but it's not fair that we have to be the teachers when we *have* a teacher," complained Amanda. "It's like saying that what we want to learn about isn't as important."

Patrick had a vein bulging in his neck, which always happened when he got upset. "Yeah. Like, 'Here's the least important stuff, but everything else you kids can figure out on your own.'"

I snuck a peek over at Amy. She was sitting on a bench off to the side, looking at her phone and eating a salad. Obviously she was listening to everything we were saying, but pretending not to. I wondered why she hadn't intervened when Dixon got into it with us. Wasn't she supposed to stop those kinds of conflicts? Or at least tell us who was right? But maybe part of sixth grade was figuring those things out for ourselves. Or maybe . . . could teachers get in trouble, the same way kids could? That was hard to imagine, but a lot of what I thought about adults had been proven wrong lately.

"They can't stop me, though," Patrick continued. "September was when it started to get chilly, back when we were little. But none of us even need sweatshirts yet! We've got to do *something* to stop global warming." We all nodded.

"Dixon probably doesn't even believe in climate change," Audrey griped.

"He doesn't have to believe in it for it to happen," the other Annabelle muttered. Then Johnson started telling us about how the oil industry replaced coal after World War II because of some plan, and then lunch was over.

We had art class that afternoon. We didn't have an art teacher, though, different parents volunteered to hang out in the studio while we painted or worked with clay or sewed a pillow. Today it was some random third-grader's mom we didn't know. She sat in the corner and read a magazine while we worked.

I wanted to sit next to Bailey, but I'd been sticking to them like glue even before realizing that I *liked* them. I thought maybe I should give them a break from me. Maybe they would start to miss me. I sat down next to Patrick instead, who was piecing together a robot out of bits of upcycled trash, since there was something we had to talk about anyway.

"Hey, if you do a climate change project, can I help?" I asked.

"Sure!" He looked excited. "Did you have an idea?"

"Noooo," I apologized. "But I know what you mean, about how it feels hotter than it did when we were little. And the fires last winter. I get panicked looking at headlines about it.

And I thought that maybe doing something to help would make me feel better."

"Yeah, I pretty much only do anything because it makes me feel better," he agreed. "Like I decided to stop eating palm oil after that video about orangutans getting their trees burned down. I felt awful, and it makes me feel better to know that I'm not making it worse. And I saw a news story about how kids our age work in factories to make clothes for almost all the stores in the mall, and that made me feel awful too, so now I only get clothes from Value Village, and that makes me feel better. Maybe I'm being selfish, maybe everything I do is to stop myself from feeling bad, but . . ."

"But at least you're doing something," I finished. "Yeah. Well, I bet we can come up with a project that is more than not-doing something bad."

"I hope so," he said, gluing a broken circuit board onto his robot.

I gazed around the art studio, deciding what I wanted to work on. My eyes happened to land on Bailey, who was working on a clay sculpture of an aye-aye. They smiled at me, and I decided that I had given them enough of a break from me. I got my own lump of clay and started to make a porcupine next to them.

We worked steadily, our knees inches apart on the art room stools more appropriate for kindergartners. I was intensely conscious of how short my fingers looked, rolling out each individual quill, nothing like their elegant hands shaping the soft clay. When they looked over at my creation and nodded approvingly, I flushed. And when they asked me to help stick on the creepy extra-long finger that aye-ayes are famous for, it was hard to keep my hands from trembling.

"Do you want to come over for a sleepover this weekend?" they asked, when the finger was safely attached.

"Yes!" I exclaimed, a surge of hope coursing through my body. "Which day?"

"How about Friday night?" they suggested. "My parents are fine with it. Dad's going to make risotto, does that work for you?"

"I don't even know what that is but it probably does. I like everything except for artichokes and blue cheese."

"Okay, well, awkward, but artichokes plus blue cheese dressing is literally my favorite meal in the entire world. But I forgive you! Neither of those things have to be in this risotto. And we can make popcorn and watch a movie, I'm allowed to stay up as late as I want during sleepovers."

"That sounds amazing. My parents always make me go to bed, even during sleepovers, because they can hear everything."

"Yeah, we had to keep it down in my old apartment, it was way smaller than your house! But now if we sleep in the living room and they're in their bedroom we could set off firecrackers and they wouldn't hear."

"Cool! I'll bring the fireworks." I spent the rest of art class attaching tiny porcupine quills, picturing the two of us lying in our sleeping bags, facing each other, talking and giggling and getting closer and closer until . . . I wondered if I was about to have my first kiss.

I walked home from school Friday, and a couple hours later Mom dropped me off at Bailey's. "Have fun, Bells," she yelled through the window. I waved at her. She looked extra pretty, and I wondered if she and Dad were going to have a date night. I also wondered if I was having a date night. But I firmly told the grasshopper party in my stomach to calm down. Being a ball of excited, nervous, crushed-out energy would ruin the sleepover. And if I pretended like I didn't like them like that, maybe it would get them to like me like that.

Bailey helped me bring my stuff up to their bedroom, which I hadn't seen the last time I came over. And of course it was perfectly decorated to match their whole deal. On one wall they had hung a big rainbow flag. On the other was a poster with a zillion different kinds of fruits and vegetables and plants. Their bedspread was zebra print, and their bookshelf was stuffed full of old books and new books.

I was curious about the plant poster, and walked over to examine it more closely. "What is this?" I asked. "A flowchart or something?"

"Oh! There's a whole series of these. Each poster is about a different taxonomy. Taxonomy is, like, groups of things, and how they're organized. This one is about different kinds of fruit."

I peered at it. Cucumbers and pumpkins and eggplants and avocados, all connected by lines and arrows. "Uh, no it's not?" I said. "I mean, yeah, those are fruit up there"—I pointed to the top, where there were apples and oranges and bananas—"but the rest of these are vegetables! And those helicopter seeds aren't fruits either."

Bailey grinned wickedly. "I have news for you, my binary friend!" They dropped their voice like they were about to utter a revealing truth of the universe. "There is no. Such. Thing. As a vegetable."

I squinted at the chart, and then at them, and then back at the chart. "Yes there is! What are carrots, then? I don't see those here."

"Carrots are roots."

"Okay, kale?"

"Leaves."

"Artichokes? I mean, they're gross, but those are definitely vegetables."

"Wrong on both counts! Artichokes are delicious and flowers."

"Flowers??"

"Yup. Broccoli and cauliflower and figs are all flowers too. 'Vegetable' is a made-up category."

That didn't make any sense. "If vegetables are made up, then why aren't fruits?"

"Because they're not!" Bailey looked triumphant, like this was a hill they would gladly die on. "'Fruit' is a job. It describes the part of the plant that distributes the seeds. Apples and oranges are fruits because they have seeds. So are pumpkins and cucumbers! And tomatoes. And those helicopter seeds. And berries. As a matter of fact, everything I named is a type of berry."

"But 'vegetable' isn't a job?" I wracked my brain to come up with something that all vegetables had in common, but I couldn't. Except that they're good for you.

"Nope! Leaves are a job and roots are a job and flowers are a job. 'Vegetable' is something people made up to sell salad mix."

"Wow." My head was spinning, which was a sensation I was getting used to around Bailey. "So you're saying that our vegetable garden is actually a . . . food-plant garden. That's cool?"

Bailey bounced onto their bed. "I think it's cool. It's a reminder that a lot of the categories people have come up with are fake. And that even if we pretend they're important, like 'eat your vegetables if you want to be healthy,' they don't always do a good job of describing or explaining the world. Like, people could look at me and be like 'She's obviously a girl because of xyz,' or 'He should be a boy because of whatever,' but 'boy' and 'girl' aren't even important categories."

I plopped down onto my rolled-up sleeping bag. "But . . . okay, I don't want to get you mad, but I have a question."

They sat up. "I won't be mad if you're asking to try to understand. I'll only get mad if you're going to argue about what I am."

I shook my head vehemently. "To understand. Okay. So vegetables are fake because they don't describe a job. And gender is stuff we've made up. But what about . . . not what you are 'really,' but don't body parts do jobs too? And those are related to gender?"

Bailey sighed. "Yeah, I know. But first of all, my body's main job is to keep me alive for as long as possible, like everyone else's, so I don't get why people are so hung up on all the other bells and whistles. I guess I'm like a tomato. A lot of people say 'You're a vegetable because I think that you're a vegetable' and some people are like 'You're a fruit because of the jobs your body parts do.' But *I'm* the tomato, not them, and tomatoes are great, so why does it even matter? You can put me on pizza or spaghetti or in a salad and one time I had tomato gelato and it was delicious. So I could be a dessert too. Who cares!"

Leave it to Bailey to make *salad* the most fascinating topic ever. Would I ever know as much as them? But before I had time to feel bad about myself, Michael's voice floated up the stairs. "Hey offspring and friend! Dinner is ready!" he called, so downstairs we went.

"So Annabelle, are you as annoyed as Bailey is about the whole ancient civilizations study?" asked Michael, spooning some risotto onto my plate. I hadn't been entirely sure what risotto was, but my shrewd powers of deduction told me that it was a gloppy rice situation.

"I don't know how you would measure annoyed," I said,

scooping up some risotto on my fork. "But yeah, I was excited to learn about stuff going on right now. Like, what you read about in the newspaper, not what we have to figure out from stone tablets and things."

"I was disappointed too," said Lindsay. "We loved Bailey's old school, and when we met with the principal, he made the Lab sound like it had the same philosophies. I guess he was trying to get us to enroll."

"And this is all his fault!" Bailey exclaimed. "I mean, the new stuff was Amy's idea, right? And then on Monday she was saying how she was told to change it back because of, like, 'community members' or something. I bet you anything it was Principal Quinn making her for whatever reason."

I didn't know the principal at all. I'd never gotten in trouble, so I only saw him at assemblies and things. But he always talked to us like we were little kids, which got on my nerves even when I *was* a little kid.

"Well, it could be worse," said Michael. "I got an email from Spectrum Families. Apparently a kid at St. Luke's came out as nonbinary and was immediately expelled."

"What?!" Bailey exclaimed. "That's terrible! What year were they? Is SF doing anything to help?"

"They're a freshman—I mean, first-year," said Michael, "and I'm not sure, the email didn't go into much detail. If you want to follow up, we can do that together."

Half my attention was working through the fruits and vegetables thing—the risotto had mushrooms in it and there were green beans on the side. I guessed that green beans were technically berries but had no idea what mushrooms would be. I wanted to ask but figured now wasn't the time. This was more important.

"Why were they kicked out?" I asked. "And what's Spectrum Families?"

"SF is the organization we were part of down in Seattle, for families that included parents or children who are LGBTQ," explained Lindsay. "And St. Luke's is the only all-boys school in Seattle. It's known for being one of the most traditional and conservative schools in the area, though it's also come a long way. They have a gay-straight alliance now, but it *is* an all-boys school. I guess technically, if a student isn't a boy, they think they have the right to expel them."

"That's terrible," Bailey said. "That poor person."

"Yeah," I agreed. "But . . . um, I have another question, but I don't want you to get mad at me for asking?"

"I bet I can guess," said Bailey. They sounded not mad, exactly, but a little prickly. "You're going to ask why a boys' school should let in someone who isn't a boy, and/or why a person who isn't a boy would want to go to a boys' school anyway, right?"

I squirmed, a little. "I mean . . . yeah. That was my question. Both of them, I guess. Is that dumb?"

"There are no dumb questions!" exclaimed Michael, but that was a thing adults only said to make kids feel better. I'd been in school long enough to know that there were some dumb questions.

Bailey shrugged. "It's not a bad question, I guess. It's true that those schools are making a choice about what gender they accept, so technically they have a right to enforce that. But I bet you a million dollars that they did it the worst way possible. That kid probably didn't want to make a big deal of it, but they were bullied so bad that the school was forced to make a decision, and instead of making their school a better place they decided to get rid of the 'problem.'" I didn't know fake air quotes could be violent until Bailey clawed at the word "problem." "I guess girls' and boys' schools don't *have* to let in nonbinary people, but they're not doing right by their students. And we don't even know if the kid wanted to go there! Maybe their parents made them, or something. And now the school is saying 'You can come here for now, but if you learn something important about yourself, buh-bye!' Instead of letting people grow and figure themselves out and have it be okay. Ugh."

"Make sure you're finding time to eat dinner in between rants, dear," said Lindsay. I quickly shoveled a bite of risotto into my mouth; it wasn't as good cold, but it was still buttery and salty. Bailey angrily took a bite, showing less appreciation. Maybe they'd had risotto so many times it was boring.

"Here's what I'll do, Bailey," said Michael. "I'll email Spectrum Families asking if anyone is supporting the student and their family. Maybe we can drive down to Seattle if there's anything going on that we can join. How does that sound?"

"Fine, I guess." They let out the angriest sigh. "But I wish there was something I could *do*. It sucks being so far away from community."

I twisted my napkin anxiously. I guessed I wasn't technically community yet, because communities were people who spent time together and talked and fought and figured things out, and I didn't know how I belonged in it yet. I couldn't be a substitute for everything they left behind in Seattle, and maybe I wasn't part of some cool family group. But I could help too.

"I wonder if my dad has any ideas," I blurted out. Then regretted it, immediately, when I saw the look on Bailey's face. They knew my dad wouldn't have any ideas. So did I. He would probably argue that the kid should make up their mind. Maybe go to a girls' school if they wanted to be a girl, but either way pick one.

"Bailey told us about your dad," Lindsay said kindly. "What ideas do you think he might have?"

Bailey wouldn't meet my eyes. They knew that he wouldn't want to do anything. "I'm not sure," I said. "I can ask." I wouldn't ask.

"I'll ask around too," Lindsay promised. "Our trans friends were so helpful when Bailey came out. Does your dad know anyone in the Seattle scene?"

I shifted in my chair. "He might? I don't know."

"He's been stealth for so long, he probably doesn't," Bailey muttered. They sounded annoyed, so I decided not to ask what that meant. Of course Michael had to butt in.

"I think your friend needs a literacy moment, B! Can you explain what 'stealth' means?"

They sighed exasperatedly. "What your dad's been doing. Letting people see him as a man, and assume that he's cis."

"Oh. Yeah, that's him," I conceded, intently staring at my placemat.

"That's certainly a valid choice!" Michael chirped. "Different people get to choose what works best for them."

"Not everyone has that choice," Bailey muttered. I wanted to know what they meant by that, but was not about to ask *another* question. I took one last bite of dinner and discovered there was a point where risotto got too cold to eat. I was learning so many things.

Michael balled up his napkin and threw it on the table. "Well, that was quite a thought-provoking meal! Bailey, Annabelle, if you two clear the table I'll take care of the cleanup. I know you have a busy night of snacks and movies in front of you."

As we cleared the table, the heft of their solid plates heavy and unfamiliar in my hands, a memory of my first-ever sleepover popped into my head. I was five, and was going to spend the night at Franka's house. Her mom ordered pizza, we ate off paper plates, and I was allowed to drink two cups of soda, which never happened at my house. But right after dinner I started missing my mom, and the idea of going to bed without her and waking up without her sent me into a sudden crying jag. Franka's mom called my mom and she came and picked me up and took me home. It took another year before I was able to try another sleepover. By that point I didn't even remember my baby panic attack, and hadn't thought about it since. But tonight I empathized with my younger self's fear of something new, and overwhelming desire for what I've always known. The problem was I was too old to call my mom to come take me home. And also, "home" wasn't what it used to be.

The evening gradually turned into a regular sleepover. After dinner we played Trivial Pursuit, not a kids' version but an old-fashioned one with questions no eleven-year-old would ever be expected to know, so it turned into a contest about who could come up with the funniest answers. Once the kitchen was clean we completely messed it up again baking a cake. I didn't understand how box cake could be so messy when all you have to do is crack an egg and add some oil and water, but it took forever to clean chocolate powder off of the different surfaces.

"Did you know that the first box cake mixes didn't even need an egg added?" I asked as I wiped off the knobs on the stove.

"Really? Like, they included dried egg and all you needed to add were the liquids?"

"Yup, pretty much," I said, proud to know a random fact that they didn't. "It didn't sell, though, and marketers figured out that people wanted to feel like they were cooking, and cracking an egg was the way to do that."

"The illusion of effort," they mused, and I nodded like that made sense. My mom made the world's best cakes, from scratch. She was the one who told me about the eggs, and how much marketing controlled what we thought was true. I thought about saying that but had a suspicion it might turn into another conversation about ~gender~, which would make me feel like a toddler pointing at every truck driving by and yelling "Truck!" while Bailey was the patient babysitter being like "Yes, that is also a truck." It wasn't a good feeling.

While the cake was cooling, we changed into our pajamas. I usually slept in my underwear and one of my mom's giant old T-shirts, but for this occasion I brought the only nightgown I owned. It was honestly too frilly for bed, but I successfully convinced my parents to buy me one after watching a slumber party movie where all the girls wore them. I thought it made me look like a princess. Of course Bailey's pj's were as cool as everything else they owned, printed with different baby animals asleep on their parents, like a joey in a pouch and a bunch of baby possums clinging to a big possum. Then we took pieces of chocolate cake into the living room and watched a movie, an old one about a vampire slayer that they eventually turned into a TV show. I hadn't forgotten that I wanted this sleepover to turn us into something more than friends, but it seemed like it wasn't going to happen right away. And the low simmer in my belly added a sparkle to the evening, a sense of endless possibility, like everything we were doing now was going to turn into a story for later.

It wasn't until much later—their parents were in bed, we were yawning in our sleeping bags—that Bailey started talking about school problems again.

"It's not right," they said, flopping back onto their pillow.

"What's not right?" I asked. They could be talking about anything, since a lot of things weren't right, and I didn't want to guess.

"None of it," they said. I was right. "Not the stuff going on in our class, or that kid getting expelled in Seattle. It's all the same problem, you know? There are so many things going on, *right now*, that are important to us, and will also affect our entire future, but they want to keep teaching us the same things that they learned, stuff that will never change. Principal Quinn wants us to learn about guys who have been dead for thousands of years, not people that are changing the world today. And an all-boys school is kicking out a nonbinary kid, but you know they would also never accept a trans boy. It's all the same. They care more about what happened to them than what's going to happen for us."

"Exactly!" I exclaimed. "Adults think that because they're in charge of everything right now, they should get a say in what our future looks like. But it's *our* future, not theirs. It's like school and our parents and everyone else is getting us ready to enter a world that doesn't even exist anymore. Or, if it does, it shouldn't. Right?"

"Right," they agreed. "Some teachers at my old school

understood that. And I think Amy does too, but clearly she can't do whatever she wants."

"I talked to Patrick during art today. He's going to come up with some kind of climate change project, and I want to help him with that. Do you want to join us?"

"Hmm." Bailey propped themselves up on their elbows. "Maybe. But you know how Amy talked about different months, how February is Black History Month and March is Women's History Month? October is Queer Awareness Month! It was a big deal at my old school—we put up posters and had guest speakers and things. I guess it's not as important as climate change, but I would be so happy if something like that happened at the Lab."

I shook my head vehemently. "I don't think that any one thing is more important than any other thing. And we need that at the Lab too."

Bailey gasped loudly and put their hands over their mouth.

"Are you okay? What happened?"

"I have the best idea!" they said. "We want to do something with that St. Luke's kid, right? What if, for National Coming Out Day, we had them come with a bunch of different out queer people to talk to our class? Maybe some of the parents from my SF group, or I could ask one of my old teachers. It would be all the different kinds of LGBTQ you can be! I bet nothing like that has ever happened at the Lab. And I bet you anything Amy would be into it."

"That's an *amazing* idea!" I exclaimed. And perfect, because

I had never heard anyone come out before until Bailey, and then my parents. Hearing other people tell their stories might give me ideas about how to talk about mine. "Would you want to be on it?"

"Nah, you're all going to get to know me. But we could find a bunch of different people, different identities and jobs and things, to talk about their lives and what it was like when they were our age—oh my gosh, we *have* to do this."

I nodded vigorously, but paused on the word "we." "Um. I mean, that is a great idea, but I don't know how much I can help? I'm still, uh, learning about all this. And I already told Patrick that I would work with him." I *could* ditch Patrick to work on something with my secret crush, but that didn't seem fair.

"Oh, that's right," said Bailey. "Hm. You can be my independent consultant! I'll tell you about what I'm planning, and any questions you have, everyone else will probably have too. You're my finger on the ground! My ear on the pulse! Or however those sayings go."

"I think you have them reversed," I said, laughing. But my laugh soon turned into a jaw-splitting yawn. "I'm sleeeeeepy," I said. "I always start sleepovers wanting to stay up all night, but it's not even one in the morning. No way I'm going to make it."

"I'm tired too," they agreed. "Okay. Let's talk about this more tomorrow, though."

We settled into our sleeping bags, talking a little longer

about nothing. Night time things. Half-awake things. I had
this strange falling sensation, not like I was falling asleep, but
like I was falling from my childhood into whatever would
come next.

chapter 13

Bailey walked me home after the sleepover. The late September morning was warm and bright. Our stomachs were full of toaster waffles. Bailey was carrying my sleeping bag while chattering about the panel idea they had come up with.

"How many people should there be?" they asked. "I don't think three is enough, but if there's six or seven people, no one would be able to talk. Four? Does four sound good? Three adults and then that high schooler? I should find out their name. And their pronouns, also, since not all nonbinary people go by they/them."

I was having a hard time keeping up, Bailey was talking so fast. "Yeah, four sounds good," I said. "Would they all be people from Seattle?"

"Unless you know of anyone here who would want to."

I shook my head, but what did I know? Maybe there were a lot of LGBTQ people in Tahoma Falls who wanted to be out. Sometimes when Bailey talked about Seattle, it sounded like another planet, not a city a forty-minute drive away. And then we were at my house. My dad came out to help me carry my things inside and gave Bailey a nod. "You two had fun?" he asked.

"Yeah!" they said. "Plans are a-hatching. Thanks for letting her come over."

"Our house is also available for sleepovers," he said, and while he wasn't exactly smiling, there was some relaxation around his mouth, and a drop of warmth in his voice. Bailey grinned, we hugged goodbye, and my throat and stomach throbbed like my crush had its own heartbeat. I forced myself to let go before they noticed anything, and my father and I went inside.

I threw my sleeping bag in the closet and my dirty clothes in the hamper. I was about to put my toothbrush back in the bathroom when Dad knocked lightly against the doorframe. He leaned against it, not quite coming in.

"How was it?" he asked.

Bailey's family is so much cooler than ours in every way, is what I wanted to say. But that wouldn't be fair. "Nice," I said. "Their dad is a good cook. We had risotto!"

"Fancy," he said. He hesitated, clearly struggling over his next question. "Do you know if . . . if Bailey told them. About me."

"Yes." His body sagged against the frame, but I couldn't tell if it was in relief or disappointment. "They told me about this group they were part of in Seattle, called Spectrum Families. For kids and parents who are gay or trans or whatever. And Bailey's mom asked if you knew any other trans people in

Seattle, because . . . um, because maybe some of them were in the group, and I said you didn't."

Or so I thought. "I do, actually," he said. "For a few months I had to go to a trans health center down there, to get my prescription. Hormones," he clarified. "Testosterone. I chatted with some guys I met in the waiting room. They gave me their numbers, but we didn't stay in touch. I wasn't ready, not with a baby, a new house, everything that happened in Arizona . . . and once things calmed down a bit I figured they had forgotten about me."

Wow. "Cool," I said. I didn't want to say anything else, didn't want to let anything else slip. This side of Dad, where he talked about anything related to his past, was so new. And like any newborn, it was fragile, as though one wrong move could break it all to pieces. But if I was careful, it would grow into something new and amazing. So we waited there, him right outside my bedroom, until he said, "Well, glad you had a good time. And glad you're back." He pounded the doorframe with his fist, gently, and as he turned away I was overcome with the urge to hug him. So I did, coming up behind him and wrapping my arms around his narrow rib cage, so different from my mom's broad warmth, and he paused, surprised, then squeezed my hands before I let him go.

It was a beautiful Sunday afternoon, so it was no surprise to find my mother outside. She was wearing her "garden dress," she called it, a light blue sundress covered in years of dirt and grass stains, and she looked like a fat Cinderella who had already found her prince but still liked to get her hands dirty.

She enveloped me in a hug, smelling like sweat and sunshine and earth. "Bells! You're home! We missed you!"

"Mooom," I protested, but hugged her back. "It was one night! Not even twenty-four hours! How could you possibly miss me?"

"You're my baby, missing you is my job."

"What did you and Dad do? Candlelit dinner, romantic movie?"

Mom laughed. "As a matter of fact, we got dressed up and went out to dinner. First time in years. It was lovely. How was the sleepover?"

I could tell Mom all about how much I liked Bailey. She would understand. But I didn't want to. I didn't feel ready. And we were already talking about so many new things, the idea of adding another topic of conversation made me want to go to bed and pull the covers over my head. And besides, if Bailey ended up not liking me back, I would rather pretend like none of this ever happened than have to explain it to my mom and have her look at me all sympathetic. That seemed excruciating.

There were other topics of conversation, though. "It was fun but also kind of a lot, honestly. I learned some interesting facts about fruits and vegetables, apparently most of these plants are fruits but some of them are other things. At dinner Bailey's dad told us about this thing that happened in Seattle, where a nonbinary kid got kicked out of a boys' school. Bailey got upset, and they want to help. They got the idea to have a bunch of out queer people come talk to my class, apparently there's something called National Coming Out Day?"

"Bless their heart," Mom said, laughing wistfully. "National Coming Out Day. I remember that. You know what, when I was in college I organized a panel, like what Bailey wants to do. This one woman talked about how she came out as femme, and that was the moment I recognized what I was."

My ears perked up. This was the perfect opportunity to ask Mom more about herself, without her realizing that I was also asking about me. "Okay, I know you met Dad through something called a butch/femme society, but I guess I don't know what 'butch' or 'femme' means. Is 'femme' short for 'feminine'? And is 'butch' the opposite?"

"It's related," Mom said, "but . . . oh, my goodness, I haven't talked about this in so long. Femme is . . . how I move through the world as a woman. Not just how I dress, but how I feel about myself. It's about being beautiful on my own terms, not because of what magazines or Hollywood says. It's about being strong, but not giving up my softness. And butch isn't exactly the opposite, but it's a way of imagining the good parts of masculinity without the bad. Does that make sense?"

"It sure does," I said. I was carefully filing away everything she said to chew over. I wanted to ask her more about how she found out who she got crushes on, and what that meant, but one big piece of information at a time was enough.

"So, an NCOD panel? Is Principal Quinn going to be okay with that? I know he doesn't usually do things that rock the boat."

"I'm not sure! Bailey hasn't even told our teacher yet. But I bet she'll be excited about it, so maybe we won't tell him. And I'm going to work with Patrick on something about climate change. I don't know what yet, but he said he would come up with some ideas."

"My little activist," Mom said, pulling me against her and kissing my cheek. "Have you told your father?"

"Have you told your father what?" my father called, crossing the yard. Mom's brow creased a tiny bit, and my heart started to beat a little faster.

"Um. I'm going to do a group project with Patrick about climate change?" Dad raised his eyebrows like he knew there was more to say besides that. "And. So. There's something called National Coming Out Day." I searched his face for signs of recognition, but he gave away nothing. "And . . . well, Bailey wants to do something. A panel. They found out about a nonbinary kid kicked out of school, and they want to get in touch with them. And find some out adults to talk about what it's like."

Dad grabbed a hoe and started hacking at chunks of dry dirt. It was uncomfortably silent for a long time, and I kept accidentally pulling up plants instead of weeds. Though I guess Bailey would say they were all plants, since weeds are plants. I kept pulling up the wrong ones, though, and was replanting a geranium when Dad finally said, "The problem with coming out is that you can never go back in. Once people know, they know."

"I'm not sure if that's true," Mom countered gently. "Back when I had woman partners, people were always asking about my husband or boyfriend. I had to come out every day, and at the time I thought that would never change."

"I wish that had been true for me," Dad grunted, pulling at a root, eyes on the ground. I didn't know how to respond to that, and Mom didn't either, so I started chattering some more about the plan to help Patrick with a climate change project, the cake Bailey and I baked, and the movie we watched. Made it sound like Bailey was a normal new friend, and we had a normal sleepover, and it wasn't going to change anything. But Coming Out Day, and everything it meant, had lodged itself in my brain, and was proving harder to uproot than a patch of crabgrass.

"You each have ten seconds to share about your weekend," Amy announced Monday, as we gathered on the rug for morning meeting. "I'll count down ten seconds on my fingers, and when it hits zero, it's the next person's turn to share."

Oh man, the pressure! I was glad to be last, sitting between Bailey and Amy, and managed to pay attention for once. Patrick said that he and his family went hiking in the Hoh rainforest. Dixon kept talking even after his ten seconds were up, claiming that his big brother was visiting from college for the weekend and snuck him into a rated-R movie. Amanda had obviously been rehearsing what she was going to say while other kids were sharing, and launched into a rapid-fire monologue that managed to include a ton of information about baking cookies, going to the mall, and babysitting for the neighbor, while ending with two seconds to spare.

Finally it was Bailey's turn. Their shirt of the day was amazing: some kind of winged creature, with words over it saying "I'm not a social butterfly, I'm a sarcastic moth." "Annabelle came over for a sleepover and we learned about a nonbinary kid who got kicked out of school and I want to organize a panel of speakers to come visit for National Coming Out Day, you said we could do that sort of thing not during social studies so is that okay?"

Amy had one finger left to fold down; it was impressive that Bailey could cram all that into nine seconds. "Let's come back to that after Annabelle shares! Annabelle, last but not least."

"Everything Bailey said! Also, I found out that risotto is delicious."

Amy laughed. "So concise! Bailey, go ahead and say more about your idea."

They explained the whole situation and their brainstorm. Amy smiled. "I love that idea, and I love that you're taking on this initiative." She turned around to look at the calendar behind her, the one crammed full of information about different Days and Weeks. "National Coming Out Day is a Tuesday. Do you think you could find speakers willing to come in the morning?"

"Sure. I haven't even asked anyone yet."

Dixon raised his hand, and I could tell from the curl of his lip that whatever he was about to say wasn't going to be good. "So, if I wanted to invite a group of straight people to talk about being heterosexual"—that word sounded so *weird*, especially coming from him—"that would be okay too, right?"

"That's called a talk show," Olivia called out, and we all laughed.

"I'm just asking," Dixon insisted. "It wouldn't hurt, and it's only fair."

We all looked at Amy. Except Bailey, who was staring daggers at Dixon. "I suppose that depends on your definition of 'fair,'" Amy said. "And 'hurt.' Maybe after Bailey's panel we can revisit your idea, based on what we learn from hearing other people share about their experiences. Does that sound acceptable?"

A ringing silence followed her words. Clearly nobody thought that sounded acceptable. But then it was time to move on.

Patrick came up to me as we were getting ready for lunch. "Do you want to eat with me?" he asked. "I have an idea for the project, if you want to help."

"I sure do! Bailey, do you want to join us?"

"Yeah, but I also want to talk about my panel with Amy. How about if we fill each other in later? You could come over after school."

"Teamwork!" I exclaimed, giving them a high-five, but I felt a pang of regret as they went over to Amy's desk. National Coming Out Day was still looming in my mind. Like the deadline for me to figure out which letter in LGBTQ+ applied to me, now that I knew that I was *something*. Helping Bailey plan for the day might give me a chance to figure it out, but asking them to constantly explain things didn't sound like helping. But I was pretty sure that I had completely invented the idea that NCOD was a rule rather than a suggestion. ACOD, Annabelle's Coming Out Day, could happen whenever I wanted it to.

So Patrick and I settled down at his desk. I opted to sit across from him, in Johnson's spot, because my skin crawled at the idea of sitting in Dixon's chair.

"Like I said, my parents took me and my brother to the rainforest over the weekend," Patrick began. "Have you been there?"

"We went a few years ago," I said, "but it was very, uh, rainy, and all of our shoes got covered in mud and it wasn't a fun hike, so we decided not to go back."

Patrick laughed. "We got entirely covered in mud, but our car has a special mud tarp over the back seat. That's part of the fun! But anyway, at one point the sun came out, and everything was *steaming* around us, and I thought about how crazy it is that we have this gigantic lightbulb in the sky that we almost never use because we're inside with the lights on all the time, and then it hit me!" He looked at me expectantly, like I was supposed to know what he meant, and all of a sudden I did.

"Solar panels!" I exclaimed. "On your house? Or at school?"

He beamed. "Well, how cool would it be if Tahoma Falls was entirely solar powered? But that would be a big project. For now I thought we could get solar panels on the roof here."

"I love that idea," I said. "We probably have to convince Principal Quinn before we do anything, right?"

"Well, first we have to do a lot of research about solar panel companies and how much they cost and why they're good. That sort of thing. We'll have to write a proposal, and then present that to him."

"Oh," I said, deflating a bit. I had imagined us marching into his office tomorrow with signs saying, like, SAVE OUR FUTURE and THE SUN IS OUR ONLY HOPE. But he was probably right. "Where should we start? Maybe we can split up the research. Like, one of us can talk about why solar power is important. One of us can go on the Internet and see if there are companies in the area who do that sort of thing. And go from there." That sounded kind of boring, but I reminded myself that we would be saving the world. Maybe. A little.

After lunch we had social studies, where we learned more about people who had been dead for thousands of years and why they were important. Amy did her best to make it interesting, but I could tell that even she didn't care, and was as grateful as we were when it was time for P.E.

It was the end of the day and Bailey and I were getting ready to go when the other Annabelle sidled up to us. She was wearing this beige overall dress that looked like a sack, with a frilly purple shirt underneath. "I like your panel idea," she mumbled. "Do you want my sister to come?"

"Your sister? I didn't know you had a sister," I said. I'd known the other Annabelle for most of our lives. How had I not known that?

"Is your sister LGBTQ?" asked Bailey.

Annabelle nodded. "She's in college. You could ask."

Bailey and I exchanged looks. The other Annabelle had been coming up with some good ideas lately. She had always been strange and spacey, but it would be interesting to see what an older version of her was like.

"Sure, can we call her or email her or something to talk?"

The other Annabelle nodded, but didn't say anything else, or move at all. We waited, and waited, and finally she grabbed a pen and Post-it from Bailey's desk, scrawled an email address, and handed it to us. Apparently the other Annabelle's sister went to Western Washington University.

"What's her name?" Bailey asked patiently.

"Sam. Okay. Bye." The other Annabelle hoisted her Frozen backpack higher onto her shoulders and left. Bailey tucked the Post-it into their pocket and we walked out into the early fall sun, inhaling the baked-bread scent of the warm after-noon.

The walk to Bailey's house was becoming as familiar as the walk to mine. Tahoma Falls isn't a big place and I've lived here my whole life, so you'd think I'd know every street. But turning left out of the school parking lot instead of right was like going to a whole different town. A coffee shop I'd never seen, a tiny free library in front of someone's house, an empty lot with feral cats that ran and hid as we walked by. My parents acted as though Seattle was this big, scary place that took days of preparation to visit, but there were whole other towns hidden inside this one too. But instead of it seeming like a wide-open field to explore, I started to feel itchy. Like I was trapped inside a maze that kept getting smaller and smaller the farther in I got.

When we got to Bailey's house, their dad was holding a tablet and positively vibrating with excitement.

"Bailey! It took a lot of triangulation, but if you would like the email address for the brave human who was kicked out of school for being who they are, I can give it to you! Their name is E, and they would love to hear from another young person like your incandescent self."

Bailey grimaced. "Okay Dad, thank you."

"My utmost pleasure! Now, I was doing some thinking, and you want your panel to be as representative of the community as possible, right? I have some ideas." He started listing off people like they were Pokémon or superheroes: an out trans woman on the city council, a two-spirit teacher in a public school, this gay dad who worked in HIV care. He kept naming people until Bailey cut him off.

"Dad! Stop! We can't get every single person you've ever met to come to our school, and you're not helping us narrow it down!"

"I'm sorry, Baileycakes," said Michael. "I'll give you two a break, and write down a few ideas while you email E and their family. You can pick from there. Okay?"

"Yeah, okay," Bailey grumbled. Michael put the tablet on the counter and went back downstairs.

"Hey, can I make a snack?" I asked. "I'm hungry."

"Oh, sure." Bailey rubbed their eyes. "Me too. That's probably why I snapped at Dad."

"Maybe!" I said, opening the pantry. I grabbed rice cakes and peanut butter and started making one for them, taking care to spread it thick and smooth. "I wish my dad was more like yours. If I yelled at him he'd send me to my room, or stomp off to his. Maybe he'd apologize hours later, but only because my mom would make him."

"Okay, but I wish *my* dad would chill. He always gets so excited! Like a puppy! It's great that he's supportive and everything, but he always takes my things and makes them his things. You know if we asked him to, he'd organize this whole thing, and there would be a dozen perfectly diverse queer people and he'd spend the whole time talking about how happy he was to have them visit and none of them would get a chance to say anything."

I cringed. "Yeah, I can see that."

"Exactly." Bailey picked up the tablet. "Here's E's email address, and we have the other Annabelle's sister. Let's get in touch with them first, and go from there."

We were sitting so close together. My hair brushed their shoulder, and I was self-conscious of my peanut butter breath. But Bailey didn't seem to notice, and my heart sank the tiniest bit. They composed the emails, explaining what we were planning, and once those were sent, we worked together on the little bit of homework Amy had assigned, an online worksheet about Greek root words, "pend" and "circ" and "poly." Then we heard the "ding" that meant someone had emailed us back.

"Annabelle's sister!" Bailey exclaimed. "Whoa, look at this."

I scanned the email. Sam said she would love to join, and that she was president of something called the "Disability Justice Council" at Western, and wanted to talk about "queering disability."

"Huh. The other Annabelle is nice, but Sam seems extremely cool," Bailey commented.

"Yeah," I agreed. But maybe the other Annabelle was actually cool and I never bothered to find out.

"Ooh, and E got back to us too!" I leaned over Bailey's shoulder to read.

Hi there Mx. Bailey:

What a nice surprise. Tell your dad I said thank you for his detective skills. It's been a truly awful time, no joke, but it's good to know that I have friends. That panel is an interesting idea. I haven't been able to go to Spectrum Families, but it would be nice to make a friend. Do you ever come back to Seattle? Maybe we could hang out.

Queerly,

E

"Aw, they sound sad and fun at the same time," said Bailey. "What do you say? Want to see if my parents can drive us to Seattle this weekend?"

Before I could answer, my phone buzzed wildly in my pocket, and I jumped a mile. It was Dad.

"Hi Dad!"

"Annabelle. Where are you?"

"Oh, sorry, I went to Bailey's after school. I forgot to tell you!"

"Correct."

"Um. Do you want me to come home?"

"Eventually, yes."

"Okay. I'll leave in a minute. Sorry."

"See you soon."

I pocketed my phone. "I should go. He sounded mad, but I bet he was worried because he didn't know where I was."

"You want me to walk you home?"

Of course I wanted them to walk me home, but for some reason I didn't want them to know that. "No, it's all right. Let me know what your parents say about this weekend, and I'll ask mine."

I was halfway home when a familiar two-door baby-blue car cruised up next to me. "Hop in, kiddo," said Mom. I slid in, the cloth seat comfortably warm against my legs.

"Did you come looking for me?" I asked.

"Nope, on my way home. But I know your father was worried about you."

"For no reason," I grumbled. "I've gone to friends' houses after school before. And he must have gotten home earlier than usual. Sorry I forgot to text, but I didn't really do anything wrong."

"I understand. We all make mistakes, but it's our job to make sure you're safe," said Mom. She was driving way under the speed limit, luckily no one was behind us or else they'd be honking. "We got you that cell phone so you could let us know where you are. You can see why he'd be worried to come home and find you gone, and not have any other information, right?"

"I guess," I admitted. "But still. I picked up when he called. He only had to worry for, like, five seconds. And I'm fine."

"I know. But you know your father is a worrier. He always thinks the worst. When you were a baby, every time you got a cold he'd take you to the emergency room. If I have a headache, he thinks it's a stroke. It's part of how he shows his love."

I sighed. "Is he going to be mad?"

"I don't think so. Give him a hug, make sure he knows everything's okay, he'll get over it."

"Okay. Um, I should probably ask you first now, then. Bailey and I want to go to Seattle this weekend. Their parents can drive us"—I hoped that was true—"and we're going to meet that kid who was kicked out of school, their name is E. We want to talk to them about visiting our school."

We were almost in sight of our house. Mom pulled onto the side of the road, and turned in her seat to look at me. "I'm okay with it. You know I am. And your father will have no good reason to tell you not to. But he might. I would never encourage you to lie, but this might be a case where you don't need to tell the entire truth. Does that make sense?"

I grinned, and hugged her as best I could despite the seat belts. "Perfectly."

chapter 14

We were halfway to Seattle, Bailey and me in the back seat, their dad driving, when Lindsay announced that she needed coffee and could we please find a drive-through espresso place.

"Do you two want anything?" asked Michael as he pulled up to the window.

"I'll have a vanilla latte," said Bailey. I asked for a hazelnut cappuccino because I liked as much foam as possible. Dad always claimed that coffee would stunt my growth, but we were in western Washington, where they practically put espresso in baby bottles. Besides, Bailey and I were already hyper enough, and a jolt of caffeine wouldn't change that. That Saturday morning was warm enough to call for iced drinks, but I liked the sensation of a hot paper cup between my palms.

At school on Wednesday, Bailey had told me that they arranged to meet with E on Saturday afternoon, at an LGBTQ community center on Capitol Hill. There was also an exhibition on octopuses at the Seattle Aquarium that they wanted to see, and since Bailey's parents had a family membership to the aquarium, they could sneak me in for free. So I took my mom's advice and when I asked my parents about the trip, I only mentioned the octopuses and the getting-in-free part. Which wasn't suspicious at all, because octopuses are awesome and I would be excited to see them no matter who I was going with. In fact, octopuses are so cool that I was worried my dad would suggest that we all go, but he said he'd use that day to clean the gutters. Mom smiled at me over her coffee mug.

The closer we got to Capitol Hill, the brighter Bailey shined. Every few blocks they'd point at something out the window and explain that that was where they once saw a celebrity, that was the library that had a huge protest over a transphobic speaker, they went on a field trip to that art gallery, one time they puked on that corner after eating some bad grocery store sushi.

This was the first time I had ever been to Seattle that wasn't either with my parents or on a school field trip to the Science Center or Children's Theater or whatever, where we'd get off the bus, go inside, stay inside, and then get back on the bus. The first time I'd been there with adults who didn't treat it like a haunted house, danger lurking around every corner. The first time I'd been there with someone who saw it as home. We hadn't even gotten out of the car, but I already didn't want to go back to Tahoma Falls.

"Here we are!" said Bailey cheerfully. Michael had to drive

around forever before he found parking, and when he finally found a spot we spilled out of the car and raced over to the community center. Everyone had to pee.

Despite my insistent bladder, I stopped short right inside the entrance and looked around. This place was so freaking cool that I wanted to move in. It was a big building with half a dozen brightly colored flags hanging across the front. I recognized the rainbow flag and the transgender flag, but others were new to me. There was a library off to the right, and across from the library was a coffee shop, and there were stairs going up and down that probably led to different meeting rooms or whatever. And the blessed bathrooms.

I reflexively looked to see which one was the men's room and which was the women's but should have known better. And I cracked up when I saw the graphics on the door: one had a stick figure sitting down on a toilet, and the other showed someone standing up at a urinal, and then the next door had both.

Bailey laughed along with me. "Simple, right? That's what they're for! What's even the point of pretending that you don't use this room to poop and/or pee?"

"I drank a whole cappuccino so maybe and AND or." We both rushed inside, luckily I only had to "or" because I didn't want to "and" in the stall next to them. After washing our hands we found their parents browsing through the library.

"Okay Baileycakes, what do you want from us?" asked Lindsay. "Should we wait with you till E gets here and then skedaddle? Do you want us to stay the whole time?"

"I think Annabelle and I should meet with E on our own," they said. "I don't know how long we'll talk for, but I can call you when we're done and then we can go to the aquarium—is that okay?"

"Totally fine," said Michael. "I'm sure we can entertain ourselves. In fact, we texted a friend who lives a few blocks from here, we're going to go see them for a bit. Let us know when you're done and we'll come get you."

"Thanks, Dad! You're the best." Bailey hugged him tight, and a bolt of jealousy ripped through me. I couldn't imagine having parents who would leave me in the middle of Seattle, about to meet a stranger (a stranger close to my age but still a stranger), and say "text me when you're done."

Bailey and I went up to the counter to order drinks. I asked for an iced mint tea, since I did not need any more caffeine, and Bailey got a bottle of fizzy lemon soda. We also decided to split a handmade pastry filled with Nutella that kind of looked like a Pop-Tart except it was a slightly lumpy triangle instead of a very smooth rectangle. When the barista asked if this was separate or together I said, "Together," feeling very grown-up, and handed over one of the two twenty-dollar bills my mom had slipped me before I left.

"Aw, you don't have to do that!" exclaimed Bailey.

"I know," I said, a little bashfully. "But I want to. I've never been on an adventure like this. Never had a friend like you. So I might as well buy you a soda." I hoped we were on our way to being more than friends, but a little voice in my head told me that *nothing* is more than friends.

Bailey put down their drink and hugged me across the shoulders, my heart leaping like a puppy. Then they picked up the plate with the lumpy triangle-tart and went over to an empty table in the corner, next to the windows. We had agreed to wear vaguely themed outfits, my goldfish-patterned shirt and blue shorts matching their white shirt with a giant squid wrapped around it and black shorts. Very aquarium-appropriate.

I checked my watch. Almost one. "Will E know what we look like?" I asked. "Will we know who they are?"

"Well, they know there are two of us and that we're both sixth-graders, and I don't see any other sixth-graders in here."

I looked around. The place was only half-full, and everyone else was an adult. A tall Black woman with long, skinny braids drizzled honey into a mug of tea. A shorter, balding white guy got up from his table and zipped his hoodie, even though it was warm inside. He looked a little like my dad, but I couldn't quite put a finger on why. Something about the shape of his face. Or his small build. Then I did a double take.

"Bailey!" I gasped, louder than I meant to, then lowered my voice to a near whisper. "Are there other trans people in here?"

They squirmed a little. "Well . . . I mean, let's not go around asking everyone to share personal information about themselves. But it's possible—this is a popular spot."

"Wow," I breathed, looking around. I wanted to announce to the entire room that my dad was trans, and my mom was femme, and I was something too, even though that would be undignified and possibly alarming. But it was overwhelming, the strong tugging sensation in my gut saying that I belonged here, that I was part of this world even if I didn't know exactly how. That I couldn't go back and be happy with my tiny world, my tiny family, even if I wanted to.

When E walked in, it turned out I had nothing to worry about; of course they were easy to spot. Not only were they the only other non-adult, they also looked like a nonbinary person who got kicked out of a boys' school. Not that I'd ever seen one before, but as soon as I saw them I was like, yup, that's who we're here for.

Okay, maybe that was mean, but it was also the first thought that popped into my head and I couldn't help it! They were wearing huge black pants, so long that the cuffs were trailing on the ground and had been worn ragged from where they were walking on them. They were also wearing a black T-shirt, way too big for them, with the words "Against Me!" printed across it in white. They were white and pale, with dark eyeliner, black nail polish, shaggy dark hair that swooped back from their face, and one earring, a black bird feather.

Their outfit might have been doomy and gloomy, but when they saw us sitting in the corner a dazzling smile leaped across their face. They waved tentatively, holding their wrist close to their body like they were worried we wouldn't wave back, but Bailey popped up and exuberantly gestured them over.

"Well hi there," they said, putting their tattered messenger bag on the floor. "Bailey and Annabelle, right?"

"None other," said Bailey, sweeping into an exaggerated bow. I decided to bob in a curtsy, and E giggled.

"Let me get myself a drink, and then we'll talk. I want sugar."

Beverage acquired (some sort of hot, foamy thing; I approved), they began talking in a light, soft voice. "I love you both already. Everything's been so messed up lately, first at school and then at home, and it's not like I was Mx. Popularity to begin with. So hanging out with other people? On a Saturday? Heaven, purely."

Bailey smiled and tapped their bottle against E's cup. "Right? Being the new kid is hard enough, and then being nonbinary on top of it? My family moved out of Seattle, up to Tahoma Falls, and if it weren't for Annabelle, I don't know what I'd be doing." I grinned, and knew I was blushing wildly. "So what happened at school? I mean, if you're okay talking about it."

"We know a tiny bit," I added, "from what they said about you in the Spectrum Families email. But also, obviously? If you don't want to go through all that again we can talk about whatever instead. Your favorite band, or ice cream or anything else." Bailey nodded in agreement.

"Against Me! and rocky road. But everyone has been talking *about* me, and no one has been letting me talk about myself, so if you actually want to hear, I would desperately love to share."

They took a deep breath, then laughed. "But also there's not much to tell! You know how it is, for them it's like 'Oh no, what do we do with this person?' and I'm like, 'Nothing? Just let me be?' Basically, I figured out I was nonbinary over the summer, my parents had assumed I was gay, so when I told them, they didn't have much of a reaction. They probably think those are the same things. And I didn't ask them to change pronouns or anything.

"St. Luke's has a Gay/Straight Alliance, so I went to a meeting and said that my pronouns are they/them. I thought it would be a safe place, you know? But the president of the club is this gay football-boy. Apparently when he came out it was a huge deal for the school and they put in an anti-discrimination thing in the handbook because of him. Anyway, he went to the principal and said that I wasn't a guy, and since we're an all-boy's school it wasn't fair for me to be there. And then the *meetings*, honey, they wouldn't *stop*, and eventually they decided that if I was allowed to stay, they wouldn't be an all-boys school anymore and would have to also accept, like, trans girls and trans boys and eventually they would have to be completely co-ed. As if that's a bad thing. So I was 'counseled out,' which, if you don't know already, is the private-school way of saying 'expelled.'"

"Cis people," Bailey said, rolling their eyes, and E winked at me.

I wanted to joke that I was only half-cis, because I was trans on my dad's side, but wasn't sure how that would fly so kept it to myself. "E, that all sucks so much," I said. "Do you want to talk about it at our school? For that panel Bailey told you about?"

E waggled their head from side to side. "It's a cute idea. But I feel like I shouldn't. I'm just getting on, you know? Still figuring out what nonbinary means to me. I don't think I'm ready to get in front of a group of people, even if they're all as cool as you, and talk about it." Boy did I know what that was like.

"I get that," said Bailey, surprising me. When had they *ever* been unsure of themself? "When I was still figuring out all this gender stuff, in the fourth grade, everyone expected me to tell them exactly what it meant to be nonbinary, and how I saw myself, and what I was going to do about it, and it was so much pressure right away when I was learning about myself. Even a few years later I'm learning new things, all the time. I think that's super smart." Wow. Did everyone go through this confusing, questioning phase?

"Agreed," I agreed. "I'm not nonbinary, but I learned something huge about my family not too long ago. It's kind of a secret, and I'm figuring out what it means for me and my life and everything. So if someone was like, 'Hey Annabelle, do you want to get in front of a bunch of strangers and explain what it all means to them?' I'd say no. Not that you *should* say no, you should do whatever you're comfortable with, I'm just saying that I know what it's like to keep some things to yourself, for a while, and we're not disappointed in you or anything." All this was true even *without* the other part, the wanting-to-kiss-my-new-nonbinary-best-friend part.

E looked dazed by this waterfall of words, but Bailey punched me lightly on the shoulder. "What she said."

We sat there for another hour, Bailey and E chattering away about growing up in Seattle, the best places for bubble tea and tacos, and whether there should be a hyphen in "non-binary" or not. I joined in sometimes, but mostly sat and listened. It was cool to see Bailey with another trans kid from Seattle; they were probably relieved to not have to stop and explain every other word in their conversation. I listened carefully, vowing that someday I'd catch up. I wouldn't be the newbie forever. And maybe someday I'd be able to help someone else figure themselves out.

"And then my mom said, 'I thought you were gay,' and I wanted to be like, 'I'm not gay, I'm t4t, which is like being super, extra, double gay,'" E finished, rolling their eyes in exasperation.

"Wait, tee for tee?" Bailey asked. I had wondered what that meant too, and it was exciting to have them ask a question, for once, instead of me.

"Trans for trans, babies, it means I only want to go out with other trans or nonbinary people."

I had barely enough time to wonder if that made me cee for tee when Bailey said, "Oh, same," and just like that my first crush turned into my first heartbreak. "I mean, I could never be interested in a cis person, you know?" they continued, as my vision focused on the crumbs left on the Nutella-tart plate, unable to raise my head, my breathing spilling over into panicked pants. "Not that I'm interested in dating right now, but still."

"I have to go to the bathroom," I announced, and rushed away from the table. Once there I locked myself into a stall and dropped my head into my hands, rocking back and forth.

"It's okay," I whispered to myself. "It's okay, it's okay, it's okay." Tears dripping through my fingers, long shuddering breaths that seemed to take over my entire body. My brain had been replaced with static, the only coherent thought worming its way through was *I'm glad I didn't tell anyone.* Then I started trying to come up with a plan, any plan, latching wildly onto the idea that if I came out as nonbinary, they'd want to date me, maybe I could do that, what did it mean to be a girl anyway, what did it matter if we could be together.

Slowly, eventually, I got myself under control. Almost calm. I wasn't nonbinary, and it was wrong to pretend to be something that I'm not just to get someone to like me. They were never going to feel that way about me. They didn't have to. I would figure out who I was, I would have other crushes, some of them would like me back, it was going to be okay, it was going to be okay, it was going to be okay, even if it took a while for that to feel true. I gathered up the pieces of my broken heart, patted them roughly into place, and shuffled back to the table.

Bailey's phone started vibrating wildly as soon as I sat back down. "It's my parents," they said reluctantly, and picked up. "Hey Dad! Yeah, okay. Sure. Okay. We're here. Bye."

"They're going to pick us up now," they said. "I'm sorry, E. I could honestly hang out with you all day, but they had already reserved us tickets to see the octopuses—octopi?—at the aquarium, and they don't want us to stay in the city too long. Rush hour, I guess, even though it's Saturday."

E pouted exaggeratedly. "I get it. Octopodes—that should be the plural, not octopi—are the coolest creatures in the entire world. Way cooler than any human being, including me."

"Well, they certainly have more legs," I said shakily, hoping my voice sounded normal.

"You don't know that!" exclaimed E. "Why do you think I wear such baggy pants? Got more legs that I can count under here."

We were laughing about that when Bailey's parents came by. "Sorry to pull you away, children!" said Michael. "But the eight-legged rulers of the deep call."

"You must be E," said Lindsay, shaking their hand. "It's wonderful meet you, Michael and I were so upset when we found out what was going on."

"Thank you," said E. They had retreated into their shell when the adults arrived, but managed a close-lipped smile. "It was cool to talk to Bailey and Annabelle. I hope we can stay in touch."

"Of course!" exclaimed Michael. "You two exchanged numbers, right?"

We hadn't yet, and once that happened, it was time to go. "Do you want a hug?" I asked E. They nodded, and their arms wrapped as tight around me as a two-limbed octopus. I was sure they held on to Bailey as hard if not harder. As we walked out of the coffee shop-slash-community center, I glanced behind me. They were slumped over the table, staring into their empty mug, slowly fading back into a lonely rain cloud.

The octopi—octopuses—octopodes? were interesting enough to take my mind off my thwarted crush. The exhibit was all about their brains, and how smart they are, and imagining what an octopus society would look like. One theory was that they are as smart as humans, but in different ways. A reason why octopuses don't have civilizations might be because they don't live longer than a few years, and because octopus parents die before their babies are born, so there's no way to pass down knowledge from generation to generation. I decided there were probably ways around that, like, having younger octopuses adopt orphan babies, but since I wasn't an octopus, they didn't bother to ask me for advice.

As amazing as the exhibit was, it was a letdown after hanging out with E. Even more of a letdown with my broken heart still scabbing over. I had been to the aquarium a bunch of times. My parents took me when I was little, and we went on school field trips there once a year. It wasn't anything new.

I wished Bailey and I were old enough to wander around the city by ourselves. Maybe that was just my lingering Feelings, but I knew it would be a different city through their eyes. Skip Pike Place Market, skip the Space Needle, see the parts of the city that my dad was afraid I'd learn about. Go into stores that sell magic spells, find used bookstores that smell like ancient paper, maybe even go to drag brunch. Or drag lunch, or dinner, or mid-afternoon snack, I wasn't picky. I wanted to experience my friend's world so it could become mine too.

But as much as I didn't want to leave Seattle, I also didn't want to be stuck in traffic for the next zillion hours. "We should be heading back," said Lindsay, checking her watch. "If we leave now, we should beat rush hour."

"It's always rush hour here," Michael said. "Make sure you both use the bathroom before we leave. Bailey, do you want me to ask if they've added a gender-neutral one?"

They rolled their eyes. "No, Dad, it's cool. I'll go in with Annabelle." As we walked towards the women's room they muttered, "He's *so* over-protective."

I shrugged, thinking of E's parents. "Could be worse."

"I knooow," they groaned, "but every kid is allowed to complain about their parents." I couldn't argue with that.

Of course, we didn't beat the traffic. There was no "beating traffic" when it came to leaving Seattle, it was always there. When it became obvious that the gridlock wasn't clearing up any time soon, Lindsay suggested that I call my parents and let them know I'd be home a little later than usual.

"And why don't you ask if your folks want to come over tonight?" Mike added. "We have a stew going in the slow cooker, and Lindsay and I haven't gotten to know anyone in town yet."

Oh gosh. I froze as my mind started racing through all the possibilities. Was this a good idea? A terrible idea? I glanced at Bailey for help, and they clearly read my mind. I was disappointed that they were never going to be my ~~girl~~- ~~boy~~-theyfriend, but that didn't make our relationship any less special.

"That's a nice idea, Dad, but you remember that Mike is mostly stealth, and doesn't talk about trans things, right? If he comes over, you have to promise to be chill."

"I'm *always* chill!" he protested. "Does that mean I shouldn't talk about things I usually talk about?"

"I don't know what you usually talk about with other adults," I said, "but . . . well, I told my parents that we were going to the octopus thing, but didn't tell them anything else. So. Um. The first part of our day would be a good thing to avoid."

Lindsay turned around to face me, her brow creased. "Annabelle, are you saying that you lied to your family about today? I'm not comfortable knowing that we took you to Seattle under false pretenses." Ugh, she sounded exactly like *my* mom when she said things like "I'm not mad I'm disappointed." Was there some book that all moms got to read called *What Tone of Voice to Use if You Want to Devastate Your Child?*

Luckily I had an answer to this one. "No no no, don't worry.

My mom knew what we were doing. She's totally okay with it, and it was her idea to not mention that part to my dad. And I didn't even lie to him! I told him we were going to the aquarium to look at octopuses. And we did."

"Hm," said Lindsay. "I'll take your word on that. No need to get all of us in trouble, and no one ended up kidnapped."

Bailey chimed in. "And Dad, can you promise to talk about sports, or the weather, or work, or anything other than how it's your life goal to be the best dad in the history of Spectrum Families?"

"How about those Mariners?" said Michael, as he extended his right hand behind him. Bailey clasped their pinky around his, and they swore on it.

"It's football season, dear," said Lindsay as I called my mom. I explained the situation, and then waited while she checked with my dad.

Finally, "Okay! Um, hang on. Mom says sure," I reported, "and what should they bring?"

"No need to bring anything but themselves," Michael said cheerfully. "Whatever they want to drink, we're not picky."

"Did you hear that? Uh- huh. I think so. Okay. Bye!"

Michael started chatting again as soon as I hung up. "I remember the first time we took you to the aquarium, Baileycakes!" he reminisced. "Your favorite was the seahorses. When you found out that the male seahorses carry their young, not the females, you wanted to stand there for hours and try to figure out if any of the boys were going to have babies."

"Like me," I mumbled, staring at those creepy white smokestacks with the word "Zymogenetics" printed on them. I didn't realize what I had said until I felt Bailey turn to stare at me.

"What do you mean, like you?"

Oh man. The caffeine had worn off hours ago, my emotions had soared and crashed all over the place, and in the warm car a wave of exhaustion had broken over me. Why did my mouth do that without asking my brain first? But I couldn't think of a way to backtrack.

"I, um. My dad. He was, he did that. Had me."

Their jaw dropped. "*Your dad* was a seahorse??"

"I guess, is that what you call it? Is that a thing?"

"It's a thing! We know some! But that's so wild. He does not seem like the type."

I slumped against the window, wishing I could snatch the words out of the air. "He isn't. But. Because my mom couldn't get pregnant, and they wanted me, he did. But he said that it was hard. And that the other trans people he knew didn't support him. That's why my mom and dad left Arizona and came here."

"Why didn't his community support him?" asked Michael. We were fully stopped in traffic by that point, and he turned around to look intently into my eyes. If this was what it was like to have a dad who talked about feelings, I was maybe glad that mine didn't.

"You know what, he . . . he wouldn't like me talking about

this. He doesn't want other people to know. I didn't mean to say it, it just slipped out."

"Understood," said Michael, turning back to the wheel. He made a zipper motion across his lips, and threw away the key.

"It's not a big deal to us," Lindsay added. "My ex-boyfriend from college had a baby a few years ago. But if your dad wanted to keep that private, we can respect that. What's said here, stays here."

If "here" was the crowded interstate between the city and the suburbs, that meant that everyone was going to find out. But I knew what she meant. She meant that this secret was safe with them, that it wasn't going to leave their family. I hoped that was true. I closed my eyes, and Michael turned on the radio, and by the time I opened my eyes again, we were back.

chapter 15

"How were the octopi?" asked Dad, as Michael ladled egg-plant stew and cous cous (which I decided after a bite was teeny-tiny pastas) onto our plates. The table was nicely set with cloth tablemats, white napkins, sparkling water for me and Bailey and wine my parents brought for the adults.

"Amazing!" said Bailey. "We got to watch a gigantic red one pry open a clam and eat it. And another tank was full of babies—baby octopuses are the absolute cutest things I've ever seen."

"And it turns out that the plural of octopus is 'octopodes,'" I added.

"Why in the world is that it?" asked Mom.

"Um . . ." Where had that fun fact come from? Oh, no. E had told us, at the coffee shop, but they hadn't explained why. And I wasn't supposed to mention E in front of my parents. Bailey shot me a Look while Lindsay saved the day before I panicked and gave up the truth.

"I think it has to do with Latin and Greek endings," she said. "The 'pus' in 'octopus' refers to their feet, and the plural for feet is 'pod,' like 'arthropods.' Does that sound right, Annabelle?"

"Yeah! That's it. It was on a sign next to one of the tanks, I think." I had to remember to thank Lindsay later.

"Did you get to see anything else besides the octo— octopodes?" asked Mom.

"Not much else," said Bailey. "But I've been to the aquarium a million times. The baby sharks and clown fish and seahorses will be there next time." I thought Bailey might have put an emphasis on the word "seahorses," but I couldn't be sure. I also thought my dad might have stiffened a little at the reference, but I also couldn't be sure of that. Luckily the moment passed without anything else unplanned popping out of my mouth, which was mostly full of spicy eggplant.

"Are you two from this area originally?" Lindsay asked.

"Oh no, not at all," Mom said with a little laugh. "We moved here from Arizona not long after Annabelle was born. We got sick of the endless sunshine and desert and wanted something completely different."

"Wow!" said Michael. "You can't get farther away from that than the Pacific Northwest."

"That was certainly part of the appeal," said my dad. "I grew up in Ohio, and Hannah is from outside of Boston but lived in Atlanta for a while. So we've got most of the country covered, between the two of us. Maybe we'll retire in Hawaii."

"I'm from Ohio!" Lindsay burst out. "Columbus, born and raised. What about you?"

"Cleveland," said Dad. "Made it to C-bus sometimes, though, nice town you've got there."

"A lot of my friends from high school moved to Cleveland for school or jobs. I wonder if we know any of the same people."

Dad hesitated. All you could hear was the scrape of silverware against plates. We were all thinking the same thing, or at least, the same general thing. How my dad was different in college—or at least, how he might have been the same, but had a different name and a different way of describing himself. How anyone who knew him then might not recognize him now, and how the people sitting around this table were the only people in this part of the world who knew that. My first impulse was to distract everyone, start talking about octopodes again or make up something from school to complain about or ask a question about, I don't know, when we could use the hot tub. But I was also curious about how my father would respond.

"We might," he said finally. "But that was so long ago, and I've lost touch with almost everyone."

"Oh, totally, I mean I graduated . . . what, twenty years ago? I wouldn't know what any of my college friends were up to if not for Facebook!"

"Facebook, right. I never signed up for it."

"You're not on Facebook?" Michael repeated curiously. "I'm both profoundly jealous *and* a little sorry for you. Hannah, what about you, are you also wasting your entire life on that dang blue website?"

Mom laughed. "Unlike my recalcitrant husband, I do have a Facebook profile, but I never update it, never look at it, and never accept friend requests. So, essentially, no."

Bailey and I mostly listened as the adults chatted through dinner. And if someone had said, "Hey Annabelle, do you want to not talk at all sitting next to your new friend who doesn't have a crush on you back while grown-ups drone on about work and home ownership," I would have said no thank you, but it was actually kind of cool. I didn't see my parents with other adults too often, aside from the grocery store or the pharmacy or whatever.

I wondered if it was a coincidence that the first time we had dinner at a friend's house was also the first time my friend and their family knew that my dad was trans. It never came up in conversation. No one mentioned it directly. But at the same time, that knowledge was flowing beneath the surface of the conversation. It even welled up here and there, through the cracks, as Dad opened up a little more, throwing in little comments that were winks to that shared information—how he sometimes had to go to a doctor in Seattle. Mentioning that he and Mom had a wedding in Arizona but got legally married in Washington. One time Michael referred to the Spectrum Families group, and while Dad didn't ask any questions, he didn't seem uncomfortable, and Mom asked some polite questions about what it was like.

It was normal. Or at least, like how I imagined normal. Like instead of my family being this vacuum-sealed package, where no one else was allowed in, we were a collection of people with our own lives and stories, breathing the same air as other people and their lives and their stories. I liked it.

When it was time to go, I was glowing with warmth, and Mom and Dad clearly felt the same.

"We'll have to do this again," said Mom. "If we find time while the weather holds, you should come over to our place. We don't have such a grand dining room"—we didn't have a dining room at all—"but we sometimes eat out on the back porch. Last barbecue of the season?"

"That would be great, thank you!" said Lindsay, grinning. "We haven't really made local friends yet—the Seattle Freeze has its tendrils up here. Say when, and we'll be there!"

"I'll grill for you anytime," said Dad. He shook Michael's hand, and we were off.

"Well, that was lovely," said Mom, as we buckled our seatbelts.

"Mm-hm," said Dad, backing out of the driveway.

"Yeah!" I exclaimed from the back seat. "We have to have them over, that was so much fun! When Lindsay said I should invite you, I didn't think you would say yes, but I'm glad you did."

"Why didn't you think we would say yes?" asked Dad.

"Uh . . ." Was this a test? "Because they know about you? And that might be weird for you?" And also because we've never done this before, but mentioning that might be too much.

From my vantage point in the back seat I saw him nod

slightly. "It's something to get used to. But it wasn't bad."
He fiddled with the radio, then said, "It was fun going to the
aquarium with you when you were little. Maybe we'll take
you again sometime. You know that male seahorses are the
ones that have the babies? We bought a seahorse blankie
when you were born. As a little inside joke. I don't know
what happened to it."

My jaw dropped. "It's packed away with the rest of her
baby things," Mom reminded him. And soon we were home.

chapter 16

When I walked into my classroom Monday morning, the first thing I saw was Johnson holding a book open in Principal Quinn's face, explaining the differences between American fighter jets and German fighter jets in World War II. The principal had this look on his face that a lot of people had when Johnson got going, a mixture of "Okay this is hilarious" and "When is he going to stop?" Principal Quinn would sometimes drop by classrooms, occasionally to talk to us about something but usually just to stand in the back of the room, smiling if anyone turned to look at him but otherwise looking awkward.

The second thing I noticed was Amy. She was sitting at her desk, holding her head up with her fingertips, staring straight down. Something wasn't right. I went over to my desk and took out a worksheet I hadn't finished yet, about the different social classes in ancient Greece, and filled in the rest of the answers, not wanting to attract the principal's attention.

My classmates slowly filtered in. Usually Amy greeted all of us, asking about our weekends, showing us pictures of her cat or following up on questions we had about work. Instead she stayed at her desk, and Principal Quinn removed himself from Johnson to say hello to everyone.

From the first day I met him I could tell that he was one of those grown-ups who liked the idea of kids, but didn't see us as actual people. When he talked to us he had this fake laugh behind his voice, like he was the one human actor surrounded by puppets or cartoon characters. When we got in trouble—like that time last year we had a substitute leave halfway through the day because Jonas had a screaming tantrum, Olivia sat in some ketchup and Felix yelled that her butt was bleeding, and Dixon and Audrey got into an actual fistfight about which was better, Fortnite or Minecraft—he would never tell us directly what we did wrong, and ramble on about "expectations" and "being helpful" and end with "do you understand?" but there was never anything to understand.

I remember the old principal, Carrie, as being kind of old-fashioned, always in skirts and jackets and pearls. That never stopped her from sitting on the floor, building with blocks, or digging in the sandbox alongside us. She must have retired, or something, and a lot of teachers who had been at the Lab for a long time left with her. And the school had slowly gotten smaller since then, more and more kids leaving each year.

Dixon was the last one to show up, and right behind him was his mom. They looked alike, same pointy chin and narrow nose, same bright blond hair, but hers was longer, pulled back into a French braid. Dixon bragged that she used to be a lawyer before she had him and decided to be a full-time mom, and I guess those habits die hard, because she was always in a pants suit and always in a hurry, even when she was cornering a teacher to complain about something and could leave whenever she wanted. She nodded at Principal Quinn, and he smiled wanly. We were a little too old to be escorted into class by our mommies, but Mrs. Brewster marched to the back of the classroom and leaned slightly against the window ledge, her arms crossed in front of her blazer. Something was going on.

The clock hit 8:30, and we were all tensed at our desks. Usually, Amy would call us to the rug for morning meeting, but all she did was lift her head up and look directly at Principal Quinn. He coughed to get our attention, for some reason, and said, "Good morning, friends. Amy invited me here to share some information with you, about making sure that this is a safe, welcoming, and inclusive environment for everyone to do their best learning." I looked over at Amy, and her lips were pressed together tightly. I was willing to bet that "invited" was not in fact the most accurate word.

"As you know," he continued, "your sixth-grade year is the capstone to everything you've learned at our wonderful school. Math, science, social studies—all of it becomes more challenging, and everything has been carefully planned and refined over many years to make sure it's the ideal curriculum for learners your age. We're so lucky that your new teacher respects all the work that went into these plans."

Hmmm. That all sounded nice, but Amy had wanted to come up with her own curriculum, and she said he wouldn't let her.

"Now, as a diverse, welcoming community"—Bailey's head jerked up at the word "diverse," and I saw Sadie and Amanda look around in confusion too—"we respect all of your unique individuality. But we also need to make sure that all of you unique individuals feel part of the same community! In this world there are so many conversations about what makes us different, but in this space all that matters is what unites us: We're all part of the Tahoma Falls Collaborative School. And that's what matters. Does that make sense?"

I scrunched up my forehead at what he was saying. It all sounded like something you'd read on the back of a cereal box. Olivia shouted, "What?" and a flurry of hands went up. Principal Quinn looked confused by our collective confusion, and of course he called on Dixon first.

Dixon didn't turn to look at his mom, who was still standing there, her arms crossed firmly, mouth puckered, but the stiffness in his neck made it clear that he sensed her as much, if not more, than the rest of us. "I think what you're saying is that we all have differences, and that no one person's difference is more important than anyone else's, right?"

"I suppose so," said Principal Quinn slowly, like he was thinking it through.

"And," Dixon continued, emboldened, "that it wouldn't be fair to have an event at school where some people are treated as if they're more important than others. Right?"

"Yes, that wouldn't be welcoming or inclusive," agreed Principal Quinn. As awareness broke over the room, a rising tide of murmurs rippled through the rest of us.

"Unbelievable," Bailey whispered. I couldn't stop thinking about E, what they were going through, and growled under my breath.

"Well, now that everything's been made clear, I can trust that you as a community of compassionate learners will make the right choice! Thanks so much for inviting me into your space, and have a great week!" With that, Principal Quinn practically ran out of the room, and Dixon's mom followed close on his heels.

As the door slammed behind them, Bailey stood up at their desk. "He's saying we can't have the National Coming Out Day panel! Because it wouldn't be 'welcoming' or 'inclusive'! Does he get how messed up that is?!"

I joined my friend, shoulder to shoulder. "That's so unfair. He's saying that we're all different, but since we all go to the same school, we should pretend that our differences don't matter!"

Dixon sighed louder than I've ever heard anyone sigh in my life. "That's not it at all. What he's saying is that it's not fair for one group of people to get special treatment over another."

"Is this about your idea for a panel of straight people? Dixon, you are something else." That was from Sadie, who stood up too.

"I want to get solar panels on the roof, are you worried that fossil fuels are going to complain about being left out?" Patrick hollered. He got up from his desk, joining the three of us. The air was electrified, and Amanda, Johnson, Audrey, Charlotte, and Jonas stood up at their desks too. Felix and the other Annabelle joined a beat later. A rush went through me, like anything could happen.

"Why are you all being so sensitive?" Dixon whined. He was sitting with his chair tipped onto its back two legs. He looked relaxed, but sounded impatient. Like he was so clearly right, and if the rest of us would get on board already, we could move on to learning about the important things, like who was in a triumvirate or whatever. "I don't want *my* identities to be left out, but you're all acting like *I'm* the one being unfair."

The room erupted in argument, but the sound of the chime cut through the din, silencing us immediately.

"Sit. Down," Amy said, steel behind her words. The eleven of us sat, reluctantly. We waited for her to start talking, to explain everything, to take a side, but there was a long, long silence. Our teacher moved to the front of the room, looking sternly at each of us in turn.

Finally, after what felt like an eternity, she spoke. "You'll notice that Principal Quinn did not give us any clear instructions. He did not tell us, directly, what to do. And as a 'community of compassionate learners,' we will make this decision in a collaborative way. Raise your hand if you are interested in the panel that Bailey is organizing for National Coming Out Day." Everyone but Dixon raised their hand.

Amy nodded, and took another long pause, and I could see her weighing all the different options. "Dixon, you've shared that this makes you feel excluded, and that your identities don't matter. Is that correct?"

"It sure is!" he said. But he didn't sound like E talking about being kicked out of school. He sounded like it was all a big joke, but a joke he wouldn't drop. Bailey put a hand on my arm, and only then did I notice how hard I was breathing, how tight my jaw was clenched. I forced myself to relax.

"All right, then. As your teacher, it's my job to make sure that everyone is included. Dixon, we're going to keep the NCOD panel on our schedule. Bailey, if you want to continue working on it, go ahead, your classmates and I are excited for it. However, Dixon, if you want to organize another event, around some aspect of your identity that matters to you, you are also allowed to do that, the same as anyone else in this class. Does that sound fair to you?"

Dixon narrowed his eyes, like he was looking for the catch. "You mean, if I want to get a bunch of straight white guys to talk about being straight white guys, I can do that?"

"According to Principal Quinn, yes."

He grinned. "Heck, yeah." An angry buzz rose up, but Amy stopped us before it could erupt. "We need to start math now. Everyone get out your workbooks. If you have questions or thoughts, you can come check in with me later, but for now we need to move on."

* * *

Here's the thing I didn't get about Dixon. When we were little, and he was the new kid, we were all friends, because when you're little it's easier to be friends with people. Like, someone takes your special pencil, you start crying, the teacher comes over and talks to both of you, and two minutes later you're fine. But the older we got, the harder it was to move past that kind of thing. And his new "I'm oppressed because I'm a straight white boy" thing was way more infuriating than grabbing the only pencil with a teddy bear eraser from the pencil bin. Even if he didn't believe in what he was saying. *Especially* if he didn't believe in what he was saying.

So when lunchtime rolled around, a bunch of us clumped up on the floor to eat. When he sat down with us, everyone splintered off into smaller groups, leaving him sitting alone in the middle of the room with his sandwich, looking confused and sad. But like, dude, that's what you get for being a jerk! For trying to ruin our plans! For getting your mom to call the principal on the teacher, which is totally what happened. The other Annabelle joined Sadie, Bailey, and me by the window, where we were whispering furiously and sneaking peeks over at Dixon, who could probably hear everything we were saying but who even cared. Patrick stopped by, gave us all fist bumps, and said he might ask Amy about the solar energy project but also could put that on hold for now and help us with the panel, if we wanted him to.

"No, you should keep going," Bailey said. "That's important too."

"Yeah," I said, "I'm still going to work with you on that, I promise. Let me know what Amy says after lunch?" Patrick nodded and took his lunch bag over to our teacher's desk.

"Are we going to let *him* do this?" asked Sadie in a low voice. She didn't specify who "he" was. She didn't have to. "The last thing anyone needs is a bunch of straight white dudes talking about how they're the *real* minorities."

"I don't know if we have a choice," I said, matching her volume. "His mom would probably bully Principal Quinn into canceling our panel, claiming that it's unfair or discrimination or something."

Bailey shook their head incredulously. "Do you think he believes that?"

"Who?" asked the other Annabelle.

"Both of them. Any of them. Are they serious, or is it all a joke?"

"I think it's a joke to him," I guessed, "but it's a joke he's taking seriously. I bet he told his mom that he was feeling left out, and she went full-on mama bear about it. And Principal Quinn is scared of her, because she's scary. So everyone is serious, but none of it is real."

"Like vegetables," Bailey grunted.

"Like vegetables," I agreed.

"Vegetables?" asked Sadie.

"I'll explain later," said Bailey.

"You know he won't, though, right?" said the other Annabelle, not bothering to keep her voice down.

"What do you mean?" asked Bailey. "He won't what?"

"You know Dixon," she said, jutting her chin in his direction. He was cross-legged on the floor, staring at the carpet and shoving Cheez-Its into his mouth. When the other Annabelle said his name, he whipped around to look at us. We pretended like we didn't notice. I saw him glance over at Amy, and I bet he was about to ask her to intervene but thought better of it. Guess the boy had some sense after all.

The other Annabelle took a minute to gather her thoughts. "He won't do it," she repeated. "He wanted to make his point. And he did. He got what he wanted, which was attention, and permission to have his own panel. But it's a lot of work, right?"

Bailey nodded.

"Once he finds out how hard it is to organize a panel, he'll give up," she continued. "Especially since he won't have help from anyone else in class. He wanted everyone to feel bad for him. So don't worry."

"That makes a lot of sense," said Sadie. "I don't see him pulling this off."

"So does that mean we keep going with the panel?" I asked. "Let him think he's won, and do what we want anyway?"

The other Annabelle nodded. I never knew she paid such close attention to Dixon's inner workings. I wondered what she secretly knew about me.

"Okay, but if you're wrong, we can't let him get away with a straight white dude panel," said Bailey. "Who *knows* what kind of jerkwads he would drag in? Probably dudes who talk about how 'Me Too' has gone too far, and how diversity is ruining video games."

"We can figure out what to do if it actually happens," said Sadie.

"What if we all stayed home sick that day?" I said.

"Yes. Freedom of speech isn't the same thing as freedom to be listened to." That was the other Annabelle. I tried not to look surprised, because that would be insulting, but that was the smartest thing I'd ever heard, and I wasn't used to hearing anything from the other Annabelle. I wondered what else I'd hear, if I started listening.

chapter 17

We spent the rest of the week working on our different projects whenever we had free time: Patrick and me researching solar power in the Pacific Northwest, and Bailey and sometimes me planning for the National Coming Out Day Panel.

Working with Patrick consisted of looking up different companies, typing information into a spreadsheet, reading terrifying and depressing articles about what would happen if we didn't stop dumping carbon into the atmosphere, and coming up with arguments to present in front of Principal Quinn. It was somehow both extremely boring and very stressful. I told myself that maybe it would be better once we got out of the research part and started making it happen, and that even if it wasn't exciting, it was still important. But a little bit of me regretted agreeing to work with Patrick on this.

Bailey, on the other hand, was having a great time planning their panel. And the other Annabelle was helping! I was a little jealous looking over my tablet with tabs of different energy companies as they laughed and chatted with Amy about what kinds of snacks to buy, but it was also cool to watch the other Annabelle coming out of her shell some more. She still didn't know how to dress, and today's Twister floor-mat-themed sweat suit was proof, but there were more important things than a fashion sense.

And I got to be part of the planning, a little. The three of us had a lunch meeting with Sadie, Patrick, and Amanda where we came up with questions we wanted the panelists to answer and topics we wanted them to discuss. I had no problem coming up with plenty of both. Bailey and the other Annabelle showed us the other speakers who had agreed to come: Besides the other Annabelle's sister Sam, we were going to hear from the Hawaiian trans woman who founded Spectrum Families with her grandchildren, a disabled femme dancer who worked with kids at Bailey's old school, and a Persian trans man who started a queer bookstore.

Of course, we also had regular schoolwork. Every time we watched a slideshow about, like, how a city-state was governed, or the status of women in ancient Greece, all I could think about was how we could be learning about Hispanic Heritage Month, or why a group called the Water Protectors had gotten arrested in Seattle, or whatever most recent illegal thing the president did and why no one was doing anything about it. Sometimes I'd look around the classroom, seeing glazed looks on everyone's faces—even Dixon's, whose entire fault this was—and wish that school was different. But I was glad we were forcing it to be different.

But on Thursday morning, Mrs. Brewster burst into the classroom, Dixon trailing behind her. "My son tells me you're going ahead with this recruitment event," she boomed shrilly. Amy had been at my desk going over yesterday's math, and our heads snapped up.

"I'm sorry, recruitment?" she said politely. I could see her knuckles turn white around the handle of her coffee mug.

"That panel! Where you'll be having adults describe their lifestyles to these children. Tell them it's okay to change their gender, when they're too young to make those kinds of decisions. I know that was *not* the agreement we reached with Principal Quinn, and frankly I'm shocked you would go against his direct order. We'll see what the board of trustees has to say about this!"

"We will not have this conversation in front of my students," Amy said firmly. "Step outside with me, Claudia, but I can only give you five minutes."

"You'll give me as much time as it takes," Mrs. Brewster retorted, and stalked out. She flung the door open and it almost smacked Bailey in the face, who sidled in when Amy held it gently open for them.

"What is going on?" they asked as they came over to our desks.

I shook my head tightly, and looked pointedly at Dixon. He was sitting at his desk, nose buried in a comic book, his whole face flaming red. The room was only about half-full, and everyone was hushed, straining to hear the argument filtering through the door.

Mrs. Brewster was shouting. Phrases like "trendy to change your gender," "inappropriate lifestyle," "what if this got on the news," and "teaching sex to kindergartners" filtered through the door. She didn't give Amy any chances to respond, and what little our teacher said came through as murmurs.

"Dixon, what did you tell her?" asked Bailey sharply.

"I didn't do anything," he mumbled.

"You must have told her something," said Sadie. "How else would she have found out?"

He wasn't looking at us, but he hadn't turned a single page in his comic book. "I . . . I said that maybe my dad could come talk. Because Amy said I could have my own panel! And they asked why, so I told them that I got what I wanted. Mom said that wasn't what Principal Quinn meant, and that it was inappropriate to have people promote their lifestyles. I didn't know. I thought it was about being fair."

Bailey stared up at the ceiling. "Unbelievable."

The door opened again. Principal Quinn was standing outside with them, and as Amy came back into the classroom we saw him walk away with Mrs. Brewster. The rest of the class trickled in after Amy, they must have been watching. You could hear the second hand tick.

Amy sat down at her desk. "Take out your math folders," she said. "Turn to today's work, and do problems one through fifteen. When you're done you can check each other's answers and then read independently."

The rest of the morning was like that. Filling out

worksheets, checking each other's work, reading during the breaks. Usually our mornings were full of discussion and argument, moving around the room, figuring things out in small groups. Not glued to our desks, writing down answers in blank spots. But we were all waiting for the other shoe to drop.

The other shoe dropped in right before lunch. Both of them. Principal Quinn's shoes, to be exact, boring brown man-shoes. He loped to the front of the classroom and cleared his throat to get our attention, but we were already staring at him, waiting for him to speak.

"Good morning, friends." He was smiling but it was forced, like the corners of his mouth were held up with toothpicks. "There must have been some confusion! As I shared before, we want to make sure this is a safe, welcoming, and inclusive community for all—"

"You said that," Bailey interrupted. "What did you mean?"

"Uh, well, um," Principal Quinn stammered. "What I mean is, it's important to work together as a school to ensure that everyone is safe."

"Safe from what?" I asked, my voice sharpened like a pencil. I had never spoken to the principal like that before, but if Bailey could, so could I.

"Well, 'safe' might not be the right word, but comfortable, and it has come to my attention that not everyone in this community is comfortable with, uh, holding events that don't conform to our stated educational goals."

Sadie raised her hand, and Principal Quinn looked relieved that someone was willing to wait instead of calling out. "Yes, Sadie, thank you for raising your hand." But the relief on his face faded as she started talking.

"So, what you're saying is that Mrs. Brewster came into the classroom, started yelling at our teacher because Bailey and Annabelle are organizing a National Coming Out Day panel that we're all excited about, and now we have to cancel the panel because she doesn't approve. That's what you came in here to tell us. Right?"

The other Annabelle was staring at her desk, her stringy hair framing her face, but her voice rang out from behind it. "My sister was going to be on it. Sam. She went here, but you didn't know her. And you're saying she can't come back because she was going to talk about herself."

I had never seen an adult look so uncomfortable. He raked his hand through his hair, bouncing up and down on his toes, and finally said, "Yes. The panel is canceled. It's in everyone's best interest. Okay. Have a good day." The laughter behind his voice was entirely gone, and he walked stiffly out of the classroom.

There was a roaring in my ears and I was sweating so hard that I could feel the slickness underneath my arms. It was all I could do not to slump over with my head on my desk. After all that work, I was going to be left alone with my questions, walking this path forever without anyone seeing me on it. A little part of me knew that was silly, that National Coming

Out Day was like any other day on the calendar. It didn't mean I *had* to do anything or *couldn't* do anything, but this felt like a sign. Like I wasn't allowed to try and figure myself out, I would always be miles behind people like Bailey and my parents and I would never find where I belonged. I wasn't even out yet and I was being forced back into the closet by some straight person. Would this be the rest of my life? I was starting to understand my dad a little better. I had wondered if he was getting more ready to talk about himself, but if this is what happened when he did, I could see why he wanted a different future for me. I hated it.

Dixon raised his hand in the silence that followed. I expected to hear some defense, some snarky question about whether he could have his straight white dude panel, but "Can I go to the bathroom?" tumbled out of him, and he dashed away before Amy could even say yes.

"Is there anything we can do?" Bailey asked once he was gone.

"I'm afraid not," said Amy.

"But that's not FAIR!" Olivia shrieked.

"You're right," Amy agreed.

"Why?" asked Jonas.

Our teacher shook her head. "Because the person in charge knows all the right words and uses them for the wrong reasons. Never say that you stand for something, and then let yourself be bullied out of it. I'm sorry, friends." And that was that.

Dixon came back from the bathroom for the morning classes, but then excused himself again for almost the entire lunch period. I bet that he was expecting us to spend the whole time ranting about him and complaining about how unfair everything was and how we had to find a way around it. But when he came back, right before cleanup, the only sounds in the room were crunching and crinkling. After lunch we had library, which was appropriately hushed, and P.E. where the gym teacher looked on in confusion as we played an almost-wordless game of basketball.

The whole day was encased in ice. Like the events of the morning had frozen everything, and if anything was too fast, or too loud, or too big, the ice would shatter and slice us into pieces. I wasn't sure what my classmates were feeling, but I figured it had to be some variation on that—like we were too depressed, too defeated to get rowdy, and that we all wanted the day to be over and hope that we could go back to normal tomorrow.

Patrick sat next to me at the end of the day. Amy had told us that it was time for sustained silent reading, but we usually only did that on Fridays. She probably wanted to give us an excuse to not have to interact for a little bit.

"Hey," he whispered. He was reading a black chapter book with a yellow van on the cover, something about saving the bees. "Do you want to take a break from researching solar panels? I know it's not that interesting right now, and maybe we want to plan some big protest about Bailey's panel instead."

I thought about it. It was tempting. Not only because I

wanted a break from spreadsheets and research. But I shook my head. "It would probably be more exciting to storm Principal Quinn's office with signs, but climate change didn't stop being important because he's a huge transphobe. It's probably good practice to care about two big things at once, right?" And I also didn't think I could handle protesting the principal's decision while pretending to be just an ally; like, "This panel is important for other people! Not me! Not this normal straight girl with two normal straight parents, I just care so much about the LGBTQ community, which isn't mine at all!" I didn't think I could fight for my rights while pretending they were someone else's.

Patrick looked relieved. "Still, if you and Bailey need help with anything, let me know. And maybe they can join us once all this"—he gestured vaguely in the direction of Dixon, and beyond him the principal's office, and beyond that the world—"has been figured out. It's all of it our lives, right?"

"It sure is," I murmured.

I didn't ask Bailey if they wanted to come over to my house after school, and neither did they. I needed some time and space to process, and I figured they did too. When the school day was over, Dixon bolted out of the room, and the rest of us trickled out slower than molasses.

"Hey," I said to Bailey, before they could turn left and I turned right. "We'll figure something out. Maybe not in school, but we could ask if the library wants to host, or the public school, or . . ." I trailed off. Bailey was shaking their head.

A person could drown in the sadness pooled in their eyes.

"I don't want to have to tell my parents, you know?" they whispered. Like speaking was too hard. "That my new school is saying that it's so welcoming and inclusive, but queer people aren't allowed to talk about their lives. And I wonder. My parents told Principal Quinn that I was nonbinary when we applied. But I bet he didn't know what that meant. Would he have let me in if he had known? Or would he have come up with some excuse to reject me? Like, 'Oh, our classroom is too full' or something? Could Mrs. Brewster get me expelled?"

"No!" I exclaimed. "That wouldn't—I mean, he might have, but now—"

"Don't tell me that can't happen!" they snapped at me. The sadness in their face was washed away by a wave of anger. "You saw what happened to E, what makes you think this place would be any different? We *know* it's not any different, and you can't pretend it is just because you're only finding out now."

I rocked back, feeling like they had slapped me. "It's—Bailey, it is different here. We're not—"

"Annabelle, I cannot right now. I'm going to go. See you tomorrow. Maybe." They turned on their heel and walked away.

I froze in place. Sadie and Amanda were walking over to me, probably to say something nice, but I couldn't take it. I gave them a weak wave and started trudging home, amazed that my legs were working.

Movement slowly cracked the ice that encased me, and the farther I got from school, the more it melted. By the time

I got home I was raging mad. Like all the anger I couldn't express during the school day steamed, bubbled, and finally boiled over.

I didn't expect Dad to be home so early, but his car was parked in front of the house, and when I burst inside, slamming the door behind me, he looked up from the kitchen table, his work laptop open in front of him.

"What are you doing home?" I asked. It came out sounding like I was mad at him, and he looked taken aback.

"The air-conditioning at the office went down. Decided to finish up the day here. What's going on, Banana?"

"What's going on is that Dixon's mom is the worst person in the entire world, he tattled on us and she came in and yelled at Amy and then Principal Quinn said that the National Coming Out Day panel is canceled because it isn't welcoming to straight people and now Bailey is mad at me because they think they're going to be expelled and I've been at that stupid school since I was a baby so that somehow makes it my fault! That's what's going on!"

"Slow down," he commanded. "Get some water."

"I don't *want* water!" I shouted. "I want to quit school or get the principal fired or get Dixon expelled!"

Without a word Dad got out of his chair, grabbed a glass from the counter, filled it with water, and handed it to me. He pointed to the chair across from him. "Sit. Drink. When you're finished, you can tell me what happened, but you may not speak to me this way."

I slammed my body down in the chair and gulped down

the water. I didn't get why adults always thought that drinking some water would fix every problem in your life or why taking a deep breath would make anything better. But for some annoying reason it worked, and by the time the glass was empty, I was a little more able to put words in order, with slightly less fire behind them.

"Okay. So what happened is, Bailey and I were planning that National Coming Out Day panel, remember?"

He nodded.

"It was going to be great. A bunch of people that Bailey's family knew from Seattle were going to come. Even a trans man who ran a bookstore!" I examined his face, wondering if he would make signs of recognition, but he didn't give anything away. "But then Dixon's mom freaked out, started yelling at Amy about how it's 'inappropriate' or whatever, and then Principal Quinn came in and said that we had to cancel it." I was skipping over a lot, but wasn't up for explaining the whole crappy situation, with Dixon and his terrible idea for another panel and how the principal wouldn't even give us a straight answer until we forced him to. But the more I thought about it, the more I heated up again, like the water I drank was powering a steam engine inside me.

No reaction from Dad. He sat there, face blank as a piece of paper. I was desperate for him to say something, anything. So I kept going.

"Bailey is upset because they think they wouldn't have been accepted to the Lab if the principal had known they were nonbinary. They got mad at me for saying they don't have to worry about that, and I keep remembering all the kids with two moms or two dads and how they only stayed a year or two before going to another school! If they knew about you and Mom, would we have been treated differently? Would teachers or other families have treated us so badly that we would have to leave?"

Dad smoothed down his beard, several times, like he was petting a dog. "Maybe now you and your friend understand a little better why I wanted to keep my personal life my own business," he finally said. And after today, I did. But that only made me angrier.

"But it doesn't have to be that way! There are all kinds of families at Bailey's old school and no one cares! They told me about a kid who has, like, four different moms, and Lindsay even told me she knows another trans guy who had a baby and they don't think any of that is a big deal!"

Dad's eyes narrowed. Oh no. I had let it slip. My stomach sank as I backpedaled desperately. "I mean, she didn't say another, she said that she knows one, and only because, um—"

Dad held up his hand. "Don't lie to me again."

"Again?" I asked, heart pounding.

"When I told you that you could share my personal information with your friend and their parents, I told you to keep that detail private." His voice was low, barely above a whisper, rasping like sandpaper. "You did not keep it private, and you didn't *tell* me that you failed to keep it private, which means that somewhere in there is a lie that you told. One of omission, or one of commission."

"But I didn't *mean* to!" I cried. I was getting so good at keeping secrets, how could I have failed at this one twice? "It was an accident, they promised not to tell anyone, but it doesn't even matter to them!"

"It's not *about* them," Dad erupted. "It's not about what those nice liberals from Seattle think, it's about *me* and *my* past! And it's about *you* being able to have a normal life and not have my history change the way people treat you!"

"Dad, no one is going to treat me differently because of—"

"You can't *know* that, Annabelle! Can't you see that now? With something like this, you can't trust *anyone*. Why do you think you've never met your grandparents? Why do you think you've never met your uncle? I never want anyone to reject you the way I've been rejected, and as much as it breaks my heart, the *only* way for that to happen is for that part of my life to be dead and buried. As soon as you started talking about Bailey I *knew* there would be trouble, and you just proved that I was right."

"Wait. Wait wait wait." My mind was reeling. "What do you mean about my grandparents? An uncle? You told me that your parents were dead and that you were an only child."

Dad's face went from angry red to shocked white so fast I thought he might be on the verge of passing out. I guess I wasn't the only one in this family who let things slip when I got worked up.

"Another secret," he muttered, half to himself.

"Another *lie*," I retorted. "Guess I got that from you."

He glared at me, but he looked more sad than mad. "It . . . it wasn't exactly a lie, Annabelle. I've never said anything that wasn't at least partially true."

My dad and I had so much in common, and he didn't even know it. I sat forward in my chair and propped my elbows up on the table. Steepled my fingers, like I was in an important meeting. "Well, I guess you and Mom never specifically said 'When you were inside her uterus' or 'Back when your father, who never used to identify as anything else, by the way,' but I guess those were lies of *omission*, weren't they."

Dad slumped over. His shoulders sagged, and he laid his palms flat on the table. "I've only ever wanted to keep you safe," he murmured.

"How is lying about my family keeping me safe?" I couldn't decide if I was angry or curious, so the question came out sounding like a mixture of the two.

"They're not dead. But they decided that I was."

Okay, now I was definitely more curious than angry. "How does that work? You didn't die."

"If I'm going to tell you this, I need a cup of coffee." He got up and walked over to the coffeepot. Poured himself a cup, added milk and sugar, and put it in the microwave. I picked at the places where the varnish peeled away from the wooden table. When the microwave beeped Dad took his mug out, blew on it, took a careful sip. Leaning against the kitchen counter, he started talking.

"My parents didn't accept me as a lesbian, but we managed

to keep our relationship going. I knew that was only because, on some level, they believed that I would get over it and marry a man, give them a grandchild, be the daughter they wanted me to be. But I hoped that, with time, they would understand why that would never happen, and they would love me anyway.

"It's funny, I had wondered if coming out as trans would improve our relationship. They wanted me to be straight, and now I was, or at least, I would be in their eyes. I told them I was still their child, I still loved them, and that while they had two sons now, my future wife could be their daughter. But my father told me that he already had one son, and he didn't want another. My mother cried, said it was all her fault, that she had failed somehow. Dad told me to get out, he wouldn't let me hurt my mother like that. So I left." He wrapped his hands around the coffee mug, held it tight to his chest. It must have been holding on to some warmth.

"And my . . . uncle?"

He snorted. "My big brother, Jonathan. He didn't mind me as a lesbian, but when I came out as trans he already had two daughters, three and five. Your cousins, I guess. The last time we spoke he told me that he couldn't explain to them that their aunt was now their uncle, that it would confuse them and upset them, so he told them their aunt was dead. Easier that way, he said. I never saw him or his family again."

My head was spinning. I had grandparents, an uncle, cousins. "What about Mom?" I asked. "Is there . . . was it the same for her? Or was that true?"

Dad heaved a heavy sigh. The slightest shudder behind it. "That's all true. She's an only child, and her parents did pass away. I wish we could have given you a big family, Bananabelle. I know we can't give you enough. But we didn't have a choice. Can't you see? All we want is for you to have more."

There was so much I could have said to him. That they were enough for me. That they didn't have to be enough for me, that as I got older, I would help build our family, in my own way.

Or maybe I could have told him that Bailey's family was proof that things could be different. That his past didn't have to be responsible for my future. That he was keeping me safe from the wrong things. But for the first time in my entire life I saw my father start to cry, so I got up from my seat and hugged him, for a long time.

chapter 18

A couple days later we were all driving down to Seattle. Traffic allowed Bailey's car to come up next to ours for a few seconds, and we made faces at each other from our respective back seats before our lane slowed and they zipped ahead.

That same Thursday that everything bad happened—Dixon's mom yelling at Amy, Principal Quinn canceling our panel, me finding out even more about my family—Bailey had gone home and cried. They told their parents everything, said they missed their old school and their old community. Michael and Lindsay decided to drive them to Seattle for that Saturday's Spectrum Families meeting. And told them to text me. When my phone buzzed I ran into the kitchen and put the screen in front of Mom's face—her hands were covered in olive oil, so I didn't want her to touch it.

"Mom, look! Bailey apologized for yelling at me!" *I'm sorry for yelling at you*, is exactly what the text said. "What should I say back?"

"Hm. Well, what are you feeling?"

I hopped up onto the counter and thought, stealing a piece of broccoli out of the salad bowl.

"They hurt my feelings and I still feel that way, a little, but also I guess they're right to be worried and I should have said that instead of being like 'No you're wrong.'"

"That sounds about right. Tell them each of those things. Maybe without the 'I guess.'"

I carefully typed out the text, read it to Mom, changed the order so the first thing they read was "You were right," and sent it.

My phone buzzed again a few moments later, and I read the text out loud.

Thanks. It was a bad day for both of us. My mom wants to talk to your mom, can she call real quick?

I held the phone up in front of Mom's face again. She washed her hands, went out onto the porch, and I don't know exactly how that conversation went, who had to convince whom, what my mom said to my dad, and what he said back to her, but what I do know is that we were following them on the highway, on our way to Seattle.

Angsty guitar music was coming through the speakers, and Mom and Dad were talking about our roof or the gutters or something. I didn't know how they could focus on boring house stuff. I was so nervous and excited and full of questions that were struggling to get out, like battering rams against my teeth. I pounced on the first lull in their conversation to try and get some answers.

"So, um, these meetings are for families with LGBTQ people in them. Do you think that anyone is going to ask what we are? Like, are you going to have to tell them, you know, what kind of family we are?"

"I'm not sure," Dad confessed. "You know this is a big step for me, Banana. I might stay back and let everyone make their own assumptions. Meetings like this are new for you, but I went to a lot of them back in the day. I wouldn't be surprised if people there recognize me. Recognize that part of me. I don't know what I'll want to say, but I promise not to lie, at the very least."

Mom turned around in the front seat. "It's complicated for me too. I haven't thought of myself as a lesbian in decades, but I'm not a straight woman, and I also don't particularly think of myself as bi. It's been so long since I've been in femme community, I'm not sure if I even count. Like your father, I won't lie about who I am, but will probably wait to see how other people describe themselves. Get a feel for the room, who's there, what it's like."

I relaxed, a little. If someone as beautiful and smart as my mom didn't have the exact right word to describe herself, maybe it was okay that I didn't either. "Do you think someone's going to ask me if I'm something?" I ventured. "Something LGBTQ, I mean." What I meant was, would I be forced to come out to prove I belonged? I almost hoped that would happen, that someone would make that decision for me, as scary as it would be. The longer I kept it to myself, the harder it was becoming to talk about, like a rope of ivy slowly wrapping its way around a tree. I needed something to help me tear it away.

But no such luck, to my mixed dismay and relief. "Don't worry, Bells," Dad assured me. "Unless the culture has changed one hundred percent from my day, no one is going to directly ask you if you belong, or why or how. Maybe if you were going to a different kind of support group, with strict rules about who could and couldn't attend, someone might try to make sure you had a specific identity. But something called 'Spectrum Families'? For kids and parents? Showing up means that you belong there, in one way or another."

"Besides," said Mom with a wink, "you're my daughter, and you got your femme sensibilities from me. Even if you're still figuring out who you are, some of my fabulousness has rubbed off on you, which has to count for something."

I grinned. We even matched, a little—Mom was in a cherry-red dress with green leaves in odd patterns, and I was in a white dress covered in strawberries. She had her purple horn-rimmed glasses, and I was wearing a purple headband. I hadn't stopped trying to wrap my mind around the fact that we weren't biologically related. But no matter what, I was every inch her daughter. Just like she promised.

"Here we are," said Dad. I looked up and gasped. We were in front of the coffee shop/library/community center that Bailey and I had met E in. I should have known.

"What's wrong?" asked Mom. "Are you okay?"

"Um. I'm fine. Got my finger caught in my seat belt." I'd tell my dad about meeting E on the drive home. This was not the time for another confession about how I had been less than honest with him. I had to remember to pretend that I'd never been there before.

Bailey's family came in right behind us. I loved it when we wore outfits that made sense together; their T-shirt said "Pi Day" followed by four rows of different pies, including strawberry. "Mike! Hannah! You beat us!" said Michael, like it was the most exciting thing in the world. "Welcome to the Seattle Center for Queer Community. Have you been here before?"

Dad nodded and I almost fell over from shock. "When we first moved here, they ran a health clinic. Easy to get your T script refilled. I've gotten it mailed for the last decade or so, but I remember coming here every few months. Always full of short guys and tall ladies."

"I didn't know they used to run a health clinic here!" Bailey exclaimed. "Where was it?"

"In there." Dad pointed to the library. "What time does this meeting start? Do we have time to get a cup of coffee?"

"We've got half an hour," said Lindsay, "but it might be nice to get in the room a little early, to make sure we can sit together."

"Plenty of time," said Mike. The adults got in line. I told Mom to get me a hot chocolate, and Bailey and I ducked into the library to poke around and whisper.

"I didn't tell my parents that I've been here before, are yours going to spill the beans?" I asked.

Bailey shook their head. "Remember they were annoyed at you for not telling? They know better than to mess things up right now."

I sighed in relief. "Okay, good. I'll tell them on the drive up. Promise." We moved over to the children's book section and started flipping through picture books, and my dad must have been first in line for coffee, because he found us a few minutes later.

"Here's your cocoa," he said, handing it over. "Bailey, your mom is getting your tea. Is there time for me to look through the library?"

"I think so!" said Bailey. Dad moved a few shelves over, skimmed the books, and slid one out.

"This was important to me," he said, showing me the cover. A stocky man in a hat smiled out at us.

"*Becoming a Visible Man*,'" I read. "Is that . . . is he trans too? The guy on the cover?"

"Yup. Jamison Green. I got to meet him once, not long after I started T. It meant a lot to see someone look the way I wanted to. Ohhh, these guys!" he exclaimed, pulling out another book. This one had a black-and-white cover, a lot of smiling men on the cover, two of them hugging each other.

"'*Transmen and FTMs*,'" read Bailey. "Um, why isn't there a space between 'trans' and 'men'? And I thought the term 'FTM' was offensive."

Dad laughed. "The only problem with this book is that it was boring. I know a few of these guys, they're cool, but this book wasn't fun to read. As for the title, well, language changes. I used to call myself an FTM. I liked the sound of it, still do. And a few of these guys said they were genderqueer, but maybe now they would say nonbinary. Makes you wonder, doesn't it, Bailey?"

Bailey cocked their head. "Wonder about what?" They sounded suspicious but also happy. Dad had never talked to them like this, so open and easy. He had never talked to *me* like this. Parts of him always felt walled off. I had always thought that was what dads were like. But his walls were coming down.

"About which words you're using now will be offensive or wrong in five or thirty years. What are future trans kids going to think about *your* gender, kiddo? Are you going to be some unfashionable old nonbinary to them the way I'm an out-of-touch old transsexual to you?" He winked, and my heart exploded. Bailey's eyes were shining with mirth. This was a new version of my dad, and whoever he was, I hoped he would stick around. Forever.

The three other parents walked over then, and Lindsay handed Bailey their drink—lemongrass tea, according to the little tag dangling down the side of the cup. "Is everyone ready to go in?" asked Michael. "Everyone's used the bathroom, got their drinks, perused the reading material? Yes? Good! Let's go." He led us up a flight of stairs, down a short hallway, and through a door.

Ever since Bailey first started talking about Spectrum Families, I had been imagining what it looked like. I assumed there would be a folding table full of snacks, and chairs arranged in a circle around a big room. I had pictured small groups of lesbian moms, gay dads, and a bunch of kids who either looked like Bailey or didn't. I figured there would be some cool hair colors, maybe some parents with not-very-parent-like facial piercings, and a lot of flannel (this was Seattle, after all). And unlike a lot of places in Tahoma Falls, it probably wouldn't be mostly white people.

I'm not saying I'm psychic, but I was right about every single detail. The snacks. The chairs in a circle. The different kinds of kids and parents, genders that I wasn't sure about, and more people of color than I think were at my entire school. Across the room I even spotted a couple that looked awfully similar to my mom and dad: a short, slim white man with a wiry beard, his arm around the wide waist of a gorgeous, taller white woman in a light blue dress patterned with white butterflies, tight around the middle and flaring out into a full skirt, a not-shy amount of cleavage. They were both watching a little kid, maybe three years old, carefully arrange Oreos and baby carrots on a plate. I wondered how that kid came into the world, if that couple's story was anything like my family's. And what it would be like to have gone to meetings like this with them when I was little, and to always feel like I belonged. A little jealousy rose in my throat and I swallowed it down. Better late than never.

"Well, well, well, if it isn't the Wicks!" exclaimed a tall, skinny Asian man, walking over with a wide grin on his face. He hugged Michael and Lindsay, and gave Bailey a high-five. "I thought you moved to the other side of the mountains, or the peninsula or something! What brings you back today?"

"We didn't go that far!" Bailey protested. "Just up to Tahoma Falls. It's okay, but I missed you all and wanted to come visit."

A flash of concern crossed the man's face, and he glanced up at the adults. Michael or Lindsay must have had one of those we'll-talk-about-it-later conversations with him using grown-up telepathy, because he didn't press further.

"Well, you always have a home here. And who's this?"

"This is my friend Annabelle! Annabelle, this is Eric, he runs the Seattle chapter of Spectrum Families. Where's Ray?"

"Diaper duty," said Eric. "He'll be back soon. And you're Annabelle's parents?" he asked, offering a hand to shake.

"That's right. I'm Hannah," said Mom.

"Mike," said Dad. "Thanks for having us."

"Of course! Everyone's welcome. Go ahead and get a snack, find a place to sit. We never start right on time, but make yourselves comfortable. Let me know if you need anything."

Only a few of the chairs had been claimed, so we put our coats and things down on six of them, all next to each other. Bailey took me around the room introducing me to people: a couple kids from their old school, teenagers, little kids. Every single time they said, "My pronouns are still they/them, what about yours?" I thought that was weird at first but it turned out that a bunch of Bailey's friends had changed their pronouns since the last time they saw each other. Introducing myself as "she/her" stopped feeling awkward after the first couple times.

I kept an eye on the couple that looked like my mom and dad. They had wrangled their child into a chair and were taking turns reading from board books. I nudged Bailey in between being introduced to friends. "Do you know that family over there?" I asked, nodding in their direction.

Bailey looked over. "Them? No, I don't think so. They might be new."

"Do you think they . . ." I trailed off, not sure if there was a polite way to end that sentence, but Bailey managed to pick up on what I meant.

"Probably? I mean, you can never know how people identify without asking them. But, yeah, I bet they have a lot in common with your parents."

"Can everyone take their seats?" Eric called over the din of the room. "We should be getting started!"

Bailey and I darted over to our chairs—the room was almost full, easily about forty people, ranging from tiny babies to some who looked like grandparents.

"Welcome to Spectrum Families!" announced Eric. "I see a lot of familiar faces, and some new ones. We always start by going around and sharing your name, your pronouns, and anything brief you want to say about why you're joining today." One last person slipped into the room, a short white guy holding a baby. He sat down next to Eric, so I figured that must be the diaper-changing husband. Dad was sitting next to me, and I heard a sharp intake of breath. He stiffened. I snuck a peek in his direction, and he was staring at the husband, Ray, I think his name was? But it was going to be our turn to talk soon, and I had to make sure I said the right thing.

Michael, Lindsay, and Bailey introduced themselves first, and more than half the room waved hello. They were like Spectrum Families royalty, and sitting next to them made me feel like I was too. Or at least, I don't know, a duchess or something. And then it was my turn.

This opening go-round had been another one of my predictions. And I kind of predicted that I would forget my carefully rehearsed statement and say something embarrassing or confusing, but for once the words came out exactly as I had planned on the car ride down. "Hi! I'm Annabelle, she and her. My friend Bailey invited me, because they thought that me and my parents would like it here. I think they're right." I was so proud of myself for coming up with that: Everything was true, nothing was too much information, and I got to tell everyone that I was Bailey's friend. Perfect.

Dad was next, and I had never in my life been so curious to hear what someone would say. He cleared his throat, but his voice was a little husky. "My name is Mike. Annabelle is my daughter. Haven't been to something like this in a long time, thanks for having us."

And Mom. "I'm Hannah, my pronouns are she/her/hers."

Dad hadn't said his pronouns, I wondered if that was on purpose or if he forgot. "I'm Annabelle's mother, and like my husband, it's been a long time since I've been to a group for my community. It's nice to be here, and I hope we're able to come back."

The fat woman in the butterfly dress was smiling warmly in our direction. Mom looked over at her, and wiped the corners of her eyes like she was dabbing away tears.

In the meantime, Dad was looking down at his hands, held clasped in his lap. Ray was staring at Dad intensely, eyes wide, distractedly jiggling his baby. But when it became clear that my dad was not going to look in his direction, he relaxed a bit, letting his eyes rest on the next person to share.

"I'm Eli," said the man who kind of looked like my dad, once it was his turn. "They/them, please." Oops, I had assumed "he." "And this is my daughter Edie, she's three. Edie, what are your pronouns?"

"She and her and hers!" Edie lisped proudly. "And my daddy is a they and my mommy is a she too."

"That's right," the woman who looked like my mom said, laughing. "I'm Vivian, she/her, but I don't mind they/them. We moved up here from Portland, and were members of the Spectrum Families group down there before I even got pregnant. We're excited to join this community."

Introductions went around the circle, and I listened closely to everyone. I was glad we went near the beginning, because what I said wasn't interesting enough to replay in my mind and I could focus on other people sharing instead of rehearsing what I was going to say. And everyone was interesting. I filed away several new vocabulary words to ask Bailey or my parents about later, and figured out a couple others thanks to context. I was surprised by how many adults went by two sets of pronouns. Did that mean I had to choose for them? I decided to not talk about anyone and listen to see how that worked.

Ray was the last to speak. "Most of you know me by now, I'm Ray, Eric's husband, he/him/his. And this is Aspen!" He held up the baby in his arms. "Aspen hasn't told us much yet, except for when he's hungry or needs a diaper changed, but for now we're guessing he's a boy. We might be wrong, though. It's nice to see some old familiar faces." Was it my imagination, or was he looking in our direction when he said that? Maybe he was talking about Bailey and their family.

"For those of you who are new," Eric began, "Spectrum Families meetings usually divide up after introductions. Adults stay here, while youths go into the adjoining room. For younger kids who want to stick with their parents, they're welcome here as well. We have a play corner set up if they're old enough for that, and Ray usually supervises. Do any of the SF kids want to explain what happens in the youth room?"

One of Bailey's friends, J.P., raised their hand. "Sometimes we split up into smaller groups based on age, sometimes we split up into groups of, like, LGBT kids with straight parents and straight kids with LGBT parents and LGBT kids with

LGBT parents. Sometimes we all hang out. It depends on the day." I hoped they wouldn't split into groups that day, it would be hard to pick which one to go to.

"Pretty much," said Eric cheerfully. "Everyone get settled. Kids can head over to the other room; adults, you're welcome to get more coffee or stretch out those old bones."

The volume in the room rose to a dull roar as everyone started moving. Bailey got up and looked at me expectantly. "You want to come to the youth room, right?"

"Yeah," I said. "I'll meet you there." They looked at me with a question on their face, but left.

"Dad?" I asked, leaning over. "Are you going to be okay?"

He cocked his head. "Of course. Why?"

I shrugged. "Wanted to make sure. Do you know that guy?" I nodded my head in Ray's direction.

"I do," he murmured. "I'll tell you about it later. But I'm okay. Go make friends."

I started to walk away, then came back and wrapped my arms around him. He patted me on the back, surprised, and Mom blew me a kiss as I retreated again.

I hurried into the youth room, a little smaller than the main room but otherwise identical, and was glad to see that everyone was milling around. I hadn't missed anything.

Bailey was chatting animatedly with kids from their old school. "Then his *mommy* came in to get the principal to shut it down! I couldn't even, who does that?"

I rolled my eyes. "You're telling them about Dixon? *He*

does that, obviously. I remember the year he brought in, like, individual lemon meringue pies for his birthday and would remind us about it every time someone else brought cupcakes or whatever. He's such a jerkwad."

Before we could catch up more, a sharp clap of hands got our attention. "All right, beans, let's check in!" announced an older white woman, with bowl-cut sandy hair, a polo shirt, and cargo shorts. She had said her name was Kelli, I remembered.

"Looking around, I don't see anyone under the age of . . . ten? Beatrice, you're ten now, right?"

A Black girl with intricately braided hair jumped up and down and said, "I turned ten last week! I got my ears pierced! Mom said she was ten when she got her ears pierced and because I'm her daughter now I can too!"

"Well, happy birthday! Since we don't have any younger kids, do you all want to hang out, or are there things going on that we want to talk about as a group?"

No one said anything, but there were so many loaded looks shooting around the room that Kelli got the hint. "Let's all grab a seat. If you want to stand, or sit on the floor, or do something else to make your body comfortable, that's fine too." She led us to the corner of the room with folding chairs, bean bags, floor mats, and pillows. I fell into a huge beanbag chair, then scooted over to make room for Bailey. Kelli was the only one to sit in a chair, I guessed because she was an adult.

We did a quick name and pronoun go-round, which I suspected was mostly for my benefit because everyone else seemed to know each other, and then different kids brought up stuff that was going on with them.

Bailey went first, as Spectrum Families royalty. "I missed being here so much. We moved to Tahoma Falls, and I don't know any other trans or nonbinary kids there. I've never been the only one before! I'm getting tired of having to teach everyone about what it means, and I worry about making people think that all nonbinary people are just like me. Like, white and female-assigned and everything. Plus there's all this bad stuff happening at our school: The principal is homophobic and transphobic and definitely also racist and ableist and everything else; this one boy's mom thinks that I'm a bad influence; and it's all . . . I want to move back here. Sorry, Annabelle. You're the coolest straight cis girl I've ever met, and I'd miss you, but it's too much."

I had been looking curiously around the room but immediately snapped my eyes to my lap. I didn't want anyone to see my face, my eyes bugging out, front teeth biting my lip hard. Hot flashes rushed through my whole body. I had never exactly told Bailey that I was straight, but I knew they assumed that I was because they spent all this time explaining their own identity and I never said anything about mine. Which both was and wasn't fair. But being called that felt like being shoved in the chest or squished under a rock.

"We miss you a lot," said J.P.

"Yeah," said a handsome brown-skinned boy. "You should come visit more often."

"Are you *sure* you're the only one up there?" asked someone else, another nonbinary kid with olive skin, dark eyebrows, and bright green hair. "I bet there are others, even transfemme kids and trans kids of color. You probably haven't found them yet." I felt Bailey bristle slightly.

"If there was a group like this up there, I could," they said. "I don't know how often I can get my parents to drive me down to Seattle. My dad acts like since me being nonbinary isn't a big deal to them, it shouldn't be for me, or for anyone else. They don't get how much I need this. Or why."

"Then you should tell them," someone said, simply.

"You should tell them," Kelli echoed.

Bailey nodded, their shoulders slumped, and passed the imaginary mic. The handsome trans boy, Juan, talked about wanting to try out for the baseball team instead of softball, and how he was joining up with some girls to break into the league because there was no good reason why those two sports had to be segregated. The green-haired one, Macy, said that eir moms were probably in the other room complaining about how hard eir pronouns were, and why e didn't want to use they/them but eir parents wouldn't switch over. I wasn't the only cis person in the room, but all the other kids talked about themselves using all these words that I still didn't know yet. Being LGBTQ was like an epic fantasy story. They had read all the books in the series, and I was struggling through the table of contents.

I wanted to stay quiet. It would be embarrassing to start talking about my not-straightness here. This was not how I wanted Bailey to find out. And everyone, even the kids younger than me, were so much more confident and sure of themselves. They knew who they were, and they knew how to talk about it. Trying to describe what I wasn't but didn't know what I *was*, in front of these cool Seattle kids, would make me feel like a kindergartner crashing a college class. I couldn't do it.

But after Bailey called me straight, hearing that kid talk about eir parents, who were gay and knew better but also weren't doing the right thing by their kid, unlocked something in me with a deep and heavy *clunk*. When Kelli asked who wanted to share next, the words came pouring out.

"I found out that my dad is a trans man and that my mom is queer and femme, and they only told me about it because I became friends with Bailey and found out about trans stuff, and now there's this whole part of my life and my family that they've been lying to me about but *also* that might make me a bad person because I know it's not my business if someone is trans, even if it's my dad, but now I don't know who I am and I don't know who they are and I wish I had always known or that I never knew and now everything is different and I don't know what to do!" And then I was sobbing.

Bailey tried to wriggle their arm under my shoulders, but it was hard because we were both lying on a beanbag, so they patted my hair. J.P. ran out of the room and came back with a box of tissues. Juan went over to the water cooler in the corner and brought me a cup of water. No one spoke, but it wasn't awkward. It was respectful. I blew my nose and took a few shaky sips of water.

"When people share," said Kelli softly, "we ask whether they want advice, or support, or to be heard. What would help you right now?"

"Um . . . I think, like, advice? Or support? I don't know, something like that."

"No offense," started Macy, "but being trans isn't anyone else's business. Even if it's your dad. So you should be honored that he told you, and not start thinking that he should have, because no one has to tell anyone if they don't want to."

"I dunno," said Juan. Macy glared at him, and I wondered if they disagreed a lot. "It's one thing to be stealth at school, or at your job or whatever. But I think this is different from that. Where you come from *is* your business, and I think Annabelle has a right to know how her family came to be."

Macy rolled eir eyes and mouthed "whatever."

J.P. raised their hand next. "It's actually unfair, in a funny way. Like, if you're a kid, you have to tell your parents that you're trans, if you want to transition or get them to call you by the right pronouns or whatever. Unless you stop talking to them for some other reason, I guess. But since Annabelle's dad transitioned before she was born, he didn't *have* to tell her. Parents always get more privacy around their lives than their kids do. I'm glad he told you, Annabelle. If you came out as trans, it would be his business, so the reverse is only fair."

"No it's not," Macy argued. "If you don't have to tell anyone that you're trans if you don't want to, that should count in every situation."

"We don't have rules for every situation yet," Juan shot back. "Everything we've come up with is mostly meant to keep us safe around cis people, not to keep secrets from your kids."

"I want to have a baby and tell that baby that they can be whatever they want because I used to be a boy," Beatrice added.

"But that's *your choice*," Macy sniped. "You don't get to make that choice for Annabelle's dad."

"Let's all check back in with Annabelle," Kelli interjected. It was probably quite obvious that this was making me feel worse, given that I had started crying again. "So, you were asking for advice. And it sounds like you wanted people to share their thoughts about two different things: whether your parents should have shared their identities with you earlier, and whether it's okay for you to be upset that they didn't. And you're getting some different opinions, which is to be expected, since there's no one right answer. What are you thinking right now?"

"I think . . ." I started, then took a long, shuddering breath. "I guess that everyone is kind of right. That it's their business to share if they want to, but also that since it's about my life too, I have a right to know. And that maybe being upset about it doesn't one hundred percent make sense but it's also okay.

Because different things can be true all at the same time. Like how green beans are vegetable but also berries. Have you told them about that, Bailey?" I asked, turning to look at them. They grinned and said yes, then leaned against me, their weight so warm and grounding that I almost forgave them for not really seeing me.

In the lull that followed, Eric poked his head through the door. "Hey, we're wrapping up in here. Are you all ready to come back together?"

"Are we?" Kelli asked the group, and we nodded. "Yup, we're ready," she said.

I grabbed Bailey's arm. "Can we wait here a minute?" I whispered. I was still trembling a little, my eyelashes wet, so Bailey nodded immediately.

Once the room was empty, they turned to me. "That was brave of you," they said. "Sharing about your parents. It must have been hard."

I let out a ragged breath. "I'm not straight," I said. It came out. Simple as that.

Bailey did a double take. "Wait, what? You—because of your parents? Or—"

"Because I have a big crush on you, or at least I did but I'm trying to get over it because you don't want to date cis people, so that means that I'm . . . I don't know, queer or bi or something. But you said I was straight back there and I'm not. I've never told anyone. Sorry."

And just like that, I had come out. To one person, but the difference between one person and no one was the entire world. I hadn't expected today to become ACOD, but it was as good a day as any other.

"Annabelle, I . . . I'm so sorry."

I started laughing. I don't know why, but every emotion was roaring through me and they had to come out somehow, and I had already shed a lot of tears. "What are you sorry for?" I got out between giggles.

"Um, I'm not sure. For assuming you were straight? For one? I should know better than to assume things. And also for not realizing you had a crush on me. And also for . . . for not having a crush on you. I mean, you're great and also cute and if I was into cis girls I would probably be into you but I'm just not! I'm sorry."

I felt the tiniest bit disappointed that they weren't going to make an exception for me, but I also hadn't expected them to. "It's okay. It's nice to know that you're not perfect either."

They shook their head vigorously. "Not even close." They paused, the hum of conversation beginning in the room next door. "I have to check: You want this to stay between us, right? Or do you want me to help you start telling people?"

"Between us," I said. "Please. There's already so much going on, I cannot handle any more conversations-with-a-capital-C."

"I get it," they said. "I knew my parents would be fine with me being nonbinary, but I didn't tell them right away. It's about you, and feeling right with yourself, not about anyone else. Can I hug you?"

We had never asked permission to hug before, but it

felt right now. Because this could have changed something between us. But it didn't have to.

"Yes," I said, and we were still hugging when Kelli poked her head in to see where we went.

chapter 19

"This is why I could never live in Seattle," Dad complained. "Too much traffic." We were only a few blocks from the community center and even the entrance to the highway was clogged with cars.

"Good thing we all used the bathroom before leaving," said Mom lightly. "And I have plenty of snacks if we need any."

I cradled my head on my seat belt, utterly spent. I was glad for the traffic. It meant the day wasn't over yet, that it was still happening.

The meeting ended with another go-round, where everyone got to share about their favorite part of the meeting or how they were feeling. Bailey said they were happy to have seen their friends, and I said I was glad to make new ones, but only because we didn't want to say what *really* happened in front of our parents. Michael and Lindsay also said that it was good to be back, and that they were going to make an effort to come more often. I wondered what the adults talked about while we were in the other room. If they were also hiding away something that had happened.

It seemed like it. Mom's voice was resonant and rich as she said that it fed her soul to connect with community again. And my dad . . . he was sitting up straight in his chair. Looking around the room. He said, "I had thought there would be no place for me in this room, and I was wrong. Thank you."

I wondered if this was going to be one of those car rides where we all thought our independent thoughts. I had enough to process that we could have driven all the way to Canada and I wouldn't mind; it would give me barely enough time to sort through everything. But Dad banged on his steering wheel and said, "The good old community center. I haven't been there in at least a decade. Last time I was there they didn't have a coffee shop, or a library. Just a lot of different offices, cubicles, one big meeting room. Must have been a huge renovation."

"Even then it was nicer than the one where we met," Mom reminded him. "The air conditioner was always breaking, and the people working the front desk never knew where anything was."

"I've been there before," I confessed. It wasn't fair to keep that from them, not when I had had a whole emotional meltdown about them keeping things from me. Though I was also keeping that emotional meltdown from them. As well as that little thing about me coming out for the first time to my new best friend that I was getting over having my first crush on. Oh well. One thing at a time.

Mom turned around in her seat to look quizzically at me.

"Arizona? Did you go to Arizona without telling us? I think we would have noticed that."

"No. The Seattle center. Dad, I was there last weekend. With Bailey. I didn't want to tell you, I'm sorry."

He looked into my eyes through the rearview mirror. "You mean, when you went with their family to see octopuses, you also snuck into the LGBT center?" His voice was mild, but I still tried to head off an explosion.

"Okay, no, we didn't sneak. And we did see the octopuses after. So I didn't lie to you, not entirely, but also I knew that if I told you the whole truth you might not let me go, or be mad at me or something."

"She did tell me, though, honey," Mom interjected. "Not where they were going, but who they were meeting. I decided to trust her."

Dad nodded slowly, processing this. We got into the carpool lane to enter the freeway and he gunned the accelerator, smoothly merging into the cars zipping up the I-5. "Tell me more," he said finally. His eyes were fixed on the road ahead.

"We found out about a nonbinary kid who got kicked out of school. Spectrum Families had sent an email about it, and Bailey's dad told us about it. And Bailey wanted to talk to them. They were like, 'Do you want to hang out sometime,' and Bailey was like, 'Yes definitely,' so Michael and Lindsay took us there to meet them. In the coffee shop. Then we went to the aquarium. I didn't want to tell you about the first part, because—"

"Because you knew that I probably wouldn't let you go, and if I did, I'd be a grouch about it," he finished.

I could only see the side of his face from my spot in the back seat, but he didn't look mad. He might have even been smiling, a bit. "Yeah. I guess," I said.

"I can't blame you," he said. "It's upsetting to learn that you didn't think you could be honest with me. But that's not your fault. It's mine."

I opened my mouth to say something, maybe "No it's not" or "It's okay" or even "Who are you and what have you done with my father," but he kept going.

"You saw that I knew someone there," he said. "From Arizona. Ray. Eric's husband, with the baby. He—well." Dad drew in a long breath, and I could see him struggle to organize his thoughts, to get the words out.

Mom put a hand on his knee. "Do you want me to explain?" she asked.

He shook his head curtly. "No. I should. Annabelle. You remember I told you about the other trans guys in Phoenix? How the group I was part of, they couldn't accept when I got pregnant? Ray was one of them. One of the worst, actually. He was married to a woman at the time, and if any of the other guys talked about being interested in dating men, he told them they weren't really trans, that they should go back to being straight girls."

"But he and Eric are married!" I exclaimed. "He's gay! Or bi or whatever. Right?"

Dad snorted. "And he had that baby, after telling me that

no real man would ever want to get pregnant, that top surgery was wasted on me, and that I was an embarrassment to the community."

"But—how—why—" I spluttered. Dad reached behind his seat and squeezed my leg.

"Before you kids came back, he pulled me aside. Apologized. Told me that he said all those awful things because he was jealous, because he was so desperate to fit in as a man that he didn't stop to think about who he truly was, and what he wanted most. He met Eric on a business trip, and fell in love. Left Arizona to be with him. And he told me—" A tear glistened in the corner of Dad's eye. He wiped it away with a finger. "He said that without me, he never would have been brave enough to have his child. That I taught him what was possible. That he's wanted to apologize for so long, and hoped that I could forgive him."

My jaw dropped. "Wow," I breathed. That was all I could say.

"And I talked to that couple, Eli and Vivian," Mom added, after a long pause.

"The ones who look like you?" I asked. Then blushed. "I mean, uh, because—"

Mom laughed. "No, you're right. Small trans guy and queer fat femme, it's a classic pairing. They're in Bothell, and are looking for community. In fact, they're going to come over tomorrow for lunch. Vivian said something about this being the last weekend before their busy season starts."

"Cool," I said. "Edie is cute."

"She's a firecracker!" said Mom. "A lot like you, in fact."

Dad shook his head, but it looked more like bemusement than disagreement. "I thought that only kids these days were going by they/them pronouns. But Eli looks like me. I might ask him—them—about all that."

I didn't know what to say to that, but had one burning question. "So you're not mad at me?" I asked Dad. "For lying?"

He sighed heavily, shook his head. "You didn't lie. And you didn't tell me the whole truth because you didn't trust me to understand. It's my job to be the kind of person you can trust with the truth. And it's also my job to trust you."

I grinned. "You know what that means! Time for my first smartphone. It'll be good for you! Prove you can trust me to navigate the wild world of group chats and social media. You're lucky I'm such a selfless daughter, giving you so many opportunities for growth."

Dad snorted. "Don't push your luck, Banana."

chapter 20

I had never seen my mom in such a state. We had plenty of snacks in the pantry, but she got up at five to bang around the kitchen, and by the time I was rubbing sleep out of my eyes she had already made two dozen raspberry thumbprint cookies and three different kinds of quiches. And our house was generally clean, but as soon as I was done with breakfast she shoved a dusting rag into my hand and told me to clean every surface I could reach, and ordered my dad to mop.

I wiped down most of the surfaces I could reach. If I recalled correctly, Eli and Vivian weren't that much taller than my mom and my dad, so I decided not to get up on a chair and do the tops of shelves because no one would see them. I tidied up the living room a little, mostly putting books and magazines and things away, then poked my head into my parents' room. My mother was in their tiny bathroom, leaning over the counter, painting eyeliner into wings. She was in the lacy slip that only went under her nicest dresses.

"Mom? You okay?"

"Yes I'm fine, why do you ask?" Wings complete, she put down the eyeliner pen and started on her hair, brushing out two individual locks on either side of her face, then pinning them up into tiny rosettes.

"No reason, just curious." Obviously the reason was that she was acting weird, but I didn't know how to say that without sounding accusatory. I didn't leave the doorway, and kept watching her put herself together.

"I suppose I am a little nervous," she admitted, looking at herself in the mirror. "It's been a long time since I've been around another queer fat femme. And they're coming from Portland. I'm sure they're so much more active in the community. I can't even imagine what kinds of drama we've missed. I want everything to be perfect, so they don't think I'm some boring suburban mom." With that, she shimmied into one of my favorites of her dresses, purple and tight with a boat neck and ruffles. "Zip me up?" she asked, and I pulled the zipper up the back. Then she put her arms around me and I hugged her gently, careful not to muss anything.

"I bet they're nervous too," I reassured my mom. "They'll probably want to know everything about how to raise a daughter as fabulous as me! And you and Dad know everything about living up here. Also you're prettier than Vivian. And Dad is handsomer than Eli. Edie is cuter than me, but that's only because she's three! So don't worry, it's going to be great."

Mom studied me seriously. "When did you become such a wise young woman?" she asked.

"Oh, forever ago. But now I need you to help me pick out my outfit, it's after one!"

By the time two o'clock rolled around we were ready for guests. I was in a dark red T-shirt dress, and Dad had changed into one of his boring white buttoned shirts. The cookies and quiche were on the counter, iced tea was in the fridge, and when we heard a car pull up in the drive the three of us went out onto the porch to greet them. A burst of pride popped inside me, that this was my family and this was my life.

I wondered if they were nervous too, because Vivian looked amazing. She was wearing a sailor dress like the one my mom had, except hers was white with blue trim and my mom's was blue with white trim. She was wearing a cute little hat over her loosely braided curls. And Eli was dressed exactly like my dad, except their button-up shirt was black. And Edie, well, it looked like they had wrestled her into a nice outfit, a dress with a frilly skirt and bows, except one of the bows had ripped halfway off and was dangling down her shoulder, and her cheeks were orange with Cheetos dust.

The two adults walked over with Edie holding hands between them. They swung her up onto the porch and Mom and Vivian immediately started complimenting each other. Eli and Dad shook hands, and I noticed that my father's shoulders were squarer than usual.

"Did you find your way here all right?" asked Dad.

"Oh yeah, I plugged your address into GPS and followed the directions." Eli's voice had a similar quality to Dad's. I couldn't put my finger on it, but I liked it.

"What a beautiful place!" Vivian exclaimed. "I wish we had a yard like this, but our property doesn't drain well, it's too muddy for grass. Eventually we'll have to get gravel or woodchips so we're not staring at a dirt pit all the time."

"I NEED TO USE THE POTTY," Edie yelled.

"Of course, sweetheart, let me show you where it is," Mom cooed. She led Edie into the house, and the rest of us followed.

I had resigned myself to babysitting for a while, while the adults talked, but after a few hectic minutes of shoes and jackets and glasses of water and telling Edie that she could have *one* cookie, not a handful, the three-year-old conked out on the couch, one of our blankets tucked over her and half a cookie crumbling in her hand. The rest of us sat around the kitchen table with glasses of iced tea, the back door open so a breeze blew over us.

"I'm so glad we were able to make this work on such short notice," said Vivian. "Believe it or not, we're getting ready for the Christmas season, and this is our last free weekend until the New Year."

"It still feels like summer!" Mom exclaimed. "What do you do for work?"

"We run a craft business," said Eli. "Wooden toys for kids. Viv is in charge of the art and design, and I get us booked at craft shows and bazaars, that kind of thing."

"You help with the art too," Vivian reminded them.

Eli laughed. "Sure, but that means spray painting over the stencils you give me. You're the creative mind in the family."

"But it's true," Vivian continued. "This is the busiest time of the year for us. We bought a house with a workshop down-stairs, and in a couple weeks we'll start going to shows every weekend. We like being able to work from home, especially now that we have a little."

"You said you were in a Spectrum Families group down in Portland?" Dad asked. "I hadn't realized there were different branches."

"Oh yes," said Eli. "We looked into it when we were think-ing about having a baby. They're all up and down the coast, even in smaller towns and cities. How long have you three been going?"

A brief pause. We knew that answering that question would leave many others open, and I was proud when Dad went for it. "That was actually our first time," he admitted. "We only learned about it a couple weeks ago."

"Your first time!" Vivian exclaimed. "How come?"

My dad hesitated, then looked at me. "Annabelle? You want to take this one?"

I raised my eyebrows. "You want me to?"

Dad smiled at Eli and Vivian. "We're among friends. Go ahead."

"Well . . ." I said, arranging the story in my head. So much had happened over the last few weeks, and I had been dealing with each new thing as it came up. I hadn't yet figured out how it all fit together as a story. But I knew where to start.

"Do you remember Bailey?" I asked. "The nonbinary kid I was sitting with, in the pie shirt? Well, they used to live in Seattle, but moved here at the beginning of the school year. And I had never met a nonbinary person before. I didn't think—" I glanced at Dad, and he nodded at me. "I didn't think I had ever met a trans person before, either."

Eli inhaled sharply. Vivian turned toward my mom, and they seemed to see each other so deeply in that moment.

"So," I continued, "because of Bailey, I learned more about my mom and dad. And they told us about the Spectrum Families group. And we all decided to go." Wow, was that the whole story? It sure felt like more than that. But maybe even the most complicated things are actually simple, when you get down to it.

"Eli, when did you transition?" my dad asked.

Eli squinched one eye shut. "Hm . . . I guess that depends on when you consider transition beginning. About five years ago, I think? At least, that's when I started hormones, but I had been going by 'Eli' for a year or so before that. What about you?"

"Twenty-three years," said Dad.

"Wow," said Eli.

"That must have been a whole different world," said Vivian. "I didn't even know I was queer then."

Dad chuckled. "It sure was different. I didn't even know how different it was until my daughter and her friend forced me to look."

There was the briefest of heavy silences. Mom and Vivian both had tears in their eyes. Eli quirked up one corner of their mouth in a smile, and Dad mirrored them.

"So, Annabelle!" exclaimed Vivian, dabbing at her eyes. "Tell us more about what it's like growing up out here. Eli and I are both from Brooklyn, but didn't meet till we were living in Portland, and we have no idea what suburban life is like. What does Edie need to know?"

"Oh, I am an *expert*," I boasted. "Let's see. Fifth grade is old enough to walk to school by yourself, and if you get lost you can flag down a mail truck and they'll take you home. I haven't found any poisonous berries—and I have eaten a LOT of berries—and I think that's about it."

The adults laughed. "We love Annabelle's school," Mom added. "It's not public, so you don't have to be in the same district. If you want to visit with Edie, let us know and we can help set that up."

"Well, we *used* to love my school," I grumbled.

Dad sighed. "Your last year is off to a rough start, isn't it, Banana?"

"Why, what's going on?" asked Eli. "You're in sixth grade, right? I remember school being the absolute worst at that age."

I shook my head. "It is kind of the worst but probably not in a normal school way? I mean, my class is small and we've all known each other forever, except for Bailey, and there aren't any bullies or football player shoving you in lockers, we don't even have lockers. Some people have zits and most of us remember to wear deodorant, so far puberty isn't as bad as everyone says it's going to be. But it's the worst because our new teacher promised us that we could learn about interesting things, like LGBTQ identities and Black history not just in February and how everything intersects, and then this stupid jerk Dixon tattled on her to the principal, so all we get to learn about are the ancient Greeks and Romans. Me and another person are working on getting solar panels put on the roof because we don't want to die from global warming when we're thirty, but who knows, maybe our principal will force us to give up on that too." I took a deep breath, a long swig of iced tea, and shoved a cookie in my mouth.

". . . Oh," said Eli. "That sure is different from my middle school experience."

"Mine too," agreed Vivian. "Annabelle, I cannot imagine being as well-informed and mature as you are when I was in sixth grade. I didn't think about anything outside of whether my shirt was too tight and wanting to kiss my best friend's big sister."

"I just played softball!" Eli added. "I don't remember anything I learned in school, but probably would if I went to a school like yours."

"And she's barely gotten started," said Dad proudly, squeezing my shoulder.

Edie started to stir on the couch, then sat up and rubbed her eyes. Her perfectly matching outfit now looked like a pile of rags wound around her body. Vivian went and picked her up, bringing her back to the table. The little girl wrapped her arms around her mother's neck, then turned to stare curiously at us.

"I'm hungry," she said. "What's for snack?"

"You've already had a cookie, but we have quiche," Dad said. "Do you like quiche?"

"I don't know what that is," said Edie crankily, staring at the plate half-filled with cookies.

"It's like a scrambled egg pie," Dad explained. I had never heard him talk to a little kid before, at least not since I was a little kid and didn't know that adults talked to little kids differently. He sounded so patient. And loving. Like a dad. Like someone who loved being a dad. Who would give up anything to be one.

"I don't like scrambled eggs with things in it," Edie said suspiciously. "Are there vegebles in there?"

Dad opened his mouth to answer, honestly, I assumed, but I cut him off. "Nope, no vegetables!" I piped up. "This one"—I said, pointing to the broccoli and cheese—"has flowers in it, and cheese. This one has leaves. And that one has a special kind of berry!" Spinach and zucchini. The spinach one also had mushrooms in it, but I hadn't figured out what mushrooms were.

"Really?" asked Edie, looking skeptically between me and the quiches. "That one has flowers in it?" She pointed to the broccoli.

"It sure does! Want to try some?" She nodded, and I sliced a thin wedge and put it on a plate for her. She broke off the tip with her fingers and shoved it in her mouth. Her eyes widened. "I never ate flowers before! It's good!" She picked up the rest like it was a slice of pizza and started happily munching away.

"Is there broccoli in that?" Vivian whispered to me. "We can't get her to eat broccoli!"

I winked. I'd explain the whole vegetables-are-fake thing to them once Edie wasn't listening. I didn't want Vivian to think that I'd been lying. Edie finished her slice, then demanded to see my room through a mouthful of crust, so I reluctantly let the adults talk without their offspring hanging around being impressive.

Edie decided that my bedroom didn't have enough toys in it, so she took my hand and dragged me outside. I could hear our parents chatting on the porch as she insisted that I watch her do somersaults and help her with a cartwheel. Dad was talking to Eli, and I had never seen him so attentive. Every line in his body was turned toward them, and he was nodding vigorously at something Eli was saying. Mom looked more relaxed, and at one point I saw her rest her hand on Vivian's smooth arm as she threw her head back in a loud laugh.

When Edie flung herself onto the ground kicking and screaming because the ladybug she was chasing after flew away, her parents started to make those "Well, guess we'd better get going" noises and stood up.

"Don't worry about her," Vivian called over. "She's just tired. She'll fall asleep in the car."

I went up onto the back porch to say goodbye. Eli shook my hand, and Vivian enveloped me in a hug. "You are a remarkable young person, Annabelle," she said, once she let me go.

Eli bounced up and down, suddenly looking much younger. "It's true! We're going to keep hanging out if only to keep you around as a role model for Edie. Your parents are cool, but that's secondary."

My mom and dad laughed. "You're welcome over any time," Dad said. "And hope to see you at another SF meeting."

Vivian groaned. "After the Christmas season. I'm glad we're Jewish, otherwise we wouldn't be able to balance all the work with obligatory merrymaking and familial obligations. But if you want to come over for Chinese food and a movie on Christmas Eve, we often host Gentiles as part of our people's traditions."

"Ooh, that sounds fun," I said.

"We'll talk about it!" Mom said. "Good luck with your upcoming shows."

They wrestled their tear-stained daughter into her car seat, waved, and drove away. The three of us lingered on the porch, nobody willing to break the spell that had been cast over us. If this was what community was like, I decided I liked it.

chapter 21

Monday morning I had my backpack on over a light jacket—it was the first day of October, and *finally* starting to get chilly. "Bye," I called, about to leave for school, when Dad poked his head out of the kitchen.

"If you wait, Banana, I can drive you to school."

"I don't mind walking," I said. "There's plenty of time."

"Then there's plenty of time for you to wait for me to finish my coffee and put on my shoes and drive my only daughter to school."

I pursed my lips and stared at him accusingly. "Why? Is something wrong? Was there a report of some serial killer snatching up schoolgirls in the area and chopping them into pieces?"

He laughed. "No reason. I wanted to spend a little extra time with you. But if you'd rather try your luck with Johnny Axe-Murderer, be my guest."

I heaved an exasperated sigh, but couldn't trample down a grin. "Fine, I *guess* I'll spend quality time with my dad. If it's a choice between that and an axe-murderer."

"But if it's a butcher-knife murderer, you'd take your chances?" he asked, gulping down the rest of his coffee.

"Oh yeah, I could take a butcher-knife murderer any day. So you got lucky today."

"I guess so." His grin matched mine; people always commented on how we had the same smile, the same dimple in our right cheeks.

On the short drive to school I kept waiting for him to bring something up. Ever since the school year started, all of our time together had been punctuated with, like, life-altering reveals, or emotional processing of that information, or unsuccessful attempts to avoid those details. So part of me assumed that he wanted to drive me to school because there was something he had been putting off telling me, or something he wanted to share about what he and Eli had discussed yesterday.

But, nope. He asked me if I thought we needed a new rug in the living room, whether we should try planting squash next year. Nothing important, but I also didn't get the sense that he was avoiding talking about something important. He was acting normal. Better than normal, to be honest.

We pulled up in front of school. I got out and was about to wave goodbye, but when I turned around Dad had also unbuckled his seat belt and got out of the cab. He came around and enveloped me in a tight hug. I must have grown in the last month, we were almost the same height now, but his arms were strong and sure around me. "Have a good day,

Bells," he murmured, and even though a dad hugging his daughter was objectively normal, I thought I was about to cry.

As the hug was ending, a harsh voice cut through the morning birdsong. "Mike Blake! I haven't seen you since June!" It was Mrs. Brewster, marching through the parking lot with her hand on Dixon's shoulder.

Ugh. She and my dad knew each other, of course, but since Dixon and I never had playdates, they didn't spend much time together. But my parents knew what she was like. Like, for a couple years Principal Quinn started a lunch service, so instead of bringing lunches we ate hot food in the gym. I guess Dixon was a picky eater, because his mom started a whole campaign to shut it down, which is why we went back to bringing our own. And one year we all learned to play the violin, but we must not have sounded good, because she sat through the entire concert with her fingers in her ears. But my parents were always polite to her, which meant that she thought they were on her side about everything.

"How are you doing? Isn't it insane that they're sixth graders this year? Yesterday Dixon was my little boy and now he's almost a man. And your Annabelle, she's turning into such a beautiful young lady!"

Dad nodded tightly. "Yup, they're getting big. Good to see you, Claudia."

"It's so great to run into you! Did you hear, I've decided to spend some time with this class in the mornings, like when they were little. Remember when we volunteered in the class-rooms all the time? I know it's normal for the lower-school teachers to need more help, but I think it's as important as they get older too, if not more so. They may not be babies anymore, but they're so impressionable! And you know, this new teacher, she has some ideas. I'm sure Annabelle has told you. Can you *believe* she thought it would be appropriate to bring in some . . . well, you know, those kinds of people, the gender people, to talk to the kids. Dixon tells me that there's a child in his class who's confused about who she—he—well, whatever it is, and the teacher is *encouraging* that!"

Dad turned slightly. "Annabelle, you go inside now. I'll see you after school."

My arms were crossed tightly across my chest. "Dad. No. I—"

He put a hand on my upper arm. It was warm. "Bells. We'll talk about it after school. I promise." And then he winked.

Dixon hurried on ahead of me. He obviously didn't want to be alone with me, which was a good move on his part. I glanced back over my shoulder, and Mrs. Brewster was still talking to my dad. His hands were in his pockets, and he was leaning forward on his toes a bit, as if he were deeply fasci-nated by everything she was saying. I was dying to know what he was going to do, but there was no good way to eavesdrop in a parking lot, so I decided to trust my dad, that I would find out later.

The classroom was buzzing when I got there. Amy was

helping Felix with his homework, Olivia and Audrey were standing at the map of ancient Greece and reading aloud the names of cities, pronouncing them wrong on purpose and laughing raucously. Johnson was sitting next to the other Annabelle, pointing to a picture of a submarine and explaining in detail how each part worked. Bailey and Sadie were already at their desks, and Dixon was sitting by himself in the reading nook.

I slid into my seat. "Hi, Annabelle!" said Sadie. "I was telling Bailey about the scary movie I saw on Friday. An old one about an evil clown. I didn't sleep all weekend!"

"Oh, I love scary movies!" I said. "That's one of the best parts about October, they're on TV all the time. We should have a scary movie marathon some weekend!"

"Count me out," said Bailey.

"You don't like them?" asked Sadie. "Do you get nightmares or something?"

"No, I *love* scary movies, but you don't want to watch them with me. I scream my head off and if I'm holding anything, it goes flying. Last time I got popcorn *everywhere*."

"Okay, but that sounds amazing. Now I extra want to watch scary movies with you!" I said. "We'd get a movie *and* a show!"

"Hey, if you want to spend hours picking popcorn kernels off the carpet, that's up to you," said Bailey.

"We have a vacuum cleaner," Sadie volunteered. "Or we could not have snacks."

"A movie with no snacks is like a . . . like a . . . like a movie without snacks," I argued. "It's not an option. If it's such a problem I'll hold the popcorn, Bailey, and you can get handfuls in between the scary parts."

"As long as you don't make fun of me for screaming every time the camera moves."

"I promise," said Sadie.

"I promise to make fun of you, but in a nice friendly way."

Bailey glared at me, but cracked after about three seconds and started laughing. "Fine. It's a deal." And just like that, I realized that my crush on Bailey was gone. They would always be the first person I came out to, and we were in each other's lives forever, I hoped. Nothing more than friends, because nothing is more than friends.

The clock ticked over to 8:45 and Amy rang the chime. As the sound of our voices faded away, the door to our classroom burst open. It was Mrs. Brewster. Of course.

Amy ignored her. "Good morning! Let's all join on the rug for morning meeting."

Dixon's mom took up her spot at the back of the classroom. Amy went through the day's schedule: math, science, lunch, social studies, P.E. We were about to go around and share about our weekends when Mrs. Brewster interrupted.

"I have a yoga class at ten, why can't you have social studies in the morning and math in the afternoon?"

Amy kept a pleasant smile on her face, but I was sitting close enough that I could see her clenched fists. "The math coach only has time in the mornings to work with students, so if we move it, both of our schedules will fall apart."

Mrs. Brewster *hmph*ed. She stayed through the end of morning meeting and through the first fifteen minutes of math before huffing out of the room. "I'll be back tomorrow," she called on the way out. "Have a good day, sweetie!" she added, and Dixon's whole head turned the color of a tomato. I almost felt bad for him.

Amy was at our desks, answering some of our questions about solving for x. "What was that all about?" Bailey whispered.

I expected Amy not to respond, or to give some fake, kid-appropriate answer. But instead, keeping her eyes fixed on Sadie's worksheet, she said, "She's decided that it's her job to make sure I stick to the approved curriculum. That's why she wanted to stay for social studies; there's nothing offensive I can do to math."

"How can she do that?" I demanded, careful to keep my voice down. "How is she allowed to barge into the classroom and tell you what to do?"

"The Lab has always had an open-door policy for parents," she reminded me. "They usually stop volunteering by the sixth grade, but technically any parent is allowed in their child's classroom."

"Like last year when my dad came in to teach us coding, remember, Annabelle?" asked Sadie. She sounded depressed.

Amy nodded reluctantly. "It's always been assumed that if

they were in the classroom, it was because they were teaching a specialty subject. Or with the younger kids, helping out with cleanup or supervising free play. But there's no real rule saying that they have to."

"But why can't she leave us alone?" asked Bailey, their voice cracking. "She won. We're not having the Coming Out Day panel. We're learning about the stupid Ancient Romans. Why is she doing this?"

"To prove that she can," said Sadie. "And to make sure that you don't try to get away with anything else."

Amy took a deep breath and nodded. "She'll stop soon. I promise. For now, I want you to try and finish these problems."

If I were a better person I'd be at least a little sorry for Dixon, even though this whole thing was one hundred percent his fault. During science we got into pairs, and no one wanted to partner with him. Charlotte was out that day so since there was an odd number he ended up with Johnson and Felix, who ignored him and did the experiment (boiling water again, but salt water this time) on their own. He ate lunch alone, and when we played dodgeball in P.E., no one wanted to get him out.

Sometimes we had guest speakers at assembly who talked about bullying, or we'd watch videos about kids being abused by their classmates, and we read books about kids who were teased or stuffed in lockers or got spitballs thrown at them. But watching Dixon hop around the gym, waving his arms, desperately trying to get someone to throw a ball at him, made me wonder if ignoring someone completely was even crueler.

Mrs. Brewster would have been thrilled by our social studies period. Amy flipped through a slideshow about Greek city-states and how Sparta was different from Athens. I paid attention for about five seconds but then let my eyes glaze over and thought about what we could be learning instead. It was the first day of Queer Awareness Month, and that single Spectrum Families meeting was more educational than all of sixth grade so far. A whole month of that would be amazing. And it was also Hispanic Heritage Month! I couldn't even imagine what we would be learning about, which was a whole problem all by itself, but a million dollars says it would be more interesting and relevant than how the Spartans were more warlike or whatever.

Besides, "social studies" was the study of society, right? Being social? All the different kinds of people who make up the world, what kinds of conflicts we have, how we get along, what we create. What could be more social studies than learning about people who were alive, and doing things, right now?

Finally, finally, the clock dragged itself to the end of the day. As we were gathering up our things, the classroom phone rang. Amy answered it, said, "Oh, hello!" to whoever was on the other end. Her eyes flicked toward me. I cocked my head questioningly, but she smiled and looked away again. She waved distractedly as we left, and her voice had an edge of excitement that hadn't been there all day.

"Do you want to come over?" I asked Bailey as we filed out. Dixon bolted to his mom's car without looking behind him.

"Yeah," they said, "but my parents signed me up for guitar lessons, so I gotta get home if I want to be the nonbinary Taylor Swift."

"You mean 'They-lor' Swift?" I retorted. We both cracked up, and they high-fived me and walked away.

The day had grown almost summer-hot, but the air had an autumnal smell of baking leaves. I stretched out my arms and took in a deep breath. Patrick came up beside me.

"Hey," I said. "Feels good to be outside."

"Yeah," he agreed. "But . . . man, I love fall. I'm sick of it feeling like summer. Want to hang out and do some more solar panel planning? I think we've gotten enough informa-tion to present to Principal Quinn, if we organize it."

"Let me check my agenda," I said, pulling a crumpled receipt out of my pocket and examining it. "Yes, I think I can fit you in, between tea with the queen and dinner with the former First Lady. Want to come over?"

"Sure," he said. "Mind if the other Annabelle comes along? We've been talking about this kind of thing, and she has a lot of good ideas."

I hesitated. I didn't want the other Annabelle that I'd been in school with for the past six years to come over. But she seemed different this year. Or maybe she was the same and I was paying attention for the first time. *Growth opportunity, Bells,* I told myself. "Sure!" I agreed. The other Annabelle was over at the corner of the grass, toeing at the dirt with her grimy sneakers like she was looking for something. Patrick and I went over to her.

"Hey A, we're going to figure out what to say to Principal Quinn about solar panels. You want to come with? We're going to this Annabelle's house."

"Yes," she said, and smiled at me. Her hair was matted in front of her eyes but she had a pretty smile, I decided.

"It takes about twenty minutes to walk to my house, is that okay?"

"Yeah," she said. "But. I live around the corner. Easy to go to my house. Want to do that?"

"Okay," said Patrick. I shrugged in agreement. We trooped around the corner, and sure enough, the other Annabelle lived in a cute little split-level house with a ramp beside the stairs that I'd looked in the direction of most days of my life. They always put up a single string of Christmas lights, I remembered, and a blow-up rabbit around Easter.

We sat on the porch and pulled paper and pens out of our backpacks. "So how do we convince Principal Quinn that the Tahoma Falls Collaborative School needs solar panels on the roof?" Patrick asked.

"We should take turns," I said. "One of us can say why we need solar panels. Another one of us can tell him how much

they'll cost to install but how good they are for the environment. And then another one of us can tell him what will
happen if we *don't* get solar panels. Which is similar to the
first part but might help convince him!"

"That makes sense," said Patrick. "Who wants to take
which part?"

"You should go first," said the other Annabelle to Patrick.
"You know so much about why alternate energy is good. And
you're good at convincing people. And Annabelle, you should
go second because you always sound so good at details.
Like, when you explain things, I understand them." I started
blushing, and frantically tried to remember when I had ever
explained anything to the other Annabelle.

"Do you want to go last?" I asked. "I don't know if I'm
good at explaining things, but we do have a lot of information here that I can recite, and I like the idea of feeling like a
successful businesswoman crunching numbers in a meeting."
I started to plan my outfit. Maybe I could get Mom to buy me
a suit jacket. Shoulders pads were the way to go.

"Yes," she said. "I want to tell him what will happen if we
don't start fixing climate change now. Scare that man into
paying attention to us." Her eyes looked hard, and fierce, and I
shivered. She was spinning a pen in between her pointer and
middle finger, and I noticed for the first time how long her
fingers were, how square at the ends. Like Bailey's. I blinked,
hard, and refocused on our project.

We plotted out our parts a bit more, making sure to record

points we didn't want to forget, but agreed that it would be more powerful if we weren't reading aloud from a sheet of paper.

"Do you think this is going to work?" I asked as Patrick stretched and stood up.

He sighed. "At the beginning of the year I thought it would. But now I'm not so sure. Especially if he sees our whole class as troublemakers now."

"But if he says no, that's still the beginning. Not the end," said the other Annabelle.

"I guess," said Patrick. "If he says no, we'll keep trying anyway." He checked his phone. "I gotta get home. See you tomorrow." He leaped off the porch steps and jogged away.

The other Annabelle and I had never been alone like this. There was so much bouncing around in my head that I wanted to tell her, but asking "When did you become a person with good ideas" was rude, and "Sorry I thought you were a weird hair-chewer, I didn't know you were full of interesting opinions" was also rude even though it had the word "sorry" in it. So I settled for saying, "I'm glad you're working on this with us. You know so much about it."

The other Annabelle shrugged one shoulder. She was wearing a terrible shirt, bright pink with ruffles, but without meaning to I pictured her in one of Bailey's outfits. It worked. "I wouldn't if not for my sister," she said. "Sam tells me a lot, and I like to listen. She says that climate justice is disability justice is every other kind of justice, and that makes sense to me."

"Huh. It must also be gender justice. And food justice. And justice for old people. And young people." I could feel myself start to go down a rabbit hole where everything was connected, and shook my head sharply to get back to the present. "Anyway. You might have learned this stuff from your sister, but it sounds like you're taking what you learned and doing your own thing with it. Which makes it yours too. So I stand by what I said: I'm glad you're working with us."

"Thanks." She met my eyes, and for maybe the first time in our whole lives we really looked at each other. We broke eye contact at the same time. My cheeks were hot.

I checked my phone, pretending like nothing happened. "I should get home before my parents start to wonder where I am. I could always text them, but then they might think I had been kidnapped and the kidnapper was forcing me to send them a text pretending like everything was fine. So I'm going to go. See you tomorrow! We have to figure out when we're storming Principal Quinn's office."

"Maybe once Mrs. Brewster leaves us alone."

"Ugh. Yeah." The other Annabelle and I had never hugged before, but the insides of my elbows itched in that way that meant I wanted to put my arms around her. But she waved, so I waved, a little disappointed, and started toward home.

I stopped by the Circle K and bought a package of the best and only flavor of Pop-Tarts—frosted blueberry, thank you very much. When I got home, I poured myself a glass of the mint iced tea in the fridge and took it out to the porch to do the rest of my homework. After half an hour my homework was almost done, I had mostly gotten the other Annabelle out of my mind, and also discovered that fake-ish blueberry and real mint was a terrible flavor combination.

Mom got home first and creaked up the porch. "Want to help me get dinner ready?" she asked, kissing me on the head.

"Sure! As soon as I finish up math." I spent another few minutes poking at the numbers, then scribbled down what I thought x stood for.

Two cauliflowers waited on the kitchen counter for me, with one of the big knives I was only allowed to use when I turned ten. Mom was up to her elbows in flour, which meant we were having paprika cauliflower soup with dumplings. Yum.

"Remind me what cauliflower is?" she asked. "It's not a root. Is it a fruit? Or a stalk?"

"It's a flower!" I exclaimed. "Well, the top part is. I guess this part is the stem. Or the stalk." I started cutting the little white florets off.

Mom looked over at it. "Huh, I guess so. There's a joke about tomatoes, right? How knowledge is knowing that a tomato is a fruit, and wisdom is not putting it in a fruit salad?"

I paused in my chopping, thinking that over. Then I put down the knife, and solemnly held up one finger in a "Hold, please" gesture. Mom stopped forming dumplings and watched as I walked over to the fridge and plucked out a chunk of honeydew from a plastic-wrapped bowl. Then I went back to the counter, grabbed a grape tomato, and stuffed both into my mouth at once. I chewed, slowly and thoughtfully, hoping that there was a wise expression on my face, or at least as wise as you could look when various fruit juices were sploshing around in your mouth. I swallowed, and delivered my verdict.

"Not bad. Maybe that isn't wisdom after all."

Mom wiped her hands on her apron. "Okay, Banana, now I'm curious." She took an apple from the fruit bowl, shaved off a ribbon, wrapped it around another tomato, and popped the neat package into her mouth. Her eyes widened. "Oh, that's good!" she exclaimed. She went back to making dumplings, I went back to chopping cauliflower, and we were coming up with different combinations of fruit salad when Dad came home.

"If it isn't my two favorite girls!" he said. He leaned around to kiss Mom, one hand on her belly, the other tugging her apron strings. Then he stole a piece of cauliflower from my cutting board. "Since you've got dinner under control, should I make the salad?"

Mom and I looked at each other and burst out laughing.

"What did I say?" he asked, grinning with us. "What's so funny about salad?"

Without a word I grabbed the apple from where Mom had left it and used the big butcher knife to carefully chop off a sliver. I took another grape tomato—we were going to run out if we kept this up—and handed both to my dad. "We're revolutionizing the concept of fruit salads, what do you think?"

He looked confused, which made sense, but ate them. He

nodded his head as he chewed. "Pretty good," he said. "Let's see."

He brought out some citrus fruits from the fridge, oranges and grapefruits, and a vine-ripened tomato. As he carefully sliced them paper thin, he asked how my day had gone.

"Ugh," I groaned. Mom motioned for me to put the cauliflower into the pot, so I did, managing to avoid splashing broth on myself. "It was boring. And weird? Mrs. Brewster came in right at the beginning and stayed all the way through morning meeting. I remember parents would do that if their kid was crying, or if they were helping out with the next lesson, but she was spying. It's so uncomfortable."

"I can see that," said Dad. "I didn't relish being ranted at by her this morning."

"The nerve of that woman," said Mom. "Cornering you in the parking lot." Dad must have called Mom to tell her about it.

"Did you say anything to her?" I asked. I didn't think Dad would say, "Well, you see, as a transgender father" to some yelling lady first thing in the morning, but I had wondered how he handled it. That must not have been his first time listening to people as they talked about him without knowing they were doing it. And then a bolt of lightning zapped through my skull. If Dad had never told me he was trans, he would have felt that way every time I talked about Bailey. Like I was talking about him, but not realizing it. And his history would have gone from something he never told me to something he wasn't telling me, which might not seem like a big deal but was the difference between forgetting and remembering.

Dad had started talking, so I forced myself to focus, even though my brain was still buzzing from that revelation. "I let her run herself out. Didn't say that I agreed with anything she was saying, but she's the kind of person who can't imagine that anyone would think differently from her."

Mom shook her head sadly. "She thinks she's protecting her son. But she's protecting him from all the wrong things."

There was a thread of triumph in Dad's voice. "She's not the only one who wants to keep her kid safe. And she doesn't get to decide what safety means for everyone else."

He was focused on the cutting board, layering slices of citrus with wedges of tomato and sprinkling them all with pink rock salt. He wouldn't look at me, and Mom was suddenly focused on wiping down the counter. They were both quiet for a moment, but it was a very full pause.

There was something going on. I remembered that phone call Amy got at the end of the day, how she immediately looked in my direction. Like whoever it was on the other end was talking about me. Or was related to me. But if I had learned anything about my parents and secrets, it was that they would tell me when they were ready, not when I asked.

Mom broke the pointed silence by talking about her day at work. Dad told me to set the table. The soup was perfect with soft cauliflower and chewy dumplings and the salad wasn't any salad I'd ever imagined, topped with dried rosemary and drizzled with olive oil. The combination was strange but delicious. There was an unspoken air of something joining us at the table, an energy I was unfamiliar with crackling between my parents, and when I went to bed that night it was with the excitement of Christmas Eve but months too early.

chapter 22

Something about last night felt so different that I wasn't at all surprised to see my dad in the kitchen the next morning and my mom at the table with a plate of eggs and toast, both of them waiting for me like we had something planned.

"Hey Bells," said Dad. "How do you want your eggs?"

I glared at him. I wasn't mad about eggs, but *something* was up. "Okay, it's no one's birthday, it's not a holiday, you're being weird, and I don't know why."

They both smiled mysteriously. "Fine, don't tell me," I said, flouncing into a chair. "Scrambled, please. And if I was walking to school I'd have to leave in ten minutes, but something tells me that at least one of you is going to drive me! For some reason! Am I right?"

"We're both driving you," said Mom. She took a careful sip of her coffee, somehow managing to avoid leaving a lipstick stain around the rim of the mug. She was dressed more up than usual, her hair styled into waves, a pearl necklace that set off her green dress with an autumn leaf pattern. Dad had dressed up a bit too, his normal button-down shirt but also a tie, his jacket draped across a chair.

"Should I be dressed up too?" I asked, looking down at myself. I looked fine but not fancy, in my gray skinny jeans and purple collared shirt.

"No, Banana, you look beautiful. Eat up." Dad put a plate of eggs and toast in front of me and I dug in. This was way better than my usual breakfast of cereal or yogurt. Whatever they were scheming, I wished it happened every day.

The last time both of them drove me to school was my first day of kindergarten. This was a random Tuesday in October. I figured that maybe if I pestered them enough one of them would crack and tell me why.

"Is there an important PTA meeting about the nut-free school policy? Are you part of a pro-nut committee?"

"Nope, food allergies are nothing to laugh at," said Mom.

"The fourth-grade parents are rebelling against the recorder program because little kids practicing the recorder is a crime against humanity and you're testifying based on your experience."

"You couldn't blame us," said Dad. "That recorder almost made us put you up for adoption."

"Oh! Principal Quinn is retiring and there's a big party to celebrate! Please please please tell me that's happening."

"He is, unfortunately, too young to retire."

"Hmph." I came up with a few more ideas, each one more ludicrous than the next, and then we were at school. Butterflies were galloping around in my stomach—I know that butterflies flap instead of gallop but that's what it felt like. Maybe it was pegasuses (pegasi? Pegasodes?) instead of butterflies, winged horses that were sometimes flying and sometimes running. Anyway, it was a weird sensation to be overwhelmingly nervous but not know what I was nervous about.

We were the first ones in the classroom. I expected Amy to be confused, flustered, maybe upset because she thought my parents were pulling a Mrs. Brewster, but she looked up and smiled without a hint of surprise. "You must be Annabelle's parents. Mike and Hannah, right? It's so nice to meet you."

She crossed the room and they all shook hands.

"Thanks so much for this," said Mom.

"No, thank *you*," said Amy. "After all, I don't have a choice in the matter, do I?" She winked.

I couldn't take it. "You *have* to tell me what is going on!" I exploded. "It's too early for parent-teacher conferences. You're clearly not mad at each other. If you don't tell me what's up, I'm going to . . . um . . . be extremely annoyed and won't stop asking until I pass out from not stopping to breathe and then you'll have to take me to the nurse's office, which will completely derail whatever your plan is, okay?" I gasped, out of breath. Making yourself pass out is harder than I thought.

"We are parents at this school," said Dad calmly. "We're allowed to join your class whenever we want, especially if it's in support of the curriculum. So that's what we're doing."

This didn't exactly clear it up, and I was about to point

that out when Johnson and Charlotte came in. Mom put a finger to her red lips. I narrowed my eyes but decided to be patient. If pumping them for information didn't work when we were alone, it definitely wouldn't work with other kids in the room. I plopped into my chair and grabbed a book, ostentatiously pretending like I didn't even notice my mom and dad in the classroom, but the book was upside down and turning it right side up did not improve my reading comprehension even a little bit.

I watched over the top of my book as everyone else came in. When they noticed my parents, they would look over at me, but I would quickly turn back to my book, flipping a page to make it seem like I was reading. It wasn't until Bailey showed up that I dropped the act.

"What are they doing here?" they asked in a whisper. For the first time they were wearing a completely uninteresting outfit, a gray shirt and faded blue jeans, and the thought tugged at the corner of my mind that they wanted to avoid drawing attention to themself. Dad caught their eye and gave them a small smile. Bailey spread their fingers in a tiny wave.

"I don't know," I whispered back. "I think it has something to do with Dixon's mom? I'm not sure, though."

Right on cue, Dixon's mom burst through the door, her son trailing reluctantly behind her. My mom and dad were over in the library corner, thumbing through books, and Mrs. Brewster breezed right past Amy to go say hi to them.

"Mike! Hannah! I'm thrilled to see you! You know, Hannah,

I was telling Mike yesterday about everything that's been going on here, I'm so thrilled to have your support." Her voice was *so loud;* no one else in the room was talking and they were all staring at the adults, except for a few kids who were staring at me. They were probably thinking that my parents were angry killjoys like Dixon's mom, and while I didn't know what they had up their sleeves, I guessed it was something she wouldn't like. The horse-butterflies (butterhorseflies?) in my stomach started to zip around faster, but I was getting excited. Like the butterhorseflies were in a good mood instead of warning me of danger.

And Mrs. Brewster wouldn't stop talking! "Of course Principal Quinn is behind me one hundred percent, we have to make sure that our children are protected from things they're far too young to know about! They're here to learn about math and reading, not about different lifestyles." She shook her head mournfully. "So few people are able to think about it logically. I'm glad you're on my side. The silenced majority, am I right?"

Now everyone was staring at them. Amy cleared her throat; the room was so still, she didn't need to ring the chime. "It's time for the school day to start, special visitors or no. Stay at your desks, please, we're going to have a special morning meeting. Hannah, Mike, do you want to join me up here?"

The smug look of self-satisfaction on Mrs. Brewster's face slowly drained away as my parents made their way to the front of the room.

"We are lucky to be in a community where parents are so invested in their children's education," Amy continued. "Like how Olivia's mother is on the school board, and Johnson's father volunteers in the library. And, of course, Dixon's mother, who enjoys observing." I didn't dare turn my head to look, but I was willing to bet that Mrs. Brewster's face was the same color as her son's, aggressively red.

"Annabelle's parents decided that since this is the second day of Queer Awareness Month, they wanted to share about their family's story, and it is our school's official policy that they are welcome to do so. Mike, Hannah, go ahead."

Dad cleared his throat. "Thanks so much, Amy. My daughter and her friend were excited about organizing a panel for National Coming Out Day, which is next week. But since that didn't end up working out, my wife and I thought that we would talk about what it's like to create an LGBT family, since I'm a transgender man and Hannah is a queer femme."

Utter joy erupted inside me like a volcano. I couldn't believe this was happening. They were coming out. No one had to pretend anymore. Bailey turned to grin at me, their face as bright as a rising sun. "This is happening!" they whispered to me. I was too stunned to say anything back, but grabbed their hand and squeezed it tight. We both turned to listen to what my family had to say.

There was a sudden *BANG* as the classroom door slammed open and then shut. Mrs. Brewster had stormed out of the room, heels clicking angrily on the floor.

And Dad started to tell his story. About growing up as a

young person in Ohio, at first telling his mom and dad that he was a lesbian, because he didn't know that there were other ways to describe how he felt. Then meeting another trans person at a student group at college, and spending years denying what that awoke in him, how deeply he knew it and how frightened that made him. He was describing the first time he went to a trans support group when Mrs. Brewster came charging through the classroom door again, Principal Quinn hot on her heels.

"Excuse me, hi there, Mr. and Mrs. Blake," the principal said anxiously, as Dixon's mom hovered behind him, arms crossed angrily. "Nice to see you, uh, today, I didn't know this was—well, I'm sure we all know that the children have a busy day of learning ahead of them, that I'm sure they're eager to get back to, so—"

"We are learning," Olivia called out.

"Yeah, we can do this instead of choice time," Patrick added. "It's cool."

"Well, uh, that's all nice, but I'm afraid we can't have parents interrupt the school day, it's not appropriate, we have to plan accordingly and—"

"The students are all quite aware of our parent policy," said Amy, a small smile tugging on the corners of her lips. "Friends, Claudia Brewster has been spending some time in our classroom lately, hasn't she?" We all nodded, vigorously.

"That's different," Mrs. Brewster screeched. "I wasn't interfering with your school day!"

"They're not interfering, they're teaching!" said Sadie.

"Like my dad teaching coding. Parents are allowed to partici-pate during the school day, that's the whole point of the Lab. No offense, Mrs. Brewster, but you just hung out in the back of the room and made comments and then left." I wanted to chime in, to defend my parents too, but I was obviously biased. And hearing everyone else come to our defense made me feel like I was flying.

"Why, you little—" Mrs. Brewster started.

"Mom!" Dixon burst out. We all turned to stare at him. I had forgotten he was even there. "Stop. It's okay. They're allowed to talk. Freedom of speech. And if you can hang out in the classroom, so can they. It's only fair. Just . . . just stop."

"I'm doing this for *you*," she screeched. "After you came home saying they were infringing on your rights, asking for special treatment, making you feel left out. I'm doing this to make sure that you get a fair chance!"

"Shut *up*," he hissed, his head now entirely in his hands, fingertips extra white where they gripped at the side of his head. "I was only—I didn't mean for—it's not—Look, it's okay. I'm okay. Please go."

"Principal Quinn, my husband and I are well within our rights to participate in our daughter's classroom, as per the school's stated policy." Mom's voice was cool and calm. "Considering that the children are enthusiastic and their teacher is willing, you have no grounds to ask us to leave. If you continue pressuring us to do so, I will be more than happy to bring this matter of inequity up with the school board. Your performance review is coming up, isn't it?"

"It sure is, my mom says there's a lot to talk about!" Olivia hollered.

"Well then." Mom leaned back in her chair and crossed her legs. "May we continue?"

Principal Quinn was clenching and unclenching his fists. Then he rubbed one hand over his face, over his hair, like he could scrub the right answer out of his brain. Finally he turned to Mrs. Brewster. "Let's go," he said.

Her eyes and nostrils widened. "You can't be serious."

He bobbed his head in what was almost a nod. "I don't have a choice. Come, we can discuss this in my office."

She turned to glare at my parents, uncountable expressions rippling over her face. "I can't believe this. You'll be hearing from my lawyer."

"I don't appreciate threats, Claudia," said my dad. "Have a nice day. Now, where was I? Oh, right. So, the first trans support group I ever went to was in the women's center. I know that might sound . . ."

And with that Mrs. Brewster huffed out. I wondered if that woman even knew how to leave a room in a normal way. We all let out a collective sigh of relief as Principal Quinn followed her, the tension draining from the room. Dixon had put his head down on his desk, but his face was turned toward the front of the room, toward my parents. I decided to feel a little sorry for him after all. It might have been his fault, but I could see where he got it from. And maybe there was a chance for him to change.

Dad went back to sharing his story. From deciding to

transition and losing his family, to starting a new one and losing his community. He didn't say anything directly about getting pregnant or having me; that must have been too much to share with a roomful of sixth graders, but he talked about how his trans friends didn't respect a choice he made, and how that affected him for the next twelve years. Mom talked too, about the feminist causes she fought for when she was younger, marching on the Capitol in spike heels. She told us what being femme meant to her, what she went through when people assumed she was straight, that she's in her mid-forties and has never stopped figuring out who she is and how to explain it to people. I already knew that National Coming Out Day wasn't a real deadline for me, and hearing Mom talk reminded me that there was never an end to learning about yourself.

We listened, rapt. When they were finally done, they asked if we had any questions, and there was a flurry of hands. Dad called on Bailey first. Of course.

"What made you decide to share your stories with us?" they asked. There was a little twinkle in their eye, like they knew the answer already.

"You did," said Dad, looking directly at them. "When Annabelle came home saying she had made friends with a new kid in her class, who was some kind of trans, everything I had been pushing away for so many years came knocking at my front door. It was terrifying. But you taught me that maybe everything I thought was true about being trans didn't have to be. And I learned how much has changed since

Annabelle was born. There's plenty I don't understand about kids these days and their genders, but I want to learn. Thank you, Bailey."

He didn't say "And thank you, Annabelle," but he didn't have to. And he might not have even made the connection that I made last night—about how I would have been talking about *him* every time I talked about Bailey, just like Dixon's mom was talking about him and his community right in front of him. And even though I wouldn't have been nasty, like she was, I would be making him feel like an imposter in his own home. I let myself imagine, just for a moment, what the rest of my life would have looked like if he decided to never tell me, but I couldn't. That wasn't a future I wanted us to live in.

Olivia raised her hand next. "Hannah! Am I femme?"

Mom laughed. "Well, I do love your dress, and it matches your nails perfectly." Olivia was in a white dress that kind of looked like a long peasant blouse with red flowers embroidered around the top, and her nails had little flower stickers on them instead of polish. "But being femme is more than your clothing. It's how you carry yourself, how you see the world, who you love and how you love them. I can't tell you who you are and what identities make sense for you, but when you're a bit older, I'll give you some books to read and some people to learn from. Sound good?" Olivia nodded, satisfied. I nodded too, to myself.

Dixon raised his hand timidly, and Dad nodded in his direction.

"Sorry if this is offensive, but . . . I mean, you look like a dude. And you're all basically a normal family, right? Why do you have to talk about it?"

Bailey hissed, and a few other people muttered their disapproval. Amy looked at my parents with a "Do you want me to handle him" expression on her face, but Dad leaned forward and pierced him with his eyes.

"I look like a dude because I am a dude. And there is no such thing as a normal family. But for a long time I thought that being honest about my life would take away everything I had. Do you think that's fair, or right? That telling the truth could ruin my life, when nothing I did is illegal, immoral, or affects anyone else?"

Dixon shook his head.

"Then why shouldn't I talk about it?"

"Well, uh . . ." He made a few other sounds with his mouth, but nothing word-shaped came out, and Dad called on Johnson next, who asked a complicated question about hormones that Dad answered as best he could.

The other Annabelle raised her hand next, and my ears perked up with interest. "People didn't see you how you wanted them to, and then you transitioned so they could," she began, looking at my dad. But then she directed her attention to my mom. Her voice was low, and rough. "But because of that, Hannah, now people don't see you how you are. Is that okay?"

Mom sucked in her breath, and Dad's mouth tightened. "That's something we never figured out," he acknowledged.

Mom put her hand over his. "I don't have any regrets,

exactly," Mom said. "But we've both had to give up a lot. Thanks to your classmates, we're learning, together, how to get some of it back."

The other Annabelle nodded seriously and tucked her hair behind one ear. "People don't always see who I am, either. But sometimes that's because I don't want anyone to. Will that change?"

"That's a big question, sweetie," my mom said. I couldn't remember what I had told them about the other Annabelle. Maybe that she never seemed quite there, didn't talk much but what she did say was weird, and I wished she had a different name. I wouldn't say any of that now. "I do know that you have a lot of time—to figure out who you are, and to find the people you want to share that with. But there's no rush. All that matters is that *you* like who you are. Everyone else can wait." The other Annabelle nodded, satisfied, and I let out a long breath.

Almost as if she heard me, the other Annabelle looked in my direction, a smile crooking up one side of her mouth. I looked down at my desk, and knew I was blushing.

There were so many questions I wanted to ask. What it was like to become a dad—not as a pregnant person, but as a man. I wanted to know if my mom was ever jealous of lesbian couples. If I was ever going to meet my grandparents, or my uncle, or my cousins. But those questions could wait. We'd get there eventually. I already knew the most important answers.

When they wrapped up, everyone applauded like my

parents were rock stars. Dixon even whistled. Amy said we could take a stretch break before math, so Bailey and I walked them to the door.

"How was that?" asked Dad, grinning. "Good surprise?"

I threw my arms around his neck. "Definitely good. Definitely a surprise." He put a hand on my head, squeezed lightly.

"Thank you," said Bailey. Their eyes were shining, like they were about to cry. "This was so much better than any panel could have been. I'm so . . . it's been hard, but, thank you."

Mom clasped Dad's arm in her hands. "Thank *you*, Bailey. We wouldn't have been able to do this without you."

"I know I haven't made it easy," Dad said seriously, "but you becoming friends with my daughter is one of the best things that's ever happened to me. And I owe you an apology. I'm sorry for how I treated you, and thank you for not letting my grumpy old trans baggage change anything about you."

"You're welcome!" said Bailey, tossing their head like a proud horse. But I could hear the emotion in their voice.

"Ugh, I am *not* ready to go back inside," I complained. "Can you guys take me home now? Say that I all of a sudden got sick? I can't handle a boring school day after this."

"No such luck," said Mom. "But I think we both feel the same way about going to work."

Amy stuck her head out of the door. "So sorry, but we have to get on with our day," she said apologetically. "If I don't get fired over this, I *will* get fired if they don't learn math."

"Go on in," said Dad, giving me a gentle shove. "We'll talk more later. Bailey, you're welcome at our house any time."

"Thanks, Mike," they said, and went in.

I gave my parents one last hug. Mom squeezed me against her belly, then pried my arms from around her waist. "Go, Annabelle. We'll talk more at home. I promise."

"No more secrets," added Dad. "This was the last one."

"Promise?" I asked.

"Promise," they said in unison. They walked back to the car, I went into my classroom, and we all got on with the first day of the rest of our lives.

epilogue

"**Dad,** stop it, I already put some on!"

"I did not go through all the trouble of birthing a child to let you get skin cancer, so you're going to hold still while I put on another layer."

I roll my eyes but don't move as he rubs some more sunscreen onto my face and neck. And to be fair, he has a point. We've been standing in our assigned spot for at least two hours. The parade supposedly started fifteen minutes ago, and apparently that means that we're going to "step off," which is parade-speak for "start walking," in either two minutes or five hours, and we won't know until it happens. The hot June sun is climbing the sky like she has something to prove. I'm holding a plastic cup from my favorite bubble tea place on Capitol Hill even though I finished it in a few gulps. There's some slowly melting ice left at the bottom, and I suck a sharp shard up through the wide straw.

Final layer of sunscreen applied, I wander over to where Bailey and E are putting the final, final, final touches on our banner. "Spectrum Families of Tahoma Falls," it says in rainbow letters, and they're carefully adding a border of artichokes, broccoli, tomatoes, and other not-vegetables. No one else will get the joke, but that's okay.

"Okay, I know I said this about a dozen times already, but you two look amazing!" And honestly they both look amazing enough for me to say it another dozen times. E has switched their all-black look for an all-white shiny suit, blindingly white eyeliner, and bleached hair. And Bailey grew out their hair a little for the occasion, and sprayed it up into spikes. They're wearing long fake eyelashes, giant hoop earrings, a real actual tuxedo shirt with the sleeves torn off, black suspenders, a black bow tie, and a poofy rainbow skirt. And their home-decorated shoes, of course. They look like . . . they look like . . . well, nothing that I can put into words, which is the entire point.

"Thanks!" Bailey says, capping their marker and jumping up. "You do too!"

"Very swamp-femme," E adds.

Mom had taken me to the Goodwill and we picked the froofiest, frilliest, most ridiculous prom dress we could find for under twenty dollars, and then cut and sewed it until it mostly fit me. I look like a fairy princess who has been living in a bog for years.

I skip away to smooch my boyfriend on the cheek. Julian looks so cute in his blue shorts and pink shirt. His rainbow bow tie is a little crooked, so I straighten it.

"Thanks, Bella," he says, and smooches me back.

"You're welcome! Happy Pride! Sam, your chair looks AMAZING." Julian's sister is maybe the coolest queer I have ever met. Cooler than Bailey, even. Her wheelchair is decorated in tassels and rainbow tape, with a huge sign affixed to the back saying "Crip Pride."

"Thanks, Annabelle! You look great too, but you're missing something." She's holding a bag of glitter in her lap, and throws a handful at me. "There, now you're part of the family." She's sparkling under a layer of glitter makeup, a half-smile like her brother's, his same beautiful brown eyes. Everyone was so happy for Julian when he came out as a trans boy in December, and I was personally thrilled to be the only Annabelle in my grade.

It turns out that the girl I hadn't liked much was actually a boy I liked a lot. His fashion sense blossomed, and his daily outfits soon rivaled Bailey's for cool-and-cute. He asked me to go for a walk after school on Valentine's Day, we got hot cocoa, he told me he always thought I was the prettiest girl in school, so I kissed him. He tasted like cinnamon. I went home, told Mom and Dad what happened, and the second ACOD went even better than the first because they immediately got all gross and embarrassing about me having a boyfriend. That was that. I started saying I was bi, but then thought that "pan" might be a better word. My parents insist that I'm queer, but mostly I call myself lucky.

Our group, the brand-new Tahoma Falls chapter of Spectrum Families, is going to march right behind the Seattle SF group. A bunch of the queer families that left the Lab over the years have joined, plus some current families that are supportive. There are also homeschooled kids, and even a few families who drive in an hour or more from their small towns east of the mountains. We meet at my mom's office, twice a month, and after every meeting at least one parent comes up to my mom or dad and tells them how important this group is, how they wouldn't have known how to get support without it, how grateful they are for my family for doing this work.

I go over to the cooler in our car, a rainbow flag hanging out of one window, the trans pride flag draped across the hood, and the femme flag draped over the back. I pull out some water bottles and walk around giving them to people who look thirsty, and take one for myself after finally giving up on my bubble tea. Eli is also plying their daughter with sunscreen. Edie is wearing a mermaid tail because why not? Mom is putting the finishing touches on Vivian's makeup.

"Yoo-hoo!" I hear a voice cry. "Come to our post-pride drag show! I'm Miss Shirley Not. It's going to be a great time!" A drag queen on Rollerblades and a banana dress is weaving in and out of the crowd, handing out flyers. She zooms over to our group and says, "Hey, kiddies! You're a little too young for this show, but you're always welcome at drag brunch. Honey, make sure you wear that outfit." She's staring at me as she says that. "You're halfway to queendom already."

I laugh, and she shoves a postcard in my hand. "What do you say, Dad?" I call over. "Drag brunch tomorrow?"

"I am *not* driving you into Seattle two days in a row," he yells back.

"I'll take the bus!" It turns out that there's a bus that goes to Seattle, with only one transfer. It took a while, but my parents finally let me start taking it if I went with a friend. Bailey and I go all the time, obviously, but I've also gone a lot with Patrick and Julian. We started going to meetings for youth interested in climate justice, after Principal Quinn refused to install solar panels. Now we have bigger projects to work on. And we haven't given up on making our local community more sustainable.

"Oh darlin', I'll come to you," says Miss Not, gliding over to Dad and circling him. "I didn't know they made 'em like this in the suburbs."

"Oh, they make 'em like me everywhere," he says, and winks. She blows him a kiss and skates off.

Suddenly there's a frenzy of motion in front of me, whistles blowing, that unmistakable look when people in line in front of you start moving. "All right, everyone, we're next!" Dad calls. "Get your signs up! Spectrum Families Tahoma Falls, let's show them who we are!"

Bailey and I race to the front and grab either side of the banner. We hoist it high and begin to march, our families right behind us.

acknowledgments

In July of 2019, I led a presentation about my picture book *When Aidan Became a Brother* at the Philadelphia Trans Wellness Conference. During the Q&A someone asked if I would ever write a book about a gestational trans dad. I was interested in the idea but wasn't sure if I knew how to tackle it, given that it's not an experience I will ever have. A week or so later, an old friend that I had connected with at that same conference was telling me about one of his friends, a new father debating whether or not to tell his daughter about his trans history, and all the thoughts and questions that brought up for me led to *Different Kinds of Fruit*.

I wouldn't have been able to write this book if I hadn't been a trans guy with seventeen years (and counting) embedded in a wide and diverse and complex network of other trans people. I can't name everyone who helped me learn about my communities, but if you're thinking "Hey, I remember Kyle from back in the day," you are part of that list, even if we didn't get along. I grew up in a place not unlike Tahoma Falls, about twenty miles north of Seattle, and went to a school called Maplewood Co-op, which shares a lot of similarities with the

Lab (including feeling isolated as a Jewish kid, like Audrey). The Seattle Center for Queer Community is an imagined version of Gay City: Seattle's LGBTQ Center. Anything I got right about that space was intentional, and anything I got wrong was also intentional.

For eight years I was the librarian at Corlears, a small, independent elementary school in New York City, which taught me everything I could ever want to know about writing for kids. Thanks to my colleagues (especially Amy-Marie, Sam, Dora, Chelsea, Patricia, Joy, and Charles), who modeled how to treat children with honor and respect. Stella let me describe her amazing shoes, Bailey allowed me to use their name, Evan gave me some interesting facts about tanks, Jasper wore a funny hedgehog shirt, Miles taught me to avoid palm oil, and Franka shows me that kids these days are extremely cool. My roots go down.

Hanne Blank's face kept floating into my mind while trying to figure out who Mom was. Kelli Dunham is as wonderful as Kelli in the book. Patrick Robbins helped me figure out the solar panels part. Alex Gelman inspired "a dad with big PFLAG energy," and Lindsay Rutledge, my best friend at work, became a real mom during the writing of this book.

Writer friends help make this career a little more sustainable. Alex Gino, the only one who's been doing this whole thing for longer than me. Robin Stevenson for our not-quite-weekly chats. Traci Sorell for being my instant favorite. Heidi Heilig for being a good neighbor. Ellen Vandenberg for your years of advice. Cheryl Klein, for giving me a chance, and

Bill Konigsberg, for facilitating that chance. Betsy Bird, for talking to me at that rooftop party (mumble) years ago. And other librarian/book world people: Robbin, T. Sokoll, Karyn, Susannah, Vee, Zev, Kate, Angie, Hannah, Riley, Athena.

My agent, Saba Sulaiman, has made so many of my dreams come true. I'm so glad you passed on my first novel in 2014, and said yes to my second one four years later. I'm grateful that my editor, Ellen Cormier, let me write more books! And thanks to the whole team at Dial Books for Young Readers, especially Ashley Spruill, Venessa Carson, and Trevor Ingerson. Ana Vonhuben and Maria Fazio came up with a perfect cover.

About two-thirds of the way into writing this book my editor was like "Something is missing between B and A," and I realized that A has a crush on B. The first rewrite went badly because I hadn't had a good crush on anyone in years, but by the second attempt I had met Damon. Thank you, bear, for the endless gummies, the lessons on beard care, and the new adventures. I could have figured it out without you, but I'm glad I didn't have to.

No specific old transsexual man inspired Mike, and no particular young nonbinary person inspired Bailey. But I know so many of both rough categories of human, and I love them both, so much. May we be blessed to learn from our history and charged to be inspired by our future.

Brooklyn, New York
August 2021